HE WAS AN AMERICAN AGENT SENT INTO THE
ENEMY-INFESTED JUNGLE, WHERE HE BE-
CAME THE NEMESIS OF THE VIET CONG. THIS
IS THE STORY OF HIS PRIVATE WAR, HIS FEARS,
HIS AGONIES, HIS BETRAYAL BY FRIENDS, AND
HIS STRANGE INVOLVEMENT WITH THE VIET-
NAMESE NATIVE GIRL HE CALLED "WIFE."
". . . A FINE, BITTER, HARD-HITTING NOVEL."

—Publishers' Weekly

Smith Hempstone

A TRACT
OF TIME

A FAWCETT CREST BOOK

FAWCETT PUBLICATIONS, INC., GREENWICH, CONN.
MEMBER OF AMERICAN BOOK PUBLISHERS COUNCIL, INC.

A FAWCETT CREST BOOK REPRINTED BY ARRANGEMENT WITH
HOUGHTON MIFFLIN COMPANY. THIS BOOK CONTAINS THE
COMPLETE TEXT OF THE ORIGINAL HARDCOVER EDITION.

LIBRARY OF CONGRESS CATALOG CARD NUMBER: 66-11226

PRINTING HISTORY
HOUGHTON MIFFLIN EDITION PUBLISHED MARCH 14, 1966
FIRST PRINTING, DECEMBER 1965
SECOND PRINTING, MARCH 1966
THIRD PRINTING, APRIL 1966

A DOUBLEDAY BEST-IN-BOOKS SELECTION

FIRST FAWCETT CREST PRINTING, SEPTEMBER 1966

PUBLISHED BY FAWCETT WORLD LIBRARY
67 WEST 44TH STREET, NEW YORK, N.Y. 10036
PRINTED IN THE UNITED STATES OF AMERICA

for

T. M.

who helped so much

"*Hereby it is manifest, that during the time men live without a common Power to keep them all in awe, they are in that condition which is called Warre, as is of every man, against every man. For Warre consisteth not in Battell onely, or the act of fighting; but in a tract of time, wherein the Will to contend by Battell is sufficiently known.*"

Hobbes' *Leviathan*

CONTENTS

ABOUT THIS BOOK

A TRACT OF TIME is a novel. It does not purport to offer solutions to the tragedy of Vietnam, although the various people in the book obviously have feelings about the situation, which they express. The time is 1963, in the months leading up to the fall of the regime of Ngo Dinh Diem, his death and that of two of his brothers. Others know Vietnam far better than I, who visited it only in the course of my work as a foreign correspondent during the period in question. In any case, the setting of the book is secondary: the story takes place *in* Vietnam; but what the book has to say, if I have said it well enough, has to do not only with that country in that particular year but with the human condition in all times of war and suffering. In short, the book is not so much about Vietnam as about trust and betrayal, love and death, desire and emptiness, within the framework of war.

It is clear that a book about men at war in Vietnam in 1963 could not be written without reference to a few historic personages. Who these are will be readily apparent. They bear their own names. Some of them, such as Diem and Nhu, flawed men but brave ones, appear in the book. Others, such as Madame Nhu, Ambassador Henry Cabot Lodge, and *New York Times* correspondent David Halberstam, are mentioned but do not appear. These people, of course, played real roles in the drama of Southeast Asia. Other characters, such as Harry Coltart, Ramsey Englehardt, John McWhorter, Ilouha, Loye, Cao Van Thuan, Yé, and General Tric Dinh Trang, are wholly fictitious, bear no relation (and are intended to bear none) to persons living or dead who may have performed similar roles or held comparable posts in Vietnam during 1963.

Finally: a word about plausibility, which has been called the morality of fiction. A woman who read parts of this book in manuscript form recently asked me if it were "real." I could only say that it was true but not necessarily factual. Some weeks later, on March 17, 1965, the following article, which I quote in its entirety, appeared in the *New York Times*:

Banmethuot, South Vietnam, March 17—The battle for the loyalty of the tribesmen in the central highlands has been resumed, with the initial success going to the Communists.

The Government of South Vietnam has taken some steps toward meeting the demands of these primitive people for a greater voice in their own affairs. The effects of this have been largely offset by new Communist pressures against the hill people, whom the French colonizers of Indochina called Montagnards, and by this government's inability to protect them from Vietcong terrorism.

Unrest among the 750,000 Montagnards led to an uprising by Montagnard troops that began Sept. 19 and sputtered for 10 days. The rebellion generated more tension than bloodshed. But for a time the Montagnards threatened to take over Banmethuot, capital of Darlac Province.

Vietnamese officials and their American advisers who work with Montagnards have seen no signs that another rebellion is building up. But in the last five weeks Communists and Vietcong units have been moving into isolated Montagnard villages and either persuading them or threatening them to support the guerrillas.

The Montagnards are of a different racial stock from the Vietnamese and speak a different language.

This, then, is their story and the story of the Americans who have fought and are fighting by the side of the people of the hills. Judge for yourself whether or not the story is "real."

S. H.

Cambridge, Massachusetts
Spring 1965

A TRACT
OF TIME

Part One

THE BROWNING

CHAPTER ONE

HARRY COLTART LOOKED along the barrel of the Browning. The post sight at the end of the automatic rifle, blackened with smoke from a smudge pot, was not yet visible. He always kept a thin, even coat of blacking on both the post and the rear peep sights. It made for clarity in the sight picture and prevented glare. He felt comfortable with the Browning. He liked the heft of it and the big, solid, dependable nature of its parts, from the sear release stop lever to the counter-recoil spring. He knew each part as you know an old familiar neighborhood, knew what each was designed to do and how it did it. He could knock down and reassemble the automatic rifle blindfolded; it was a thing it gave him pleasure to do. Sometimes you came across a bad Browning, usually a demonstration model that had passed through too many untrained hands. An automatic rifle was complicated, like a person, he thought. If people who did not know about it or care about it monkeyed with a Browning too much, the rifle sometimes went sour. But this was a good one. Harry Coltart respected it and believed in it. It had never let him down. He felt good about having it now, although he wished he could see the post sight. Nor could he see the ford, although the lumpy stillness of the dawn was full of the murmuring of the stream, groping its way down from the flinty hills and across the sodden clearing, searching querulously for the rice paddies of the plains. The clearing beneath him and the ford were wreathed in fog, a wispy, motionless haze which hung in tatters on the bushes and collected in dense patches along the banks of the stream. Off to his left, in the coarse stubble which led down to the grassy margins of the ford, Harry heard a rustling noise, huge and irregular, as if a leather-shod man with big feet were walking hesitantly through dry leaves, unsure of his direction. A cock partridge courting his hen. Harry knew it was minutes until sunrise and thought how strange it was the way sounds seemed magnified at this hour. Was there really such a thing as a

15

pre-dawn hush, a momentary pause when creatures withdrew into themselves in expectation of the miracle of the coming of another sun? Or was it just that a man's pre-dawn thoughts were such that he created the hush inside himself? Harry shivered and shifted his body on the dew-soaked ground. After weeks in the hills, he had lost weight, and malaria had made him sensitive to damp cold. Early mornings were cold in the mountains, whether you were in Vietnam or in the Alleghenies back of Staunton. He rubbed his hand slowly along the Browning's gas cylinder tube and the steel felt like ice under his fingers. The waiting was the bad part. Once the fighting started you no longer were conscious of the beat of your heart. There was too much to do. But now, waiting in the silence for it to happen, he could feel his heart thumping in his chest. The dawn air was clean and sharp in his lungs and he sucked it in greedily to quiet his heart. The air had a fresh taste of apples to it. Later the tropical sun would chase the freshness from the air and draw from the jungle other stronger, fetid odors, smells of rotting vegetation, decaying wood, and long-standing, shaded water. But now, as the corpse-white light filtered into the clearing, the air tasted new to him, as always that of every hunting dawn had, and he breathed deeply and with gratitude, knowing what was to come.

Harry Coltart went over in his mind the details of the ambush. It was a simple plan and thus a good one. It was when you tried to be too complicated that things went wrong. There was no place for the baroque in partisan warfare. They would let the advanced guard and the mass of the coolies cross the ford. When he saw the radioman, he would fire and Yé's montagnards at that signal would open up on the coolies as they scrambled back toward the ford. A burdened man could not cross the stream lower down. It was too fast and deep there. Any coolies who tried to get out that way would have to dump their loads. The important thing was to scatter the supply train, kill the radioman, and destroy his set. Too many SCR-300s, old sets captured by the Chinese in Korea, but still useful to the Vietcong, were getting through to the Mekong delta. As soon as the radio had been destroyed and the coolie train broken up, Yé was to post a covering ambush while he and the rest of his tribesmen withdrew into the jungle. Rendezvous at the Hill of the Two Brothers. The plan had seemed clear to everyone. There was nothing to do but wait.

The wind had risen slightly and the sun was beginning to burn away the wisps of fog when the first scout waded into the ford. He was a short man with very long, black hair which hung down almost to his shoulders. His black cotton shirt and shorts were ragged and he looked as if he had been in the jungle for a long time. It was not just the length of his hair and his ragged clothes but the way he moved, his knees slightly bent, his elbows close to his sides, his eyes lizard-busy. The Viet stepped gingerly into the ford, feeling with his toes for rocks. Then he splashed quickly across and up the bank, his thickly muscled, hill man's calves shining with pearls of water. Once across the stream, he paused and eased the rifle which he carried slung over his shoulder. He looked directly at Harry and the American held his breath. Then the scout hitched his rifle and loped out of sight down the trail paralleling the stream.

The first coolie, dressed in the same fashion as the scout, dressed as every Vietnamese peasant dresses, but bent under a huge A-frame loaded with something wrapped in leaves, felt his way tentatively into the ford. In midstream he hesitated for a moment, his knees bent under the load, his brow pressing against the head-strap, then cupped his right hand and scooped water, like Gideon's men, to his open mouth in an unbroken motion.

It all happened so quickly that later Harry was uncertain of the sequence of events. The echo of the premature shot reverberated in the hills and Harry heard startled, gutteral shouts, the noise of resisting underbrush giving way before running bodies, red-breasted parrots screaming in the trees, beating the air with their wings. Harry's muscles contracted nervously at the shot, and in the ford, water still streaming from his cupped hand, the coolie straightened up, dropped his load and stood motionless for an instant, frozen in wide-eyed surprise. Harry cursed quietly to himself as he brought the post sight of the Browning to rest on the man's stomach. He exhaled half a breath, squeezed the trigger and felt the Browning shivering like a live thing against his cheek, thrusting into the socket of his shoulder. With his left hand he pressed down on the stock of the automatic rifle with all his weight, the metal tab of the hinged butt plate cutting into his shoulder, feeling the surge of power as the bipod bit into the ground, kicking chunks of loose dirt into the air. The gun's stuttering, deep-throated bark hammered against his eardrums but he was conscious of it only as a central theme, authoritative and insistent, stitching an atonal discord of shots and cries which welled up out of the empty clearing. He knew he was firing needlessly, expending too many rounds, but still in his angry frustration he held down the trigger, firing into the underbrush which hid the coolie train. Harry could see the stream below him through the wisps of whipped fog which rose to mingle uncertainly with smoke from the guns of the montagnards. But he could no longer hear the murmur of the brook where it broke from the cleft at the top of the valley and tumbled down over the smooth, bone-white pebbles at the ford. The coolie lay face down in the ford, the flow of the stream tugging at his ragged clothing. The A-frame lay broken on the mud of the bank, leaf-wrapped packages of rice strewn in the grass. The coolie had been hit in the stomach. He held his left hand clasped to his belly. With his right he clawed feebly at the slippery bank of the stream. His legs twitched spasmodically, but he could not bring his knees up under him to bear his weight. The sight of the coolie struggling in the stream seemed to excite the montagnards. Harry could see little geysers of water rising from the stream around the dying man. The montagnards hooted and laughed. Harry laid the post of the fore sight on the spot where the coolie's neck joined the trunk of his body, touching the trigger gently. The coolie jerked suddenly under the impact of the slugs, beating the water around him into a froth. Then he lay still, all his tomorrows draining from his mouth in black, convulsive gouts. The montagnards kept firing at the body.

The scent of apples was gone from the air and with the first faint waves of heat came an odor of gentle decay, of the damp dung of forest animals, wet bark, and stagnant water, punctuated by the acrid, sensual smell of burning cordite, the scent of war. The momentary nausea which had gripped Harry at the sight of the life leaking out of the coolie in the ford left him. He felt blood pumping through his veins and a red haze of almost sexual excitement seized him. "Go, baby, go!" he whispered to the Browning, sighting an indistinct movement in the underbrush beyond the ford, squeezing the trigger, holding it down, the automatic rifle squirming against his shoulder while half a magazine of shell casings whirred past his right ear like brass locusts in flight. He heard himself shouting, felt the rigidity of his legs, his toes digging for purchase, swallowed the copper taste of pennies. In his search for a target, his eyes returned to the coolie lying dead in the ford, one forefinger pointing accusingly at the uncaring sky. This one would smite no Midianites. The excitement drained out of him, leaving him empty and spent. He shook his head hard, as a retriever shakes water from itself, as if to rid himself of the dregs of exultation and nausea. The premature shot had bitched the ambush. One coolie, and perhaps the lead scout, was dead. With luck possibly one or two other Viets had been hit. He swore to himself. The rest of the coolies, the radioman and his precious SCR-300, by now would have faded back into the jungle. Firing from the far side of the stream indicated that the Viet fighting men had moved forward through the retreating coolies. Soon the Viets would begin feeling their way up the ridges on either side of the montagnards, groping for position while the center laid down a base of fire. Suddenly Harry felt very tired. The failure of this one ambush, he knew, in itself meant little. But he could not disregard its larger significance. The resistance movement among the Koho was fragile, a delicate flower which demanded the sunlight of many victories. He and Yé were virtually its only roots. Englehardt had cautioned him in Saigon that the resistance movement in its early stages could sustain few defeats. The dead coolie mired in the ford signified his second failure in five actions.

Harry hunched his head back into an imaginary carapace as the underbrush around him crackled and snapped, whipped by a burst of automatic fire. He felt his bowels loosen. It was a personal thing, a highly individual dilemma, to have bullets fired at you. Not just in general, not just in your direction, but at you, Harry Coltart. The Marines didn't teach you about that at Basic School. Nor had the Agency much to say on that score. How it felt to sense death, to smell it searching for you like a dog snuffling for a buried bone, was a tightly kept secret. Those who knew never talked about it, although the mark of their knowing was plain upon them to another who knew. Perhaps the memory of that knowledge was so unspeakable that a man's ravaged nerve ends healed over with scar tissue which could not, would not break to allow the truth to be spoken. It was better that way. If you did not talk about it yourself or have to listen to others do so, you could learn to live with it. Harry had met that truth on an ice-honed Korean ridge called the Punch Bowl, had carried it deep within his stomach for nearly a dozen years. He had a notion that it might be one of the reasons he was in Koho country instead of practicing law in Charlottesville. And now in the leaden flogging of the living trees around him, that truth came back to him, mocking and terrible. Harry pressed his angular frame harder against the ground in search of cover, until the balled fear lay crushed against his spine. With an effort of will, he forced his face up, away from the protecting earth, swinging the chattering barrel of the Browning around, protesting with his own fire against the death seeking him out. He could see no Viets, but he fired into the face of the jungle until the Browning went silent. He cursed, punched the release button, caught the magazine as it fell, rolled over onto his left side and jammed the empty magazine into his rucksack. In a single, continuous motion, as practiced as the genuflection of a priest, he snatched a full magazine from the rucksack, rolled back into firing position, slapped the magazine into the underside of the Browning, and fired.

Even as he hammered away at flitting shapes and waving underbrush, his soldier's ear told him that the volume of fire was heavier now to his left, where the low ridge swung around from the source of the stream and climbed to become the hill from which Yé's group of montagnards were firing. Over the din of the guttural shouts of the tribesmen, the bark of guns, and the whistle of crossbows, the whining of ricocheting bullets and the distant scolding of parrots, Harry could hear the Viet leader urging his men on with high-pitched cries. *"Tien! Tien!"* That shout of "forward! forward!" had echoed through these hills and rolled across the lowlands of Vietnam for nearly twenty years. An entire Vietnamese generation had grown up with it. The French had heard that cry at Dienbienphu and now, Harry thought, it's our turn. And the little yellow men kept coming, most of them, like lemmings, pressing to their deaths, as if driven by some elemental urge. He had seen them at that frozen reservoir in Korea, at Yudam-ni and Hagaru-ri and Koto-ri, when the bugles sounded in the searing cold of night and the squat peasant soldiers in quilted cotton uniforms came on in waves. He had seen them come with their urgent bugles and, in a sense, he guessed he had dedicated at least a part of himself to fighting those bugles. He did not pretend to understand the seemingly atavistic urge which brought the peasant soldiers on to die. He knew it was not enough to say that Mongol cavalry on shaggy little ponies sweeping across a frozen Korean lake, any more than Vietcong terrorists, answered that cry of *"tien"* only out of fear. That was a politician's lie.

He knew that with fear you could force men to don uniforms and bear arms, but not to fight, not to fight well enough to win. Harry sensed that something interminate was bursting out of China and into the southern rice bowl. Deformed and terrible though it might be to western eyes, it had about it a certain terrible majesty. It spoke to men whose brittle lives never had held significance for anyone other than themselves, men whose heritage always had been hunger and pain, driving them on willingly to their deaths. Harry sensed that pulsing, elemental drive in the jungle around him and suddenly felt defeated and alone. It was no good. He raised his whistle to his lips and blew three short blasts.

From his hill off to the left, Yé acknowledged the signal with an answering whistle. Good old Yé. The Koho chief would have to hold the left for five minutes until the others could break off contact and he could set up a blocking group at the edge of the forest beyond the rice paddy. Harry guessed the old man could do it. The hills were his and he knew them. A man drew his strength from the soil of his birth and on it he could do what he had to do. Slowly the fire from Harry's hill died down as the Kohos slipped away one by one into the forest. The Vietcong fire from beyond the stream was light. Most of them, Harry guessed, were trying to overrun Yé's position. The lead-thrashed trees around Harry lay broken and silent, sap oozing from their wounds. The coolie still lay where he had fallen in the ford, the gentle current playfully tugging his long, black hair, leeches dark on his broken body. A man born to bear burdens would carry no more. "*Tien, tien!*" came the cry from the left and with it a new volley of fire. Harry squeezed off a final, long burst into the jungle's expressionless face, jumped to his feet and ran back down the narrow, winding trail in a half-crouch, the Browning cradled in his arms. As he ran, he ejected the empty magazine and forced home a full one.

This time he did not bother to pocket the empty magazine. He kicked it aside as he ran for his life.

CHAPTER TWO

THE GOING WAS EASY, the land tilting gradually as the ridge wore down into a mountain rice paddy, and as he sprinted into the clearing Harry outran his fear. In the center of the paddy was a longhouse. No one was there. The ironwood stakes which supported the floor platform had collapsed and the longhouse lay broken on its side, like a beached fish. As he ran past the longhouse, Harry ducked his head without breaking stride and peered into its gloomy interior. It smelled empty, devoid of life, wholly vegetable, as if it had been abandoned for a long time. The paddy had become exhausted, its strength drained from it by a succession of rice crops, and the farmer had moved on to slash and burn another clearing from the forest. Or there had been a tiger. The fighting in the hills had not been intense enough to drive a man from his paddy. The Vietcong had enjoyed the passive cooperation of the hill tribes for many years. In any case, you did not abandon a piece of rice land because of the war. The war was a fluid thing, not a constant condition of life in the hills. Some times the war came briefly to a range of hills and the peasant farmers drifted off into the jungle. Then the war went away and the peasants returned to their paddies. The war was a thing you could live with and grow accustomed to as a condition of life, like pain, and a man did not easily abandon sweet soil until he had flayed it and flogged it and rendered it barren. But a tiger was enough to make a man go, Harry knew.

The going was easy across the paddy because the bunds were broken and the land lay parched and thirsty under the rising sun. Harry ran effortlessly, the big Browning slung over his narrow shoulder, its weight thumping against his thigh, and then he was out of the clearing and back in the cool of the forest. There he found two montagnards squatting under a tree, their eyes fixed on the opposite side of the clearing, their rusty Japanese rifles cradled in their laps. They were not of Yé's village.

"Get ready to fight here," he said to them in halting Koho laboriously learned from Ilouha, "so that the others can pass through us." Living with someone was the way to learn a language, and Yé's daughter had taught him well, although he still did not feel as at home in the language as he did with Annamese. The two montagnards, short, brown men with heavy brows, high cheekbones, and eliptical eyes, said nothing. They rose to their feet, stretched, and moved off silently, away from Harry and the distant popping of the guns. The American shook his fist angrily at the retreating figures and dropped to his knees, setting the bipod of the Browning at the right edge of a fallen tree trunk, so that the trunk gave him both cover and concealment. He would have to provide covering fire himself, at least until Yé and his group arrived. He had no way of knowing how many of the montagnards were still on the far side of the clearing. As he thought about this, half a dozen Kohos appeared at the edge of the forest and ran, singly and in pairs, across the paddy toward him. All of them were barefoot, some naked except for a breech-clout and an iron bangle. Others wore ragged, black shorts of cheap cotton. Some carried crossbows or blowpipes, the traditional weapons of the hills. Others, wealthier men, had rifles, ancient muzzle-loaders, British Lee-Enfields, or Japanese pieces. Only one American Garand had found its way to Yé's village. As the Kohos sprinted across the clearing they ran bent slightly at the waist, their knees loose, their eyes either on the ground or constantly shifting from side to side. They came silently and effortlessly, gliding over the paddy, the sun buttering their brown bodies. Harry watched them come, trying to engrave on his mind the pattern of their coming, with the pale sun and the green of the forest behind them, the abandoned longhouse toppled on its side. It was something he wanted to take with him, to remember, to keep when it was all over. There was always, he had found, something you wanted that way, something that summed it up for you and that nobody could take away. On the other side of the paddy, the firing fell off and then died away except for a few isolated shots. There was nothing in the warming air but the humming of insects, the far-away terrified chattering of gibbons, the scolding of parrots, and the weight of his failure black upon him.

Yé materialized among the trees at the far side of the paddy, hesitated for a minute at the edge of the clearing, and then came on fast. Harry watched the chief bounding across the paddy, his muscles bunched in the broad-jumper's crouch. On his bare chest bounced a greasy, leather pouch containing his amulet, a tiger's collarbone. He was tall for a hill man, perhaps five feet eight, and heavy through the chest, like a swimmer. He ran with one shoulder ducked low, his left arm cradling the burp gun given him by the Vietminh in the time of the French. Often Harry had wondered about the gun. To a montagnard it was a princely gift. What had Yé done to earn it? Betrayed a French Groupement Mixte leader? Provided important information? Or was it just the price the Vietminh had been willing to pay for the benevolent neutrality of the Koho at the time of Dienbienphu? He had asked Yé about it but the chief had been evasive. What would the Vietcong pay Yé to deliver him up to them? Plenty, Harry supposed. Always you lived with the threat of betrayal and it was not a pleasant thing. That and the sense of isolation, of separation from your own people, were the hardest things about running a partisan operation. Despite his status in the tribe as Ilouha's man and Yé's blood brother, Harry did not quite trust the Koho chief. There was too much he didn't know about Yé. But Harry realized he had to depend on him. There came a point when you could not go on alone, when you had to trust someone. There was no one else; he had only Yé.

The Koho chief broke stride when he saw the American lying with the Browning behind the tree trunk, and dropped to the earth beside him, breathing deeply and regularly.

"I have left a two-man ambush on the trail," he said.

"Good. And the others?"

"Mlene takes his men toward the plain. He will meet us at the Hill of the Two Brothers."

Harry nodded. The withdrawal at least was going well. For a people which for centuries had lived as part-time brigands, the breaking off of contact with an enemy, perhaps the most difficult of all small-unit actions, seemed to present few problems. The last of Yé's men had cleared the paddy. They stood waiting in groups of twos and threes in the cover of their jungle, their breath coming easily, their faces blank, their dark eyes scanning the far side of the paddy for signs of the Vietcong. There was no time to waste.

"We've got to get out of here. A couple of men must stay here to cover us," Harry said.

"No," Yé replied, shaking his head, his eyes averted.

"Why not? Suppose the Viets follow?"

"They will not follow for long. The men don't want to stay. They want to go back to their longhouses."

Harry swore under his breath. First the premature shot and now this. The Koho partisan movement was dissolving before his eyes.

"You're chief, Yé. You know as well as I do that someone should stay for a few minutes."

"The men do not want it," Yé repeated.

There was not much time. Harry studied the expressionless mask of the Koho chief's face, brown and wrinkled as a walnut. Harry could read nothing there. Neither love nor hate, neither loyalty nor betrayal. He saw only a broad forehead, widely spaced black eyes, high cheekbones, and a great slash of a mouth, these features framed by a tousled mop of greasy, black hair beginning to go gray. Harry sighed in exasperation.

"Go on, then. I'll cover," he said, sinking down into firing position again. This is something, he thought, which is going to have to be sorted out. Something was eating at Yé and the other montagnards, something that had to be put right if Englehardt's plan was to succeed.

Yé barked orders in the guttural language of the hill men and the half-naked Kohos loped wordlessly down the trail and out of sight. The old chief crouched down beside Harry.

"I will stay with you, Erohé," he muttered, using the name the Kohos had given him at the ceremony of blood brotherhood. Harry nodded, pleased.

"Who spoiled the ambush?" he asked.

"Later. There are men." Yé pointed with his chin, as was the fashion of the hill tribes, in the direction of the clearing. A lone figure, doll-like in the distance, broke from the cover of the forest, ran a few yards across the abandoned paddy and dropped out of sight onto his belly. Another man, clad like the first in black shorts and shirt, followed him. In the shadows of the trees, other figures flitted, working their way around the clearing to the left. The Vietcong leader was no fool, Harry conceded. He was taking no chances. The main body would not cross the paddy until the scouts had shown that the opposite piece of forest was empty. There would be no chance for a second ambush.

The American set the post of the fore sight to the right of the spot where the first man had disappeared and set the change lever of the Browning at the slow cyclic rate of fire. The doll-like figure rose suddenly into the fore sight, the post almost covering it, and hung there for an instant. Harry squeezed the trigger gently and the Browning stuttered, ripping the silence of the clearing. The scout spun around, bent over slowly, as if to pick up something he had dropped, and pitched forward onto his face. Harry could hear the nervous chatter of Yé's burp gun as the Koho chief opened up on the flanking party working its way through the trees to their left. The second scout lying hidden in the stubble of the abandoned paddy popped into view like a marionette and dashed forward in a low crouch. Harry pivoted the Browning and fired a short burst, but the scout already had flung himself into the grass. Harry could see the grass swaying slightly in the windless sunlight as the scout rolled away from the spot where he had thrown himself down. Harry adjusted the peep sight slightly for elevation, sighted in carefully on the spot where the swaying grass ended, and squeezed off a burst. From the other side of the clearing came answering shots, showering him with bark, broken twigs, and leaves. Harry panned the forest's edge, his forefinger hard down on the trigger, emptying the twenty-round magazine. Yé was firing steadily, his lips moving soundlessly, his naked body quivering to the rhythm of the burp gun. Harry reloaded quickly.

"Let's get out of here," he shouted. The Viets would keep their heads down for a while. Most of them seemed to be armed coolies, territorials, which explained their high shots. Recruits always fired high. He had gotten a glimpse of only two men in the gray cotton uniform of the Vietnamese People's Army.

The Koho chief turned toward him, his eyes questioning. Harry placed his finger on his own chest, then pointed at Yé and down the trail. Yé pointed back at him, indicating that the American should go first, and continued firing. Harry nodded, wriggling backward, dragging the automatic rifle after him, until he was deep in the undergrowth. Rising slowly to his feet, he slung the weapon and ran. Behind him he could hear Yé firing a long burst and the answering patter of shots from the Viets. Harry ran hard, pumping his forearms, conscious of the twenty pounds of Browning slapping against his thigh, his eyes pinned on the winding trail, watching for roots and *punjis*. He was afraid of *punjis* and hence very much aware of the possibility of the trail being studded with them. The sharpened slivers of bamboo could pierce an army boot. And the human excrement in which they were dipped almost always caused the wound to go septic. The path climbed slowly and Harry's breath whistled through clenched teeth as branches and lianas whipped at his face and bare forearms. Crickets were calling in the heat of the underbrush. His throat felt dry, caked with dust, and in his mouth was the taste of blood and sweat. His nostrils were full of the smell of rotting vegetation and of the mold which lay on the forest floor. *Punjis*, he reminded himself, got to watch for *punjis* and roots. When he reached a curve in the trail, he realized that Yé was behind him, running easily, his brown shoulders dappled by the sunlight which filtered weakly through the forest's canopy. Short of wind, Harry slowed his pace and finally stopped and stood leaning on the automatic rifle, his breath rattling in his chest, his lungs bursting.

The hill man padded up to him, sweat glistening on his hairless chest.

"The others have gone this way," the chief said, pointing up the trail. "The Viets, if they come this far, will follow them. We'll leave the trail here."

Yé motioned Harry past him, down the hillside into a deep gully choked with secondary growth. The Koho chief followed him after carefully rearranging the undergrowth where they had left the trail. Then he shouldered his way past the American, slipping and sliding down the slope and into the damp bushes. The bushes concealed a dry watercourse scarred by the delicate hooves of mouse deer. The undergrowth arched together above the watercourse, forming a hot, airless corridor through which the two men scuttled. The dry rivulet angled back toward the abandoned rice paddy and then cut away sharply, falling in shelves. It was hard work carrying the big Browning in the watercourse. Soon Harry was conscious only of the stifling heat, his labored breathing, and the scrape of his boots on the rocks. He could no longer hear firing. We're out of it, he thought to himself, we made it. When the watercourse branched, creating a small clearing, the Koho chief turned and motioned to him to stop.

"It is safe. Rest."

Harry propped the Browning against the bank of the watercourse and sank gratefully to his knees, gasping for breath. He slumped back against the bank, conscious of the cloud of gnats attracted by the sweat on his face, and filled his lungs with air. Yé squatted on his heels, oblivious to the insects, tracing cabalistic designs in the sand with the butt of his burp gun. The two men averted their gaze from one another, conscious of the thing which lay between them, wounding their thoughts. The American was the first to speak.

"What happened at the ambush?" he asked.

"Someone fired too soon."

"Yes. Who? Why?"

"Perhaps Hone. Perhaps Mouhi. It was a mistake."

"It was not a mistake."

"No, it was not a mistake."

"Why then?"

"To warn the Vietcong. Many believe this fight is not for the Koho." The old chief spoke slowly, deliberately, seemingly absorbed in the designs he was etching in the sand of the watercourse.

"But you believe?"

"Perhaps, Erohé. Sometimes I'm not so sure." Yé shrugged expressively and spat a red stream of betel nut juice at a scarlet-hooded gecko which had emerged from a pile of rocks. The lizard retreated hurriedly.

Harry felt his face twisting into a mask of exasperation under his matted, filthy beard. He had been through it so many times with Yé, with the other Koho chiefs. One more time.

"The Viets are your enemies, Yé."

"Why, Erohé, tell me why?"

"Because they are Communists. Because they will enslave you. Because they will steal your land and make cattle of you. You know all this." As he enumerated each point, Harry unbent a finger from his clenched fist and when he had finished held the three fingers close to Yé's face, as if to force the truth on the chief through the physical proximity of his hand. Yé wrinkled his brow and studied the designs he had etched in the sand, as if hoping to find there the answers to the questions which afflicted him.

"Communists? We do not know what this means. Your words may be true but we do not know it. What we do know is that the *Yoane,* the yellow Annamese of the plains, have been our enemies since these hills were young. The Vietcong come from the north, from the mountains. From that direction we have not been threatened since the time of the men you call Mongols. And who amongst us can remember that time?"

"I speak the truth. The Viets . . ."

"We do not know it, Erohé. What we do know is that you are a *Boc,* a high-nose from beyond the bitter water, whose home is not this place, while many of the Vietcong are of our blood. You serve the *Yoane*, who always have been our enemies. These things we know. And for this . . ."

"But you know . . ."

Yé raised his hand and Harry fell silent.

"And for this reason," Yé continued, "many believe that the Koho should not fight the Vietcong. But come," he added, rising to his feet, "soon the sun will be high. It is better to travel now and to talk later."

Yé sniffed the air and listened intently for a minute, his head cocked to one side and his forefinger to his lips. Satisfied, he nodded to the American, slung his burp gun and set off down the dry watercourse.

While the two men walked in silence, the younger man following the older, making the long loop which would bring them to the rendezvous at the Hill of the Two Brothers, Harry thought about what Yé had said. He had thought about it a hundred times before: in Saigon during the briefing for the mission, at night on the sleeping-platform with Ilouha warm at his side and the fire painting flickering ghosts on the longhouse walls, on long treks through the hills with Yé and the young warriors. It was something he never really stopped thinking about, consciously or unconsciously, because he sensed that on his resolution of the problem depended the success or failure of his mission. What Yé had said, Harry knew, was the kernel of the whole problem of organizing the hill tribes, the montagnards as the French called them, to resist the Vietcong. And Englehardt, in his methodical, professorial fashion, had convinced him that it was essential that the hill tribes should be persuaded to fight. As Englehardt said, what the newspapers persisted in calling "the Ho Chi Minh trail"—as if it were a turnpike instead of a huge tract of broken country through which literally hundreds of trails wandered—funneled through the core of the montagnard country. Over these trails from North Vietnam through the Koho hills to the Mekong delta came much of importance to the Vietcong in their struggle against the Diem regime. Nobody from Englehardt on down pretended that the Vietcong would collapse if the supply routes through the montagnard country were cut. The rebellion already was self-sustaining, despite the pap that State fed to reporters like John McWhorter for daily regurgitation to their readers. That was a point that troubled Harry. He half suspected that there could be no American victory in Vietnam and he disliked persuading primitive tribesmen to commit themselves to a losing game. How was it Englehardt had put it? That there was a difference between losing and not winning? Yes. His hulking, gray-faced superior had suggested that a condition of permanent stalemate might be possible and desirable. It was one of the good things about working for Englehardt. He had the reputation for being not only an honorable, intelligent man but a patient one, one willing to talk through a problem until a logical, ethical solution presented itself. And then he let you think that you had come up with it. Men liked to work for Ramsey Englehardt. And when you thought about it, even if one had to lose, it was important to lose as slowly as possible, to buy time to dig in further to the south, in Thailand and Malaysia. The problem was that, perhaps understandably, neither the Annamese of the plains nor the montagnards of the hills, after twenty years of virtually continuous bloodshed, had much interest in buying with their blood time for ramparts to be built further to the south. There had to be a more immediate reason than that. He had made a start with Yé, but only a start. If the Vietcong supply trains were to be stopped, he had to do much better than that. The coolies could not carry much. They ate almost three-quarters of the rice they brought with them on the long march from the Red River delta. But they did bring important spare parts for radios and mortars, SKZ recoilless rifles, compasses, field glasses and fuses. And the Ho Chi Minh trail acted as a conduit through which technicians and cadre leaders flowed south and selected South Vietnamese Vietcong moved north for training. Free movement through the montagnard country gave the VPA battalions a link with the outside world, a contact which prevented them from feeling isolated and alone, sustaining their fiercely held belief in ultimate victory.

And if the montagnards didn't fight, Harry knew, those men and supplies were going to keep coming. You couldn't interdict those trails through air strikes. There were too many trails and the cover was too thick. In any case, the coolies could move by night. Diem's regular troops couldn't cut the trails. The plainsmen, the Annamese, were out of their element in the hills. They didn't know the country and they didn't like the people. To the Annamese, the montagnards were *moi*, savages, animals to be shot on sight. The sentiment was mutual and Diem's troops could expect no help from the hill tribes. Only the montagnards alone could do the job and it was up to him, Harry Coltart, to convince them that it was in their interest to do it. Englehardt was depending on him and he didn't intend to let the old man down.

What we've got to do, Harry thought, is to recreate the circumstances of the twelfth century, when the montagnards fought with the Vietnamese against the Hindu Chams. But that was a long time ago. Hemmed into their barren hills by a circle of Annamese forts, the only lowlanders with whom the hill tribes had come in contact in recent centuries were tax collectors, Annamese soldiers living off the land, and the occasional trader. Nor had the French helped much. Out of a curious blend of imperial necessity and sentimental attachment, they had administered the montagnards separately from the rest of Indochina, thus reinforcing the hill tribes' inherent sense of isolation and antagonism toward the Annamese of the plains. The past provided at best a shaky foundation, Harry thought as he swung along in Yé's footsteps, for building a pro-Diem movement among the montagnards. But it had to be and it was his job to build that alliance with gold, promises, and, if necessary, threats. That, as Englehardt would have put it, was the name of the game.

And yet Harry knew that the little brown man in front of him was no fool. Yé would do what seemed to him best for his people and Harry respected him for that. That was what he himself wanted for them, too, he guessed.

CHAPTER THREE

NEITHER THE KOHO nor the American had spoken in the two-hour march from their resting place in the dry watercourse. It was safer to keep the silence of the forest unbroken. For Harry, in any case, walking was a time for thinking, not talking. If you talked, you destroyed the rhythm of the walk. But if you kept quiet and looked and smelled and thought, you fell into a swinging gait which, if you had to, you could keep up all day, aware of your weariness only when you stopped. It was something his father had taught him. Yé's pace had been easy and regular, the distance-eating stride of a man who walked much and knew precisely where he was and where he was going in the maze of broken hills. Yé never held a straight course but followed the easiest path, preferring to walk further rather than to break the pace to push through an obstacle. Finally the older man stopped and held up his hand, the sunlight glinting on the knotted muscles of his shoulder. He tested the wind with a pinch of pollen pulled from a piece of grass, listened intently for a moment and then gave a low, doglike bark. There was silence, Harry conscious only of his own heavy breathing, and then the roebuck's cry was repeated twice from the slopes of the low hill rising out of the forest before them. Yé uttered the coughing bark again and walked on, motioning to Harry to follow.

The montagnards were waiting in a fold in the hill. They squatted on their hams, picking their teeth with slivers of wood, or lay on their stomachs under the bushes, their dark, Polynesian faces expressionless and patient. Harry remembered his initial surprise at the range of pigmentation found among the Koho. Those with the purest Polynesian blood were the color of copper. There were few of these. Most of the Koho were darker, sharing the blood of the Negrito peoples their ancestors had absorbed.

None of the montagnards spoke as Harry and Yé walked among them. The American slumped to the ground gratefully, conscious now of his fatigue, and fumbled in his shirt pocket for a cigarette. His khaki shirt was cold and black with sweat and his calves were tight with weariness. He lit a cigarette and inhaled deeply, aware of the scrutiny of one of the hill men, who studied his actions as if seeing them for the first time. Harry blew a smoke ring and winked at the montagnard. The man laughed and covered his mouth with embarrassment. You slay 'em every time, Professor Coltart, Harry thought to himself. But you're losing the bloody war. Yé sauntered among his people, speaking to several in low tones before returning to Harry.

"We can return to our villages now," he said.

"Casualties?"

"Djero, of the village of the cliff, will not return. He was one of those I left on the trail."

"I'm sorry. Others?"

"Mektoub, of my own people, he of the small longhouse, a bullet in the shoulder. The shoulder is broken."

"Let him come to me when we reach the village."

One man dead and one wounded out of a band of twenty-three. A fair exchange for three or four Vietcong dead, even if the radio had not been destroyed. But a fair exchange was not good enough. The Koho were few and when a people is few, each death diminishes the whole by more than one. He had seen it before. It happened with animals, was happening now in the States with condors. When a species falls below a certain numerical level, a collective sadness, a premonition of doom, seems to fall on the survivors and they no longer reproduce enough to sustain the death rate. A hunter had been lost, perhaps two if the shoulder proved to be badly broken. And Mektoub was the son of Hamon, the *patjao*. It was not a good thing. After Yé, the sorcerer was the most powerful man among the Koho. If Hamon lost interest in the fighting, the partisan movement among the montagnards was finished. The dead man's brother or his uncle would inherit his wives and children so that neither wombs nor stomachs would remain empty. But the loss still would be felt. Each hunter would have to track in a wider arc, bring home more meat. Sacrifices would have to be made so that the spirit of the dead man might be appeased and leave the longhouses in peace. Hamon would see to that. For the moment, some walking remained to be done and Harry was anxious to get going before he stiffened up.

Most of the montagnards already had drifted away into

the forest in twos and threes to return by different routes to
the three villages which had sent men to the ambush. Nobody
had to tell them to do that, Harry thought. The hill men had
been hunters and hunted for so many generations that they
did by intuition that which more sophisticated men had to be
taught to do.

Finally it was their turn. Yé led the way, with Harry
behind him. Helped by another montagnard, Mektoub followed, holding the arm of the wounded shoulder tight against
his stomach. They skirted the base of the Hill of the Two
Brothers and entered a forest, the air heavy and sweet as
honey, thick with the humming of insects, the calling of
secret birds. As they climbed, the forest gave way to a
vertebra of hummocks and these to flinty hills, washed by a
new rain and smelling of iron. The men climbed slowly under
a white sky, the healing sun warm and good on their backs.
After many weeks in the hills, Harry still was unsure of his
sense of direction, although he judged that they were not far
from Yé's village. His lack of skill in this respect was, he
knew, a matter of vast amusement to the Koho. The smallest
Koho boy could hunt for hours in any direction from his
longhouse and still return unerringly to it.

Soon Harry recognized a new texture to the air and tasted
on the wind faint smells of smoldering wood. And then he
saw the longhouses of Yé's village. There were nearly a
dozen, although they seemed fewer. Raised a few feet above
the earth on wooden pilings and scattered among the trees
at the edge of the clearing, the longhouses created the impression of being rooted in the ground, of growing from it, of
being a part of the forest around them. The village appeared
to be empty but gave off a lived-in smell of warm ashes, water,
and excrement. The ground around the tall sacrificial bamboo
pole, at the base of which lay rotting offerings of rice and
fruit, was empty. But the hardness of the earth pounded by a
year of bare feet conveyed the essence of human occupation,
of life. As the four men walked across the clearing, Mektoub
hanging on the arm of his friend, the women, children, and
old men materialized silently on the edge of the forest which
had hidden them, the old men rheumy and querulous, the
children naked and big bellied, skittish as wild animals, the
women bare breasted and serene, their loins wrapped in
lengths of coarse, black cloth bought with forest honey from
Annamese traders.

Harry's eyes searched for Ilouha and found her, a sturdy,

high-breasted girl the color of burnt cinnamon, about whose
lips played the faintest trace of a smile, as if she cherished
within her a knowledge secret and good, as if laughter waited
only upon a pretext to show itself. She was a little too heavy
by American standards, Harry had to admit, and he had
noticed a new plumpness about her in recent days. Or was
it just his imagination? Under his gaze she was firm and
rounded, built to give pleasure and to bear children, to work
and to laugh. She had Yé's wide brow but her nose was finer,
her lips fuller and she lacked his stolidness. Even in repose
Harry found a quality in her both rhythmical and electric
which kindled something deep within him. As Harry leaned
on the automatic rifle, her eyes met his and returned his joy
with a shyness almost mischievous. With unhurried steps she
walked toward the men, a gourd of water in her hands, her
head high and her back as straight as a lance. Inclining her
head slightly to Harry, in a token of wifely submission, the
girl took the Browning from his shoulder and handed him the
gourd.

"You have come," she said.

"I have come, Ilouha."

"I see you, Erohé."

"And I you."

Harry gave the answers required by the Koho greeting and
raised the gourd to his lips, the water spilling down his working throat and onto his sweat-stained shirt.

"You are tired."

"Yes, we have walked far. Boil water. Mektoub is
wounded."

The girl nodded and walked away, the Browning slung over
her shoulder, her firm hips swaying under the thin, black
cloth. Although she had good breasts, small but rounded and
high, Harry seldom noticed them any more in a sexual sense.
He guessed it was because all the Koho women went naked
above the waist. But the swing of her bottom under the black
cloth when she walked or pounded manioc had a way of making him want her with an urgency he never had known before.
Now he was tired and did not want her. But he watched her
as she went and it gave him pleasure; and it came to him that
the nameless village which for weeks had been little more to
him than a clearing in the forest where he lived to do a job,
had become his home in a sense which he did not completely
understand but which he felt very deeply. He thought about
it as he walked to the small longhouse which he shared with

Ilouha, thought about it and then left it, conscious of the more immediate problem.

Harry scrambled up the log which acted as a ladder to the platform, bent low and scuttled crablike into the longhouse, ducking his head to avoid the ridgepole. A fire smoldered, as it always did, on the three flat stones which comprised the hearth, its flames reflected on the metal of the Browning. He would clean the rifle later. He had showed Ilouha how to swab out the barrel, but not how to field-strip it. In any case, Harry had no intention of letting her take over the cleaning of the weapon, although she always tried to do it. A soldier stopped being a soldier when he let someone else clean his rifle.

Ilouha had put water on to boil and gone down to the stream for more. He rinsed his hands in another gourd. It had taken him a long time to persuade her that she mustn't use water for cooking or drinking which had been used for washing. She remained unconvinced, he knew, but accepted his order as just another relatively harmless *Boc* eccentricity. But, he thought as he rummaged in the shadows for the spare rucksack containing his first-aid kit, he could not get her to cook outside the hut. At least the fire kept the bugs down and, having had two malaria attacks, he was not anxious for a third. His eyes smarting from the smoke, Harry left the hut and sat smoking at the forest's edge, watching the young boys bring in the goats from the jungle, while the weariness drained out of him. He was going to have to talk it out with Yé, he decided.

When Ilouha brought the boiling water, Harry called for Yé and Mektoub. They came and with them old Hamon, the *patjao*, Mektoub's father, a shriveled wisp of a man with shrewd, hard eyes, the sticks of his arms and his greasy, gray hair festooned with bones and feathers, the certificates of his trade. The two older men helped Mektoub, his lips trembling with shock, to sit against a tree while Harry bathed the wound with a cloth dipped in warm water. He was conscious always of Hamon's red-rimmed eyes upon him, watching his every movement. He said a silent prayer as he examined the wound. It was not too bad, he thought. Broken but not too badly. The bullet had smashed the right collarbone and veered upward, nicking the shoulder bone and emerging from the back just under the bone. It was hard to say if the shoulder bone was shattered or just cracked. But at least, he thought to himself, I won't have to dig for the slug. Hamon was making small clucking noises deep in his throat as he studied his son's wound. Later, Harry knew, Hamon would do what he felt the situation required.

Harry took a pair of forceps from the rucksack, dipped them in the boiling water, and began to daub the edges of the wound with a ball of cotton soaked in alcohol. As he worked, he began to talk, squinting in concentration.

"What of the T'ai, those who live far to the north under Ho Chi Minh?" he asked, addressing neither Yé nor Hamon, casting the words between them.

"There is news sometimes," Yé replied.

"You know they are taxed, that their young hunters are taken for the militia, that their chiefs are voiceless and cast aside like broken gourds? That their *patjaos,* even the great ones, are scorned?" This last for Hamon's benefit.

"We have heard these words," Yé replied. Hamon grunted noncommittally.

"And you believe them?"

Hamon spoke: "We do not know. Here the Vietcong make no trouble. They pay for what food we give them. They pay for news. They pay for young hunters to scout for them. They leave our women alone except for those given to them, as Yé has given Ilouha to you." Yé nodded his head in agreement.

"But when the Annamese come into the hills," Yé interjected, "they take our food, even when our granaries are almost empty. They break our laws. They use our women. They take our young men for the army, when they can catch them. Always it has been so."

Harry pursed his lips in annoyance as he worked on the wound. It was not going to be easy to persuade Yé. He knew there was justice in what the Koho chief said. The Vietcong had handled the hill tribes diplomatically. The honesty of the Communist tax collectors was legendary. Sometimes Harry thought in despair that the Vietcong officials were the only honest ones in Vietnam, although he knew this was not true. There were plenty of good government officials. And it was precisely these whom the Vietcong went to great lengths to assassinate. The bad ones they allowed to live. As for their own people, a corrupt Vietcong official did not last long. They shot him. It made a great impression on the people. And on the officials.

"The Vietcong treat you well now," Harry said, "because they believe you are foolish and will help them against the

Yoane of Saigon. But if they beat Diem and win this war, it will be another story, Yé. As the T'ai now know."

"You believe this?" Hamon asked.

Harry finished disinfecting the wound, spoke a few words of comfort to Mektoub, pulled a pair of tweezers from the first-aid kit, and dipped them in the hot water. He turned and looked steadily at the sorcerer.

"I believe it. That is why I am among you."

Yé stood up, spit enormously and with apparent satisfaction, and shifted his weight from foot to foot before he spoke.

"Yet you *Bocs* have lied to us before. When your people first came to these hills, before the time of my father's father, who also was a chief, you said that our hunting grounds would be ours while bamboo still grew. Then came the rubber planters . . ."

"Damn it, Yé, those were the French, not Americans."

"They were *Bocs,* high-noses like you, my son. The planters came and they cleared the forests at the roots of our hills and drove away the game. They took our best rice lands, drove us higher into the hills, and laid a tax on us."

"But this was years . . ." Harry interrupted before Yé would wave him into silence.

"Let me finish. When the *Bocs* came back and drove away the Japanese, when I had first become chief, there came the time of war against Ho Chi Minh. You *Bocs* told us we should fight against the Vietminh, that we should be free of the Annamese if we did this. When the fighting stopped, we were not free. *Yoane* troops came here from Saigon and Hué. They made us pay tax, took our food, used our women. We have been betrayed many times, Erohé. Shall we be betrayed again?"

Harry did not answer immediately. He picked carefully at the wound, using the tweezers to extract the splinters of shattered bone from the quivering flesh. Mektoub said nothing, his fingers gouging the ground, his dark eyes blank, his mind in a distant place.

"Hear me, Yé," Harry said finally, choosing his words carefully. "I came to you three months ago because I had heard that Yé was the greatest warrior among the Koho, a chief who had much wisdom. I heard that Hamon was the most famous *patjao* in the hills. I brought gold and presents for all your people from the emperor in Saigon, Diem, whose children the Koho are. I shared your fire, Yé. You gave me

Ilouha, your daughter. Together we have seen and done many things. In all this has my tongue ever proved crooked?"

Yé turned to Hamon and the two men conversed together in a dialect Harry could not understand. The American threw the tweezers into the calabash of hot water and examined the wound carefully in the failing light. It seemed clean. He dusted with penicillin the small hole where the bullet had gone in and the ragged bloody lips of flesh were it had come out. Mektoub had fainted. It was just as well. He had to try to set the shoulder.

"It is as you say," Yé conceded, "you never have lied to us, Erohé."

"Then hear me now," Harry answered, "when I say that not only the Koho but all the peoples of the hills, the Rhadé, the Stieng, the Jarai, the Halang, even the Sadang far to the north, must fight the Vietcong. If you do not, you will die slaves."

"And the Annamese?" Hamon asked. "Diem, the emperor in Saigon, who has taken the religion of the *Bocs*?"

"Diem has promised that you shall be free."

Yé shook his head in disbelief.

"Does this mean," the chief asked, "that no Annamese soldiers will come among us? That no roads will be cut into our hills without our leave? For this is what freedom means."

Harry lowered his head and hesitated before speaking. There had been, as Yé charged, too many betrayals.

"I don't know," he said slowly, his eyes fixed on Yé's.

"This is what we want, Erohé. We want the word of Diem and of the great *Boc* soldier in Saigon, that the Annamese soldiers will stay out of these hills, that no roads will be cut, that we shall be left to rule ourselves according to our own law. And we want your word, Erohé, that their promises will be kept."

"Without this," Hamon added, "we will agree to nothing."

Harry worked on the shattered shoulder, sweating with concentration, feeling for the break, lining up the bones as best he could. It was said that a montagnard never forgot a friend or forgave a foe: if he could heal Mektoub, Hamon's support might be won.

"This is a big thing you ask, Yé." The Koho chief nodded, toying with the amulet dangling from his neck. The tiger's floating collarbone was a potent charm and it had worked for Yé, preserving him, protecting his people in times more difficult than those the oldest man in the tribe could remember.

"It is a big thing. But without Diem's pledge and your word, the Koho will not fight. If the Koho do not fight, then the Rhadé and the other tribes will stay in their longhouses. This is in my heart, Erohé."

Harry bandaged the shoulder tightly, binding the arm to the wounded man's side. It would have to do. He could do no more. The American slumped back into a sitting position before he spoke.

"I cannot say these words, Yé, because it is a big thing, too big for me to say. Perhaps I will go to Saigon to find the answer."

"It would be well to do this, Erohé. The men went to the ambush today only because I urged them to do so. But they will fight no more without this word of freedom. Now go to your longhouse, my son. Hamon and I will see to Mektoub. Ilouha awaits you."

Harry trudged across the clearing and climbed the log to the platform. He was glad that it was over. When he lay down on top of his sleeping bag in the longhouse, he realized how much the fighting, the long march, the dressing of the wound, and the talks with Yé and Hamon had taken out of him. He would clean the Browning in the morning. He was very tired, tired with the aching weariness which comes with malaria, dysentery, isolation, and failure. It had been a tough three months and now he was on the verge of losing it all. And if the partisan movement collapsed, he would be letting down not only Englehardt and himself but failing the Koho. He had convinced himself that it was necessary for the montagnards to participate in the fight against the Vietcong if they were to share in the fruits of victory. As he watched Ilouha stirring the evening meal of manioc paste and strips of rubbery, highly spiced chicken, he realized how much she and Yé, yes, and even old Hamon, had come to mean to him. The Koho and the hills in which they lived had become a part of him. He was not sure how these relationships were to be resolved in the years to come. One did not, after all, become a hermit living in a Southeast Asian rural backwater. He was not made that way. Nor was he capable of lying to himself about Ilouha. The liaison had been formed initially for political reasons. But she had soon proved herself to be useful and comforting. Finally, he had found himself, as he came to know her as a person, becoming increasingly fond of her, conscious of a need which she both inspired and satisfied.

Ilouha had given herself to him shyly at first, perhaps fearing

that he, the *Boc,* might spurn her, perhaps unsure that the desires of such a tall, fair-skinned, yellow-haired person could be
quite natural. Together they had made the discovery that she
was a young girl—not more than sixteen, Harry reckoned,
for the Koho women aged quickly and Ilouha's firm body had
nothing of age to it—and he a man with needs and desires
which she could satisfy. They had given each other joy and it
was a very simple thing. Like most simple things, Harry
thought, it is not readily available where I come from. The
difficult problems we can handle in the States. It's the simple
ones which get away from us. As to what he meant to Ilouha,
he was not sure. He sensed that he gave her sexual pleasure,
although Ilouha did not know the American woman's emotional shorthand for expressing this. He felt that she was
grateful to him for the consideration which he showed her,
although she appeared a bit perplexed, perhaps a little worried,
about the fact that he never beat her. And he suspected that
she took pride in his role as hunter, killer of men, counselor of
chiefs. Whether or not she viewed him as her husband forever and the father of her children he did not know. For
himself, he knew only that he was happy in her healing laughter, redeemed in the suppleness of her young body. Thinking
this, he watched her, thinking well of her, while she sat stirring
the stew over the fire, humming quietly to herself. Neither
spoke, but in the gathering darkness of the longhouse, they
were aware of each other's presence and glad in it. It was a
simple thing.

Harry ran his hands over the matted hollows of his cheeks.
His blond beard must be long now, and very dirty. He had not
looked at himself in a mirror for nearly a month, but he knew
that his hair and his beard were long, that he was dirty and
very thin. He chuckled as he looked at his hands. He had
always been very fastidious about his nails. These were
ragged, broken, and black with dirt down to the quicks. The
backs of his hands were covered with scratches, one of which
had gone septic. When last he had looked at his reflection, it
was just after the second malarial attack and a bout with
dysentery. He remembered the sense of surprise and mild
shock with which he had greeted the face in the cracked hand
mirror. It was the face of a stranger. It had not been Harry
Coltart of Leesburg. Not old Judge Coltart's son. The man in
the mirror was a large-eyed, gaunt stranger whose skin, beneath the dirty blond stubble, was drawn tightly, like vellum,
over the bones of his face. It was the eyes that had struck him

most. They were large, luminous, staring, almost a little
mad. They were the eyes of a silent man, a man isolated from
his own people. He realized then that he had been long among
the Koho, perhaps too long. Later he had broken the mirror.
He hoped it did not mean bad luck.

He was very tired and sleep was close. But there remained
Saigon and Yé's pledge to be thought about. Saigon. The
Caravelle and clean sheets and all the hot water you wanted.
Espresso on the Rue Catinat, with the delicate, flower-like
Annamese girls cycling by in their pastel-colored trousers
and figure-clinging *ao-dais*. Books to read, newspapers from
the States delivered to your room in the morning with the too
strong coffee and brioche, and weekends at Sans Souci with
Marc. Harry knew that he was lousy, ridden with intestinal
parasites, and shot through with malaria. It had been a long
time since he had enjoyed the pleasures of Saigon and he
realized that he wanted them.

The business of the pledge was another thing. He was
certain in his own mind that Yé meant precisely what he had
said, that the Koho and the rest of the hill tribes would not
fight unless they had a firm promise of autonomy from Saigon,
a pledge which he himself would guarantee. It was not, he
decided, something he could get around by making alternative
offers to Yé and Hamon. What had happened at the ambush
indicated that there was no real enthusiasm among the montagnards for the partisan movement as presently constituted.
They had to be given more of a stake in the fight. Yet he was
not at all sure that Ngo Dinh Diem was prepared to go that
far, although Englehardt had convinced him that the Vietnamese president was aware of the complexity and importance
of the montagnard situation and anxious to do what he could
to bring the hill tribes into the war. It was a question of how
far Diem was willing to go. The easiest thing, Harry reckoned, would be to give Yé his pledge and then work to see
what could be done to make the promise good. But he could
not bring himself to do that. And it was not just a question
of the old man on the porch at Leesburg and what he would
have done and said. His father's time had passed and with it
had died many of its values. Dostoevski had asked: what son
does not desire his father's death? And that went for the
father's values, too. But some still remained. The Koho had
bound him with their trust. It was easy enough to give one's
word if one could keep the problem in the abstract, and it was
a cardinal rule of his work that all problems should remain

abstract, all relationships impersonal. Yet neither Ilouha nor Yé nor Mektoub, with his wrecked shoulder, nor even villainous, old Hamon with his red-rimmed, lizard's eyes, were abstract any more. For him, even the country had changed. The Koho hills now were more than just a map coordinate. He knew the people who lived in the hills and the secret places where the water ran swift and white and he knew how the hills smelled and looked in the early morning light, when the sun came up out of the South China Sea, and the forest was just beginning to stir.

All this created a problem. The answer to that problem lay in Saigon and there, he reckoned, he would have to go. Because this time he wanted to be very sure that all the cards were on the table. As Yé had said, there had been too many betrayals.

When Ilouha came to him with the food, he had almost dropped off to sleep. He refused the food and pulled her down beside him. She stroked his cheek gently and ran her fingers through his hair, whispering to him. He could feel her moving close to him to give him warmth, pulling the blanket of roebuck hides over them. The fire flickered low but did not go out and, comforted by the warmth of her next to him, he slept.

CHAPTER FOUR

HARRY COLTART LAY naked on his bed on the sixth floor of the Hotel Caravelle. He had taken three showers and now he felt almost clean and very tired. He had shaved and, as he glanced at the mirror fixed to the opposite wall, he realized that several years had disappeared with the beard. The man in the mirror, so nonchalant in his knobby, white nakedness, looked quite young, except for his slate-gray eyes. The eyes had a flat, inert quality to them. They did not seem to reflect light. It was as if they had once looked upon something and, having seen it, resolved never to look again. He noticed that this peculiarity, this personal form of stigmata, made some people, particularly his fellow countrymen, ill at ease, as if they feared he might tell a foul joke in mixed company. The French did not seem to mind so much. They were an old and defeated people, used to death, as were the Vietnamese. But to Americans it was unpardonable for a man to walk around with death written in his eyes. Indecent exposure, Harry thought. He wasn't quite sure when his eyes had acquired this quality. Perhaps it had always been there. But he knew that Korea had effected a fundamental, almost chemical change in him. Or was the whole thing a figment of his imagination, an attempt to dramatize himself? He knew he had that weakness, had fought against it for years. He recognized that this tendency probably had more than a little to do with his joining the Agency, with his crazy need to play Lawrence to a bunch of reluctant Southeast Asian "Arabs." Get off it, he muttered to himself. Yé was no Faisal, Englehardt no Storrs. The whole concept of the montagnard movement was narrow, restricted, small scale. Always had been. Never had there been any question of autonomy or nationhood, nor could there be: the hill tribes could not run a county council, let alone a nation. They were, when all was said and done, a montage of ignorant, dirty savages bound together only by their distrust and hate for the Annamese. And yet, and yet

44

. . . To hell with it, he thought to himself. I'm back in Saigon and I'm going to enjoy it. I'm going to get a straight answer from Englehardt to a straight question and that's all I can do. With mock seriousness, he raised his glass in a toast:

"To each Don Quixote, his own windmill," he proposed to the naked man in the mirror, and the man with the lifeless, gray eyes drank with him, his dead eyes peering at him over the edge of his glass.

The Virginian, luxuriously comfortable on the mound of pillows, sipped his beer and watched the Vietnamese workmen whitewashing the old opera house outside his window. The grotesque old building now housed Ngo Dinh Diem's rubber-stamp national assembly. The assembly was not in session and it did not really matter if it ever met again. It was just window dressing, probably always would be no matter who sat in the president's palace. Every new country needed a national assembly, an airline, and a steel mill. It didn't really matter if the assembly met, if anybody rode the airline, or if the mill produced steel. They were just talismans, fetishes, like Yé's bit of tiger collarbone, symbols designed to prove you were nobody's slave. Trouble was that not everybody at home understood that. All the good people at home seemed personally hurt when the locals didn't make proper use of these things. And the locals sometimes struck out in blind unreasoning anger when the fetishes failed them. It was all most unfortunate.

Harry liked the assembly building. Its high, white walls and gray, slanting roof of corrugated iron pierced by circular windows gave it a humorously antiquated, nautical look, as if it were a Vietnamese *Merrimac* stranded on a shoal of hooting traffic. The painters had climbed to the roof on rickety fifty-foot bamboo ladders spliced together with pieces of rope. The ladders swayed so much that some of the men had to steady them at the bottom while the others scrambled up. Finally there was only one man left on the street and nobody was left to hold the ladder for him. He did not come up, but squatted on the sidewalk watching the whirl of the traffic. The workmen crouched on the roof, laughing and talking. One of them leaned far out over the street, swiping at the facade with a brush tied to the end of a bamboo stave, one of his mates holding him by the seat of his ragged trousers. The others horsed around, pretending to push the man who was holding the workman doing the painting. Harry watched them with a terrible fascination, sure that the rotten cloth would give way. Finally, he forced himself to pull his eyes away.

I would like to lie here all day, he thought, clean, and tired, and comfortable, sipping beer, then have a pitcher of martinis and a steak brought up to the room. It would be better to eat in the room rather than going upstairs. He did not want to go upstairs to the Champs Elysees. Although the food was good, he did not like the restaurant's lying, panoramic view of Saigon, with all the stench and blood erased. Every night the city was peppered by grenades and plastiques, and people died full of pain and anger and dull surprise. The next morning, if you were up early and liked to walk the streets before the town was awake, you found them lying face down in the blood-spattered gutters, their guts leaking out, or floating, big bellied, like obscene fish in the canals. Later, before the Americans were up, the police scraped the bodies off the streets or fished them out of the canals with long gaffs and carted them away. After the police had gone, very old women with lined faces splashed water on the sidewalks and swept down the cobblestones with long, sure strokes of homemade brooms. That way, when the boutiques opened and the American wives came to shop, no one was offended.

None of this seeped through the highly polished glass of the Champs Elysees' picture windows. The explosions, if you heard them, were muted, drowned in the music of the orchestra. Not that the explosions weren't appreciated when they were heard. The women seemed to find them stimulating. Harry remembered one of the first nights he'd been in Saigon. A large plastique had exploded on the Rue Vernier, near the Banque de l'Indochine, quite close to the hotel. The conversation in the restaurant had hushed for an instant, as if everyone had taken a deep breath at the same time, and then broken out again in a higher, gayer key. On the faces of the women Harry had seen a flush of color, a new glitter in their eyes, an indefinable sense of excitement in their motions. One, a pretty Frenchwoman with the face of a child, had placed her hand in her escort's, squeezed it tightly and looked up into his face with such an expression of carnal desire and promise that Harry had looked away quickly, as if he had seen something obscene. Early in the morning he'd walked over to the Rue Vernier. The bomb had exploded among the market stalls, the force of the concussion puffing out the flickering oil lamps, the light of which he remembered as playing on the faces of the market women as if they'd been painted by a Vietnamese

LaTour. The bomb had been a big one and the explosion had pounded the marketplace into a jelly of squashed mangoes, splinters, melons, vegetables, human flesh, and excrement. The sphincter was the most dependable of muscles. No matter how suddenly death came, it always seemed to find time for its final, expressive protest. You could not surprise the sphincter. It was never off guard. Since that morning, Harry had gone no more to the Champs Elysees.

He would have liked to lie on his bed at the Caravelle all day, and then to have the steak and martinis brought to the room. But he knew he had to see Englehardt. Englehardt would know by now that he was in Saigon and would wonder why he hadn't come. At the "safe" village at the foot of the escarpment he'd radioed for a helicopter and gotten one within an hour. The chopper ride to Bien Hoa had been a matter of minutes. Then a quick shower, a change of clothes, a brief report to Murkland, the communications man, and another chopper to Saigon. Murkland would have been in contact with Englehardt by now. Harry wondered what Englehardt would say to Yé's demand. Englehardt attached great importance to the closing of the mountain trails. But whether he could get Diem to agree to autonomy for the montagnards was another question. Even if Diem did make such a promise, how was he to know that the pledge would be honored? When you got right down to it, it was Harry Coltart who was going to be giving his word to the hill tribes. Englehardt, he decided, would be able to tell if Diem was lying. He had known the President since the days when Diem had been an anti-French nationalist. And what about Englehardt? How far could he be trusted? Harry smiled at his own scepticism. Ramsey Englehardt could be trusted all the way. Harry knew that. Englehardt had proved that in Guatemala when the Dos Lobos operation had fallen apart. He had demonstrated it again at the time of Budapest in the Kiernan affair. Earlier in the year, Englehardt had pulled Thompson out of Laos rather than seeing him blown. That was why everybody liked to work for Englehardt. You could trust him. Harry had spent nearly half of his ten years with the Agency working for Englehardt and he knew enough to trust him. If Englehardt said Diem was acting in good faith, then he was.

The thought made Harry feel better. He finished his beer, got up and dressed quickly. The sooner he got onto Englehardt the better. Although he had no papers with him, he checked the room out of habit, took the elevator to the lobby, and walked quickly out into the street.

"A taxi, please, Abdullah," he said to the Senegalese doorman, "to the A.I.D. building."

"Oui, monsieur." Abdullah blew importantly on his silver whistle and Harry saw again the coolie floating on his stomach in the ford, the current tugging at his shorts. He erased the scene from his mind with annoyance. He was becoming too filled with associations, his memory crowded with enough recollections to last a lifetime. It is a part of our problem, he thought. We see too much and we know too much and finally there is no part of us left for living in the present. It was not a good thing.

"C'est ici, monsieur."

He tipped the Senegalese and crammed himself into the blue and cream Renault. The damned thing, like all Saigon's taxis, seemingly had been designed to carry two midgets and a briefcase. Abdullah spoke to the driver in his wonderful Afro-Vietnamese French patois and the man nodded, engaged the gears with a jerk, and pulled out into the stream of traffic, disregarding the languid, formal gestures of the little, white-clad Annamese policeman standing on his podium under a red and white striped umbrella.

The Rue Catinat was jammed. Peugeots and Citroens, their horns blaring, jockeyed for position with a huge and gaudy Buddhist hearse built on a truck chassis. A Frenchman with a wispy, existentialist beard, his buttocks like fat sausages in his abbreviated shorts, his shirt open to the navel, whirred by on a motorcycle, past a long column of olive-green American military trucks. Some of the trucks towed rocket launchers. Hardware. That always was the American answer to a deteriorating situation. But you couldn't defeat a grievance or kill a lie with a rocket launcher. If we're losing this war, Harry thought, it's because we're using the wrong weapons. The huge vehicles dwarfed the tiny Annamese perched behind their steering wheels, making them look ineffective and child-like. Behind the trucks were two jeeps loaded with American Special Forces officers in combat fatigues and jaunty green berets. For them the war was a postgraduate course in their craft, a prerequisite for promotion, an opportunity to prove their competence. Just like Spain, Harry thought. Vietnam gives us the chance to test our men, our tactical theories, our weapons. Most of the Vietnamese, unfortunately, could not regard the war in this light.

The sidewalks of the Catinat were wide and gracious, built
to accommodate tables. But there had been no tables on the
sidewalks for years. The Vietminh and the Vietcong had seen
to that. Now you drank indoors, behind wire mesh screens
designed to deflect grenades. The sidewalk was jammed with
Annamese businessmen in tightly cut French suits with narrow
cuffs and shoes with pointed toes, and girls in pastel-colored
silk trousers and hip-hugging *ao-dais,* slit to the thighs on
either side, their faces protected from the sun by mushroom-
like hats of glazed straw tied under their chins with velvet
ribbons. Harry wondered how many of them were filles de
joie. Most of the prettiest ones were, he reckoned. With
thousands of Frenchmen still in the country and sixteen
thousand young American soldiers on hand, there was an
inflated demand for pretty Annamese girls. White women did
not do well in the tropics. They either became hard, angular,
and shrewish, or they got fat and sluggish. But the Annamese
girls remained delicate as birds, remote, cool, enticing.
Threading their way through the businessmen and the girls,
coolies jogged, shouting for gangway, balancing on their
shoulders springy bamboo yokes from either end of which
bobbed baskets filled with fruit, fish, or vegetables. In the
garden running between the double avenues of the Rue
Catinat, sidewalk photographers with ancient cameras mount-
ed on tripods snapped pictures of shy Vietnamese lovers;
armed police looking for plastiques strolled in pairs among the
bicycles parked in the public racks, and vendors hawked bal-
loons towering above them like twenty-foot multicolored
mushrooms. An old Chinese amah, dressed in black trousers
and high-collared white jacket, stood under a banner exhorting
Vietcong terrorists to surrender, each hand firmly grasp-
ing a wriggling little French boy dressed in a sailor suit.
The amahs, Harry thought, with their broad, high foreheads
and their hair pulled back tightly and wrapped into a small
bun, always manage to look prim, intelligent, and stern.
Away in the distance, beyond the formally trimmed hedges
and palm trees of the garden, on the other side of the flower
market, stood the barbed wire barricades and tanks parked
outside the Gia Long temporary palace. The old palace had
been virtually destroyed in the last abortive coup. It lay in
ruins over by the cathedral. Through the open window of the
taxi, a rich olfactory mosaic composed of urine, fish, vegetable
matter, sweat, and sunlight hit Harry in the face. The busy
street echoed with the blaring of horns, the tinkling of bicycle

bells, and the shouts of the pedicab coolies and sidewalk vendors. After months in the hills the din and jostle of the Catinat
was both fascinating and startling. In the hills, things were
much simpler: you slept, you ate, you made love, you walked,
you killed. That was all. In this city where your shoes
sprouted green whiskers of mold overnight if you forgot to
leave the light burning in your closet, things were different,
more complex. Yet it was here, in the city, that the fate of
the mountain people was to be decided. Here there was
room for neither Don Quixotes nor windmills. It was Englehardt and Diem who held the keys to the kingdom.

He paid off the taxi-driver and clambered out of the
Renault.

CHAPTER FIVE

HARRY WROTE ENGLEHARDT'S name and his own on the printed visitor's slip and, as an afterthought, scribbled "rural water supplies" on the line marked "purpose of visit," rather than leaving it blank. The young Marine guard, Germanic with his shaven head, heavily starched khaki shirt and well-pressed blue trousers, accepted the slip without comment, glanced at it and dialed three digits on his telephone. Through the double doors which opened onto the platform at the back of the building, Harry watched without interest coolies unloading large and apparently heavy sacks from an A.I.D truck. It had nothing to do with him.

"You can go up, sir," the young Marine was saying, "second floor and to your left. Room 204. Return this slip when you leave, please."

Harry nodded, stuffed the slip in his pocket, and walked slowly up the steps, thinking about what he was going to say to Englehardt. He found 204, knocked twice and opened the door.

"Mr. Coltart?" inquired a plump American woman turning from her typing. "Go right in. Mr. Englehardt's expecting you."

He tapped on the door to Englehardt's inner office and entered without waiting for a reply. The heavy-set man had risen from his desk and was halfway around it, his hand extended in welcome, before Harry had closed the door behind him.

"Harry! Good to see you! Sit you down! Coffee, or something stronger? You've been having quite a time with your Hatfields and McCoys!" Englehardt wrung his hand vigorously and rumpled a shaggy mane of gray hair with the other, his blue eyes sparkling and merry.

"Coffee'll be fine, Mr. Englehardt." He's put on weight, Harry thought, and he looks tired. Englehardt's fleshy face was pale and lined, and there were dark circles under his eyes.

51

Harry sat down in the chair next to Englehardt's desk. The older man returned to his seat, picked up the telephone, and pushed one of several buttons at its base.

"Julia," he said, his eyes still fixed on Harry's, "let us have a couple of coffees, will you?" He raised his bushy eyebrows at Harry in interrogation.

"Cream, no sugar, please," Harry said.

"One black, one white, no sugar in either, Julia." Englehardt replaced the receiver and smiled.

"From the looks of you, you could use a bit of sugar, Harry. When you're as old and fat as I am, every calorie ends up right here," he said, patting his belt buckle. "But you, you're young and you burn it off."

"I've gotten out of the habit."

"Yes, and picked up some new ones, according to Murkland." Harry flushed.

"You're the one who told me to take a Koho woman if Yé offered me one." The older man laughed easily, fumbling with his tobacco pouch.

"Just pulling your leg, son. How's it going up there? Your first reports looked pretty encouraging, but we hadn't heard from you for some time. You're okay aren't you, Harry? Physically I mean." Good old Englehardt the mother hen. He always looked after his men.

"Sure, I'm fine. My stomach gave me some trouble until I got used to the chow, and I had a bit of malaria. But I'm okay now."

The door opened and the plump secretary entered carrying a brown plastic tray.

"Our coffee. Julia, this is Harry Coltart."

Harry got to his feet and shook hands. When the door had closed behind the secretary, he lit a cigarette and waited for Englehardt to pick up the conversation again. He didn't want to have to talk about the montagnard question until he had to.

"Now, then, Harry, what brings you here?" Englehardt asked. "Problems?"

"Yes. A bit of a problem." Keep it straight, he said to himself, keep all your cards on the table. Englehardt will play it square, just as he did in the Kiernan affair. Everybody in the Agency knew how Englehardt had backed up Kiernan in his refusal to make contact with Imre Nagy unless he could give the Hungarian rebels firm assurance of military assistance.

"Right. Shoot." Englehardt leaned back in his chair, his eyes on Harry.

"It's the Koho. Yé says they won't fight unless they get autonomy." He studied Englehardt to see what effect his words might have, but the older man's face registered neither surprise nor emotion.

"That's a big order. Can't you talk them out of it?"

"I don't think so. And if the Koho don't fight, none of the other tribes will." Englehardt struck a match and lit his pipe. He's getting old, Harry thought.

"I don't know that Diem will buy that."

"That's what they want."

"Mmmm. McPherson and Eisenberg say the same thing about the Jarai and the Sadang. It makes things damned difficult. How've things been going up to now?"

Harry inhaled deeply and snubbed out the cigarette in a large, silver ashtray on Englehardt's desk. He recognized it as the one Englehardt's people had given him after Dos Lobos.

"Not too badly. The whole thing's hinged on Yé. And Ilouha's made a big difference. With the language and all," he added lamely.

Englehardt nodded, a smile playing at the edges of his mouth.

"A woman can be a help. But don't go getting yourself involved emotionally, Harry. You're a pro and this Koho thing is just another job for you. Remember that."

"I know that." There was a brief uncomfortable silence.

"Good. Keeping personalities out of it is one of the hardest parts of our business. But if you don't, you'll get burned the way Tom Kiernan did. And I'm too close to retirement for another deal like that. Now: what about your operations?"

"Things went well at first. But the last couple have flopped. The Koho just aren't interested unless they can get a pledge of autonomy. You know how they feel about the Annamese."

Englehardt stood up and paced slowly back and forth in front of the window, the striped light through the Venetian blinds playing on his bowed head.

"Sure, I know. I also know how the Tyroleans of the *Alto Adige* feel about the Italians. I know how the Karens and Kachins feel about the Burmans, the Kurds about the Iraqis, the Berbers about the Algerian Arabs, the Masai about the Kikuyus."

The older man walked over to a large wall map of Vietnam and stood studying it, his back to Harry, his hands clasped behind him.

"I could go on indefinitely, Harry," he continued. "Every

country has its ethnic minorities. And every ethnic minority has grievances. But they each can't have a separate state. It wouldn't make sense."

"It makes sense to the Koho," Harry countered, "and we're the ones who're asking them to fight."

Englehardt returned to his chair.

"Listen, Harry. This just isn't the time. Diem is in trouble. The reporters and half the people at the embassy are after him. Nhu's strategic hamlet program isn't working out. Something's going on with the Buddhists and I've a pretty good idea what it is. Your friend McWhorter, I might add, isn't helping much."

"McWhorter? Is he here?" When he'd seen him before, McWhorter had been based in Hong Kong.

Englehardt nodded.

"Based here now, lives at the Caravelle. He's playing footsy with the Buddhists. They're using him and the *Express* for their own ends, ends which don't happen to coincide with those of the U.S. government."

"Some aspects of the Diem regime are pretty shady, sir," Harry replied. A flush came over Englehardt's puffy cheeks.

"Damn it, Harry, I know that. I also know the man's strong points. He's tough, intelligent, and has the will to fight. Finally, I know, if John McWhorter doesn't, that there's no alternative to Diem."

Harry held no strong views on the subject. He knew that the newspapers and the people back home had a tendency to throw their hands up in horror at the actions of any authoritarian regime, and Diem's certainly was that. On the other hand, what Englehardt said made sense. You had to work with what you had. That Vietnam existed at all was a tribute to Diem. When he'd returned from exile in America, there'd been no functioning administration, no executive machinery. The army had been completely demoralized, the police and the internal security forces in the hands of the Binh Xuyen river pirates, who'd bought the concession from the old emperor. The Cao Dai and Hoa Hao sects, Harry recalled, had been in control of most of the country not held by the Communists. Handed a truncated country cut off from its northern industrial base, Diem had been saddled with a million refugees fleeing from North Vietnam. Somehow Diem had shaken up the army, crushed the sects and the river pirates, established an administration, and absorbed the refugees. Rice and rubber production, Harry knew, was way up despite the war. Government revenues had doubled, school enrollments had tripled, as had health facilities. Yes, he had to admit that Englehardt had a point. Diem might not be loved but he was both respected and feared. He fulfilled the one basic prerequisite of any national leader: he ruled. And there was nobody else in sight.

"We could lose this war," Englehardt continued. "And if we lose it, we've lost all Southeast Asia, from Cambodia to Indonesia. Diem is our only hope, Harry. So the Agency is with him right down the line."

"And what about my montagnards?"

Englehardt chewed his knuckles, studying Harry carefully before he spoke.

"They won't fight without autonomy? They can't be bought with something else? Gold? Guns?"

Harry shook his head.

"What do they want, specifically?"

"A promise from Diem that government troops won't come into the hills without their permission. A veto on road building. Regulation of Annamese traders. Recognition of tribal law as valid in the highlands. And they want my word that Diem will keep his promise."

Englehardt gave a low whistle. "It's asking a lot, Harry."

"They know that. They say we're asking a lot from them. They don't see that they've got much of a quarrel with the Vietcong."

"I see."

"One other thing," Harry added. "I think we ought to play this one completely straight. If Diem won't cooperate, tell me and I'll do what I can to keep the Koho in the war. But I'm not going to make them any promises we can't keep."

"You feel pretty strongly about this, don't you?" Englehardt said.

Harry nodded. "That's the way it is."

Englehardt pushed his coffee aside untasted and strummed on his desk with a pencil, his eyes on the ceiling.

"Well, McPherson and Eisenberg say about the same thing. Neither the Jarai nor the Sadang seem much interested in the fighting. But it'll take a helluva lot of doing. Tell you what, how long has it been since you were in Saigon?"

"About three months."

"You're looking a bit frayed about the edges. Take a week's leave. Beat up the town. Go see your friend Michaud. Shoot a tiger, get laid. Meanwhile, I'll see Diem. Maybe I can talk him into it."

Harry knew it was the best he could hope for. If Englehardt put it strongly enough to Diem, the President might come through. Having McPherson and Eisenberg's reports to substantiate his own should help.

"The Koho want a straight answer, sir. They deserve one."

Englehardt eyed him carefully and then wagged a finger reassuringly.

"I'll get them one. Be back a week from tomorrow. If Diem'll play, I'll know by then."

Harry rose to his feet. "I'll need papers," he said, "for Michaud's."

"I'll have money and movement papers sent around to you at the Caravelle tonight. Now get out of here. I've got work to do."

"Thank you, sir. Thank you very much." He'd done all he could for Yé, for Ilouha, for all of them. Now it was up to Englehardt. He closed the door behind him, nodded to the secretary, and walked downstairs, turning in the slip to the Marine guard.

As he walked out the gate of the A.I.D. compound, another man entered, walking fast, his eyes on the ground, and the two men collided.

"Sorry," Harry said.

"Harry, you old bastard, welcome home! Still peddling rural water supplies?"

"Hello, John, how are you?" Harry asked.

"Not bad. Look: I've got an appointment at the pagoda in half an hour. But I'm free after that. What about lunch at the My Canh? Meet me at the Caravelle and we can share a taxi."

He had nothing else to do.

"Sure," he said to McWhorter, "the Caravelle in an hour."

CHAPTER SIX

LOYE THE RHADÉ gave no sign of acknowledgement when
Phan Duc whispered to him that he was wanted at the pagoda.
He maintained the rhythm of the unloading, not indicating
that he had heard. He had learned not to question or to dis-
cuss instructions when they were relayed by Phan Duc. To
do so produced no further information, perhaps because the
man knew no more. But Loye knew that what Phan Duc
told him came from higher up and was meant to be obeyed.
Many strange things had he seen and heard in the months he
had been in Saigon, working on the loading platform of the
American Aid Mission, and he sensed that much more was in
store for him before he could return to his hills with the news
that the *Bocs* were gone, Diem's puppet government overthrown, that a new age had dawned. What that new age
might bring he could not say, but he was sure in his heart that
it would be better than the old. Were not the Vietminh and
the Vietcong one? The first had fought to oust the French,
the second was sworn to defeat the Americans and Diem,
their puppet. Did not the Vietcong stand for that which every
Vietnamese wanted: rights for ethnic and religious minorities,
an end to corruption and venality, the crushing of the land-
lords, the lowering of taxes? Sometimes Loye wondered
whether the Vietcong would be able to do all that it intended,
to fulfill all its promises. There was so much to be done and
so little with which to do it. Yet he knew from the lectures
he attended at night in the lumber godown in Cholon, the
Chinese sector, that history fought on the side of the people.
The comrades had warned them that the new age would
come neither easily nor quickly, but they promised that inevitably all the peoples of the world would know justice and
plenty. It was the task of each of them to hasten that day. In
the evenings after the lectures, as he lay curled on the floor
above the bicycle repair shop, in the small room which he
shared with four other comrades, Loye often thought of that

57

distant age, proud that there was a role for him to play in the achieving of it. Few of the Rhadé understood the meaning of the movement. Many of the hill tribes still harbored reactionary sentiments as he, to his shame, once had. But even he, he who had borne arms against the Vietminh, had been redeemed by the movement. So should they be redeemed. One day the people of the hills would take pride in the name of Loye, he promised himself. All that was bad, and there was much of this, would have to be swept away. But the good could be retained. His personal dream was of schools. There would be a school in each village and no montagnard child would grow up, as he had, unable to read and write, ignorant of the world and the Party. He was not yet a member of the Party but he was very close to membership and he wanted it badly. He knew he was making progress. Comrade Tran had complimented him more than once on this. Soon he would be permitted to join. Loye knew he must fight and study and work for the coming of the new age, but still he longed for the hills of the Rhadé, for the forests of his youth, for his people, for the life of the longhouse. It had been many years since he had been back and the absence of these things was a dull ache in his chest. He did not sleep well in Saigon with its noise and its bustle, its heat and the indecent proximity of the Annamese comrades with whom he shared the stifling room above the bicycle shop. It was in those night hours that he ached for the coolness of the hills. Although he now knew, as the Party had taught him, that the Annamese were his friends, not his enemies, as the *Bocs* and old chiefs had told him as a boy, he hungered for the company of his own people. Even as he toiled on the loading platform, Loye hungered for his people, as an unlucky hunter hungers for the liver of the roebuck which eludes him. He put the thought out of his mind angrily. He would have to report himself to Comrade Tran, and the revelation that he still harbored reactionary tribal emotions would set back his progress toward Party membership. Comrade Tran would be very disappointed.

So he was to go to the pagoda. Phan Duc had not said whether he was to go at noon, when work stopped on the platform, or to wait until the end of the day. He would go at noon. The Party did not like to be kept waiting. Meanwhile, he kept to his task of unloading the big American trucks. They contained rice in sixty-pound sacks marked with a pair of clasped hands. It was his job to tell Comrade Tran when a big shipment of rice arrived and, if he could, to discover the destination of outgoing shipments. Phan Duc, who had worked longer on the platform than he, was a very clever man. Phan Duc had been able to get hold of the key to the rice godown long enough for a wax impression to be made. Loye knew that other comrades entered the godown from time to time and defaced the markings on the sacks or added Vietcong symbols to the bags. Phan Duc said that sometimes the comrades added something to the rice that made the people who ate it ill. Usually, he said, this was done only to rice allotted to military garrisons. But sometimes other people ate the adulterated rice. When they became ill, they blamed the Americans. Or they feared to eat the American rice when it was given to them again. In either case, they were made aware of the power of the Vietcong.

Loye wondered if they grew much rice in America and if the lives of the peasants were hard. None of the Americans he had seen looked like peasants. They were all very large, bigger even than the French. Loye had never seen a French peasant but Comrade Tran had told him that there were such people. He supposed that this was right, because he had seen many French soldiers at the time of the fighting against Ho Chi Minh. Not just officers but common soldiers like himself. All of the Americans seemed to be officers. Perhaps there were no peasants in America. He would ask Comrade Tran. Comrade Tran had been to Singapore and was a very wise man. He would know. After the war is finished, Loye thought, I will go to Singapore. But first I will go back to the Rhadé hills and build a school. Then I will go to Singapore.

The work on the loading platform was hard but Loye liked it. There was a rhythm to it and a pleasure in seeing the trucks emptied and the sacks piled neatly on the platform. He did not feel like a coolie, because he had the other job, the important task of telling Comrade Tran about the rice shipments. It was just another way of fighting, Tran told him. Still, he was a soldier and he would be glad one day to get back to the business of fighting. Work on the platform was almost restful after the delta. Loye knew he had not been of much help to his battalion in the delta. All of his fighting with the French against the Vietminh had been in the hills. The fishlike life of the swamps was strange to him and twice he had fallen ill. Still he had learned much that was new to him and had repolished the knowledge the French had given him. He knew how to lay out the aiming stakes for a mortar, how to level the bubble in the sight, how to drop the heavy shells down the pipe. He could fire the SKZ recoilless rifle and build a simple box-mine. Machine guns and grenades he had already known about. He had learned to keep his head down when an airplane flew overhead, because he now knew his face reflected light. They had shown him how to fire at the planes they called helicopters, leading them a bit as a hunter leads his quarry. Having served with the French, he was a better shot than most of the Vietcong, he thought with pride. Also there was much that he could teach the Annamese comrades about man traps, although many of these could be used only in the forest, where you had trees from which to hang the traps. Those of the pit type were useful in the delta, however. Perhaps I do not have to be entirely ashamed of my performance in the delta, he thought to himself. Otherwise, why should I have been assigned to the tactical school in Cholon on nights when there were no indoctrination lectures at the lumber godown? Of plastiques he knew very little, for this explosive was a thing of the cities and he had not fought in the cities. He was just as glad. He did not like the idea of leaving a bicycle loaded with plastiques in a crowded market. He would do it if he were ordered to, he guessed, but he did not like the idea of women and children being killed. He had not had to do these things. Saigon for him meant working on the loading platform, conveying information about the rice to Comrade Tran, attending ideological lectures, and studying at the tactical school. Of these he preferred the last. It meant that he might someday get a command of his own, a small one, of course, but nevertheless a command. This he wanted. He was a soldier, not an Annamese coolie. The tactical course was almost over and the comrade who taught it was pleased with him. Perhaps it would not be long before he got his command. He had, after all, been a corporal once.

The summons to the Xa Loi Pagoda meant nothing to Loye. He was not a Buddhist and never had been in the pagoda, although he trotted by it every day on the three-mile journey from his room above the bicycle shop to the loading platform. Nor did he know what connection the pagoda might have with the Party or with the National Liberation Front within which the Party worked. Comrade Tran had told him that the headquarters of the National Front was in Saigon but he had not told him where it was or mentioned the names of the leaders. Loye did not want to know. Comrade Tran dispensed information the way a miser hands out gongs and studded shields, grudgingly, fearfully, almost bitterly, as if he were personally diminished by the giving of the information. Although Loye sometimes suspected that Comrade Tran pretended to be protecting information which he did not have, to give himself importance in the eyes of the younger Vietcong, Loye approved of his reluctance to speak. If you fell into the hands of Diem's police, it was better not to know too much. The lights burned all night inside the sad, gray walls of the Sûreté, and Loye knew what went on inside those walls. Occasionally bodies turned up on the rubbish heap outside the walls of the Sûreté. Once Loye had helped to carry away one of these bodies. The comrade had had only bloody sores where his fingernails had been and his body was covered with small burns. His teeth were broken into ragged slivers and the man's scrotum was swollen to the size of the sweet melons the old women sell in Cholon market. This was the work of the man they called Mong Le. There was no one in Saigon who did not know his name. Sometimes it was better not to have too much information.

There was much that Loye did not understand about the organization of the movement. He knew that men who were not Communists held high positions in the National Liberation Front. He knew that many who fought with the Vietcong or at least cooperated with it were not Communists. But Comrade Tran had explained that Party members held all the vital posts within the National Liberation Front, all the important Vietcong commands. The Party, Tran had explained, was the spearhead in all things. Could the Buddhists of the Hoi Phat Giao Nam Viet, whose headquarters Loye knew was the Xa Loi Pagoda, be a part of the National Liberation Front? Could the two organizations be the same thing? He did not know; perhaps he was about to find out.

When the Annamese foreman blew his whistle at noon, most of the coolies threw down the sacks of rice they were carrying, curled up on top of them and went to sleep. Those who had rice squatted in the shade against the wall of the compound and chewed their rice with the stolid concentration of hungry men. Those who had no rice never watched the eating of those who did, not wishing to make them feel uncomfortable. Although that portion of his wages which he did not turn over to Comrade Tran for the Party was enough to provide him with rice, Loye never brought food to the compound. Even though the men did not look, he did not like to eat in the presence of men who had no food. In the hills, he who had no food had a right under the laws of courtesy to eat with those who did. But in the city it was different. The city knew no law.

Loye wiped the sweat from his forehead and showed his work pass to the guard at the entrance to the A.I.D. compound. He did it only out of habit and courtesy: the guard was a Party member and knew him well. It had been with the guard's help that Phan Duc had been able to make the impression of the key to the rice godown. Turning left, Loye walked the short block to the wrought-iron gate of the pagoda. The gate was guarded by two young bonzes in saffron-colored robes, their heads shaved. Both men looked very strong and carried wooden staves. Loye guessed that, like most of the monks in the pagoda, they had been bonzes only for a short time. Comrade Tran had told him that it was usual for every Buddhist to spend at least a few months sometime in his life as a monk. Even Buddhist members of the Vietcong did this. Often it was convenient for a man much sought after by Mong Le's Sûreté to seek the sanctuary and anonymity of the saffron robe. Loye had seen the famous one-columned pagoda in Hanoi and knew that Ho Chi Minh's Communist regime had restored the damage done to it during the war against the French. But he also knew that the Party regarded the monks as social parasites. Not being a Buddhist, this attitude did not shock Loye. Buddhism was nothing to him, but he admired the Xa Loi Pagoda. With the many curlicues on its towers and the pieces of brightly colored glass cemented into its yellow stucco walls, it struck him as a building of true grandeur. The montagnard schools of his dreams resembled it in many respects.

Loye did not know who he should ask for at the pagoda. But a fat monk was sitting cross-legged by the steps leading up to the entrance to the building and Loye walked up to him.

"I am Loye the Rhadé," he announced. The fat bonze said nothing but gestured to one of the young monks guarding the gate. The young monk led him wordlessly into the cool darkness of the pagoda, through a warren of passages. The building was full of yellow-robed monks. Some squatted, talking together in low tones. Others sat alone in silent contemplation, their eyes staring and unseeing. Still others sat copying manuscripts at a long row of rough desks. From another part of the pagoda came the clashing of gongs and a wailing chant. Once through an open door Loye saw two bonzes, their shaven heads and bare shoulders glistening with sweat, working a creaking machine which spat out pieces of paper with words printed upon them. Finally the young bonze opened a small, unmarked door, entered and motioned to Loye to follow him.

In one corner of the room, which was lit by a single electric bulb hanging from the ceiling by a cord, a very old monk, so thin that his limbs stuck out from under his yellow robe like sticks, sat cross-legged on the floor. He was smoking, taking deep, long pulls on a bamboo pipe with a silver bowl. Another bonze was hovering over a spirit lamp, preparing another pipe. Loye recognized the acrid odor of burning opium and, despite himself, felt an expression of contempt working its way across his face. He glanced guiltily around to see if anyone had noticed this breach of manners.

A middle-aged bonze sat at a wooden table. Muscles rippled under the skin of his naked left shoulder and Loye guessed that, like the guards at the gate, this one had not always been a monk. Clearly he was an educated man, Loye noted with a mixture of envy and respect, because the table was littered with papers and pencils. As the man at the table studied him, Loye saw that he had a hard, thin mouth and wide-set, intense eyes. This one, Loye thought to himself, is a leader. You could tell not only by the eyes and the mouth but by the way the man held his head. He was accustomed to giving orders, not taking them. The bonze pushed aside the papers upon which he had been working and motioned Loye to a rickety chair beside the table.

"Take this one away," he said to the bonze at the spirit lamp, indicating the old man in the corner, "and see that he gets as much as he needs."

"You do not approve of opium?" he asked, addressing himself to Loye, while the other monks shuffled from the room on sandaled feet. He spoke in Annamese, with the accent of Hué.

"No."

"Nor does the Party. But it has its uses. That old one was a Communist when you were nothing but a naked puppy playing in your father's longhouse."

Loye said nothing. It was possible he had made a mistake but he was not going to listen to talk of "naked puppies."

"He is old and broken now," the bonze continued, "like a toothless tiger. But he has one more service to render to the Party, the final service. There is no need for him to suffer unduly. The opium will make it easier for him."

Loye did not understand. "Who are you?" he asked.

"That need not trouble you. You may call me Comrade Thuc, although that is not my name. You are Loye the Rhadé?"

"I am Loye."

Loye searched desperately in his mind for what he might have done to warrant disciplinary action. He could think of nothing. Relieved, it came to him that the interview might have something to do with a new assignment. The bonze shuffled the papers in front of him and pulled from the pile one which he placed before him. He studied it for a minute and then spoke, his eyes still fixed on the paper.

"You are of the southern Rhadé?"

"Yes, but the Party teaches us not to think in terms of tribes."

The bonze made a gesture of impatience. "Yes, yes. But your home *is* in the south of the Rhadé country? Your father *is* Cheo, chief of the country to the south of Banmethuot?"

Loye did not like the direction of the interrogation. There always was the possibility that he was to be held hostage for the good behavior of the Rhadé. Had he been in the position of the bonze, he conceded, he would have taken such a step long before.

"Yes," he answered, "Cheo is my father. What's happened to him? Why are you asking me these things?"

The bonze ignored his question and continued to study the paper in front of him.

"You know not only your own country but that of the Koho?"

Loye relaxed a little. It was only an intelligence interrogation. The bonze only wanted information about the highlands.

"The Koho are our cousins. In my youth we often hunted with the Koho, with the people of Yé." How long ago that seemed! Yet even now a Koho girl was promised to him. One day he would return to the highlands to claim her. The thought of the dry-season hunts with the Koho brought to him anew the longing within him for his land, his people.

"Good," the bonze said. "You, too, have a service to perform, Comrade Loye, one which will require courage not of the type which comes from smoking opium."

Loye noticed a trace of a twinkle in the bonze's eye as he spoke of the opium. He was not a bad person, and surely a leader. Loye felt proud that such a one should interview him in preparation for a new assignment.

"I am ready," he said.

"Your record, despite a few reactionary lapses, has been good. I note that you have applied for Party membership. It is the feeling of Comrade Tran that ideologically you are not quite ready for this honor. But you are close. If you do well on this assignment, the matter will be reconsidered. Now: you were captured in the T'ai country of the Democratic Republic of Vietnam in 1953, while acting as a scout for a French Groupement Mixte d'Intervention?"

"Yes." They never forget it, Loye thought, and they never let you forget it.

"And re-educated in Hanoi?"

"Yes. At the Special School for Ethnic Minorities."

"Good. You have received instruction in Party doctrine and have attended the military leadership school at Ankhé. Later you served with a Chu Luc division of the Vietnamese People's Army in Zone V and in the Mekong delta. Comrade Bao tells me that you have been doing well in your tactical course."

Loye felt a flush of pride on his face. He held himself a little straighter in the rickety chair. "Thank you, Comrade," he said.

"Always you have followed. Now you are to lead. How does that strike you?"

Loye could contain himself no longer. He jumped to his feet, placed his hands on the table and leaned across it toward the bonze.

"I am ready, Comrade. I am ready to lead," he said excitedly.

"Sit down. You are not ready. You are being given the job not because you are the perfect man for it but only because you are the best available for this particular task. In any case, there will be many people from whom you will still take orders, your political officer for one. Remember that. Never forget it. Those who lead must also follow. Do not let your pride get the best of you, Loye."

Loye sat down, chastened but still excited. A command! It was what he had wanted. The bonze was speaking again.

"Your people, not just the Rhadé, but all the hill tribes, continue to show reactionary tendencies. Some of them go so far as to give active support to the Americans and Diem's puppet government. This must stop."

Loye said nothing. The reluctance of the montagnards to

give active support to the Vietcong was something of which
he was deeply ashamed.

"This is not entirely the fault of your people," the bonze
went on. "The colonialists kept them locked in their hills.
They used vicious lies to teach you that the Annamese were
your enemies. Why did they do this?"

"To make it easier for them to rule us; to put off the day
when all Vietnamese will be brothers under Ho Chi Minh."
The bonze nodded with satisfaction.

"Exactly. And now the American imperialists are employ-
ing the same tactics. They have sent agents among the
montagnards to try to stir them up against the Vietcong,
against the National Liberation Front, against the Vietnamese
People's Army. They do this thinking the hill tribes are stupid
and can be bought to fight against their brothers in an unjust
war."

"Is there fighting now in the hills?" Loye asked. He did
not dare to think that the bonze was going to send him back
to fight in the highlands. To have a command and to have
it on his own ground was all he could ask for. He tried to
suppress his excitement.

"There is some fighting. The Americans and their lackeys
are trying to stop the coolie trains coming down from the
north. Like the French before them, they will fail, but for
the moment they are causing us some concern. That is why
I have sent for you."

"What can I do?" He knew he had it now. He knew he
was going home. It took a conscious effort of will to concentrate on what the bonze was saying.

"Few of your people have had military training. Yet this
is an assignment which must be given to a local man, for both
political and tactical reasons. You served with the French
and you've fought well since your re-education. You will
take over command of the 301st Sector. It will be your job
to protect the coolie trains in the Rhadé country, in that of
the Gar, and in the northern hills of the Koho. The last
portion of your sector is particularly important. Can you
do it?"

"I can do it, Comrade." Loye felt an immense warmth for
the Party. It gave a man a task to do that meant something
to him. He would not fail the Party. One day he might be
given all of the highlands to command!

"Good. Your main problem will be the Koho part of your
tor. The Americans have sent an agent there. The Koho

call him Erohé, the elephant. You will find him a worthy opponent. He lives with Yé's people and has taken Yé's daughter as his woman."

The bonze's words struck Loye like a blow. For a moment he could say nothing.

"She they call Ilouha?" he asked, knowing the answer, fearing it, but having to have it.

"Yes. I thought this information might be of some interest to you. She had been promised to you, had she not?"

Loye nodded. She had been but a child. The emotion he felt was not jealousy but antagonism toward him they called Erohé, who had stolen what belonged to him by right and custom. It had been a long time ago, but he had not forgotten the girl, for in the hills time means little. Lost was the chance to link the Koho to the Rhadé by bonds of blood, lost because of the American.

"Good," the bonze said, "this will give you a personal interest in the affair. In addition to guarding the coolie trains, I want you to win Yé away from his alliance with the *Boc*. If you can, kill the white man or discredit him in Yé's eyes. Both, if possible."

"This *Boc,* this Erohé, is he now in Yé's village?"

The bonze pushed the papers aside.

"No. He is here in Saigon now. But he will return."

"Why not kill him now?" Loye was anxious for the *Boc's* death. It would be to him as honey from a forest tree to see the *Boc* die.

"Because it is not enough to have him die here," the bonze asserted, drumming with his finger on the table for emphasis. "To kill him, to defeat him here would mean nothing, because the Koho would not see it happen. He must be killed, defeated, discredited in the hills, where the lesson will not be lost on the montagnards. Do you understand?"

"Yes, Comrade." The bonze was right. To see a thing was worth far more than to hear about it. If Erohé were killed here, the Americans would only send another agent. Loye could see that. The important thing was to create such a climate among the Koho that they would refuse to accept another American agent.

"Good. Tomorrow Comrade Tran will bring you a new identity card. Also money. You will take a bus to Nha Trang. There you will be met by a man named Yan. He is half-Koho. He will guide you to your base in the hills."

The bonze stood up, indicating that the interview was over.

"How will I know Yan?" Loye asked.

"He will have a broken pipe-stem in his mouth. Now you must go. I am expecting a *Boc* visitor, an unwitting ally in our struggle. Good luck to you, Loye. The Party has great hopes for you." Loye scrambled to his feet and bowed slightly.

"Thank you, Comrade Thuc," he said. But the bonze already had settled back into his chair and was poring over a paper, the folds of skin on his shaven scalp knotted in concentration.

Loye suppressed a twinge of indignation at his abrupt dismissal. He was to have a command. He was going home. That was all that mattered.

Part Two

THE BONZE

CHAPTER SEVEN

NGO DINH DIEM SAT silently, lost in thought, at his huge, bare desk in his soundproofed office at the Gia Long temporary palace. He had just come from Mass and was in a contemplative mood, the tips of his well-manicured fingers joined in front of his lips as if he were still at prayer. With a sigh, he roused himself from his reverie and pressed a button on his desk. A disembodied voice answered in French from a speaker next to the button.

"Ask my brother to come in," Diem said. Another day begun. He realized that he was tired, that after nearly ten years in power, he was beginning to lose interest in the process of government, in the prosecution of the war. In the early years, there had been a thrust to it, a challenge in the reconstruction of his shattered country. Ruling now seemed to be a question of trying to settle interminable quarrels. Squabbling among the generals. Jealousies within the family. Disagreements with the Americans. He was sick of it all and increasingly had come more and more to depend on Nhu to handle the day-to-day running of the government. He did not know what he would have done without Nhu. Yet the Americans were trying to make him give up his younger brother. The upholstered door opened quietly and Nhu entered, a folder bound with blue leather under his arm, a faint smile on his thin lips. The younger man bowed slightly in front of the President's desk and, at a wave of Diem's hand, seated himself in the straight-backed chair which stood to one side. Although the office was only dimly lit, Nhu wore dark glasses, which gave him the appearance of being masked. He was dressed in a dark suit, which became his slight build, and a conservative tie.

"You slept well?" Nhu inquired.

"Moderately well, thank you. And you?"

"I was up a good deal of the night. Business with Mong Le."

"Well, what have we for today?"

"Here is a resumé of yesterday's operations. And a police report on Buddhist political activities. And there are several appointments." Ngo Dinh Nhu pushed the folder bound in blue leather across the desk to his brother.

"Tell me about it. I don't feel like reading now." One day's resumé was much the same as another's, a catalogue of minor military actions, a listing of villages taken and lost, an account of death and betrayal. He was thoroughly sick of it. Nhu retrieved the folder from the desk, opened it, and scanned its pages while he talked.

"Most of the news is bad. The number of incidents mounts daily . . . here, in the Mekong delta, along the Cambodian frontier. Only Hué is quiet."

"Thank God for Can and Thuc." Can, by western standards, was an ignorant man. His brother had never been outside the country, held no academic degrees, and ran central Vietnam like an old-style war lord. And only there were the Communists finished and on the run. If only I had another like him for the delta, Diem thought to himself. Nhu could do it, but he needed Nhu in Saigon. Part of the credit for the stability of central Vietnam rested with old Thuc, Archbishop of Hué. His elder brother had used the machinery of the Church skillfully in the cause of family and nation. Too skillfully, perhaps. It had cost Thuc the See of Saigon and a cardinal's red biretta, for the Holy Mother Church did not relish being used. There was a time, he mused to himself, when I thought of entering the Church. And it might have been better so. Nhu was the one with the greatest desire and capacity to rule.

"Yes, thank God for Can and Thuc," Nhu was saying. "But the war will not be won or lost in Hué. It will be won here in Saigon, in the delta, and in Washington. I wonder if you should consider going to Washington, or sending one of us, to sound out the Americans' intentions?"

It was a thought, Diem conceded. The continuation of American aid was essential and in recent months he had sensed a weakening in Washington's support for his regime. For all their marvelous technology, Diem thought, the Americans are just big children, obsessed with their civilization of gadgets. And like children, while capable of great generosity, they tend also to be irrational, impatient, inconsistent, unwilling to accept unpalatable facts. It was almost more dangerous to have them as friends than as enemies. And often less profitable. Yes, Nhu was right; somebody should go. But who?

"Perhaps," Diem said. "But I can't go and I can't spare you. The Vatican would not approve of my sending Thuc. Can is unsuitable. What about Tran Le Xuan?" Nhu's wife was as clever and as tough as any of them. She could do it. Nhu scratched his head, his brow wrinkled in concentration.

"That might be an idea," he conceded. "Madame Chiang at one point was able to accomplish a great deal for the Nationalists. A pretty woman appeals to the Americans' sense of chivalry."

"We can decide about this later. What's the Buddhist thing you mentioned?" Diem asked. Nhu snapped the folder shut and replaced it on the President's desk.

"We have information that the Communist bonzes are planning some new sort of demonstration. We don't know its nature but it appears to be important. Whatever it is, it's going to happen soon."

"What steps have you taken?" the President asked.

"I've doubled the guard here and put more riot police into the streets. Until I know the nature of the thing, there's not much more I can do."

"What is the source of the trouble?" Diem inquired, pivoting slowly in his chair.

"The Xa Loi Pagoda. The Hoi Phat Giao Nam Viet is involved."

"Why not raid the pagoda and arrest the leaders of the association?" Religious toleration always had been the rule in Vietnam. If there was trouble with the Buddhists, it could only be a question of a few dissident leaders. These could be dealt with.

"We considered that," Nhu answered. "But it would play into the hands of the Vietcong. Most of the leadership of the association is not Communist. The important thing is to find out definitely who is behind the plotting. With wholesale arrests, we'd run the risk of splitting the country along religious lines."

Diem nodded in agreement.

"That must be avoided at all costs. We've enough on our hands already. What about the Americans?"

"Pressure is building up against Kennedy," Nhu asserted.

"How is this?"

"The Vietcong has been extremely clever. It is using the American correspondents here, particularly McWhorter of the Washington *Express*, to create the illusion that yours is a Catholic government oppressing a Buddhist nation."

Diem clenched his fists in irritation. "Why not pull his visa?" he asked.

"Possibly. But it would provoke an unfavorable reaction in Washington. Perhaps something unfortunate, for which the Vietcong could be held responsible, might happen to him?"

Diem glanced at his brother to make sure that he had understood him correctly. But the younger man was studying the design on the carpet.

"Only in the last resort," Diem replied.

"Yes. The last resort."

"Anything else?"

"More unrest among the Hoa Hao, the Cao Dai and the other sects. The agent the Americans sent to the Koho returned to Saigon today, so something may be up among the montagnards."

"These situations can wait, can't they?"

"Yes. The main thing is the Buddhist plot."

"Keep after that. Do what you want with prisoners already in your hands or those you can pick up quietly. But no wide-scale arrests, no raid on the pagoda. Not yet."

Nhu nodded.

"By the way," he said, "there is one more thing."

"Well? What is it?" Always there was something. One never had the opportunity to read, to reflect. He was anxious to get back to *Bajazet*. There were some amusing parallels between the plot in the seraglio of Murad IV, as depicted by Racine, and his own situation.

"Speaking of the Cao Dai, General Trang is waiting to see you. And General Duc Xien."

"What about?"

"The command of Saigon. Fung Lao must go. One could put up with his corruption and his inefficiency but now he begins to think of himself as a man on horseback."

"What are you going to do with him?"

"I had in mind an ambassadorship."

"All right. But nothing too good. Perhaps a Central American country. Whom do you prefer between Trang and Duc Xien?"

"Duc Xien is the better soldier. Trang will die only by a silver bullet."

Dien laughed. He remembered fat old Trang well, and

the allusion to the silver bullet was well taken: Trang was not famed for his incorruptibility. On the other hand, he was clever and without political ambitions. Duc Xien was both young and vain. Such men could be dangerous.

"If you have no preference," Diem said, "I think I would say Trang. He strikes me as more dependable."

Nhu shrugged his narrow shoulders.

"All right. Since he is Cao Dai, I'd just as soon have him here where I can keep an eye on him, until I get to the bottom of this unrest among the sects. I'll send him in. What shall I do with Duc Xien? He'll wonder why he's been called in."

"Tell him to come back tomorrow and I'll give him a decoration. It will flatter his vanity."

Nhu smiled. "He has most of them."

"Well, then, a cluster for his best medal and a nice citation. You know what I mean."

"I'll take care of it. I'll be back at noon to talk about this afternoon."

Nhu bowed and let himself out the door. Soon, Diem thought, I can get back to *Bajazet*. He admired Racine greatly for the faultless nobility of his alexandrines, for the simplicity of his diction, the psychological realism of his characters, and the skill of his dramatic construction. Odd that even educated Anglo-Saxons, such as the American ambassador, could not appreciate him. He supposed this was attributable to the difference of dramatic conception between the classical tragedy and the English drama. Yet he enjoyed Shakespeare immensely, at least the histories. Odd. Slowly he became aware of a huge bulk standing in front of his desk. General Trang. Yes.

"Good morning, sir," Trang said.

"Good morning, General. Sit down."

"An honor, an honor," Trang mumbled, lowering himself onto the protesting chair. He was tall for a Vietnamese, but very fat, his stomach bulging under the khaki jacket, the left breast of which was a rainbow of decorations. His strong chin was softened by a roll of fat which gave his face the appearance of running without interruption into his neck. The mouth was slack and moist, the lips of a voluptuary. But the iron-gray hair incongruously was cut very short in the military fashion, creating a false note in the man. His eyes were quick and beady, shifting constantly around the room, greedily devouring the richness of the furnishings, seeming to evaluate each of the few art treasures which were the room's only adornment. Diem noted with distaste that Trang was sweating. A bead of perspiration wobbled at the end of his fat nose and brown stains were spreading under each arm of his jacket. Fascinated, Diem studied the drop of perspiration on Trang's nose.

"I am considering a new command for you, General," Diem said.

"A new command?" Trang asked.

"Yes. Would you like that? You've been in command of II Corps, have you not?"

"Yes, my President." He's not sure of himself, Diem thought. There's a note of uncertainty in his voice. He's afraid I may have tired of his corruption, that I may be sending him to the delta or to the Camau peninsula. Let him dangle for a bit.

"These are difficult times, Trang, times which require the utmost in loyalty, honesty, and efficiency from the country's leaders, civilian and military."

Trang pulled a handkerchief from his pocket and mopped his brow. The bead of perspiration continued to teeter at the end of his nose. Diem had an almost uncontrollable desire to tell him to wipe it off.

"If it's that little business of the pay accounts you're speaking of, sir, I can explain that. My aide . . ."

Diem waved his hand in amusement. Trang really was nervous.

"It's not that, Trang. I have assumed that you had nothing to do with that. No, it's far more important than that: I'm considering giving you the Saigon command."

Diem could see the glitter in Trang's eyes. Already he's estimating how much the appointment will bring him, Diem thought. It would be wise to play upon this emotion.

"Thank you, sir," Trang said.

"The change will become effective immediately. Fung Lao is to be an ambassador. How long you will hold this post depends on you. It affords many, shall we say, opportunities."

Trang smiled, displaying a great mass of gold teeth.

"There are also," Diem continued, "great responsibilities. Upon the shoulders of the Saigon commander rests the fate of the nation, the defense of the presidency. He who is not vigilant, who does not energetically prosecute the war against subversive elements both within and without the army, cannot hope to enjoy for long the opportunities which this post affords."

He thought he had made his point. Trang was not a stupid man, neither was he lazy, despite his huge bulk. He would do a good job if he understood that his future depended upon it, that he would be constantly under surveillance. Trang was the sort of man with whom one could work. He would restate the position once more.

"You have never been to Central America?" he asked.

"No, my President."

"Nor I, but I understand it is an unpleasant place affording little opportunity for one who must think of his family's financial future. That is where Fung Lao is going. I depend upon you to be worthy of your new assignment."

Trang hoisted himself to his feet and snapped to attention.

"Thank you, sir. I'll do my best."

"I know you will. That will be all, Trang."

Trang saluted and withdrew. Diem made a mental note to take the general's aide away from him. Trang is an ignorant man and a venal one, the President thought, but at least he's safe. He's too old and shrewd to see himself as head of a junta. And now, he thought with pleasure, Racine.

CHAPTER EIGHT

As THE TAXI RATTLED over the cobblestoned street toward the My Canh, Harry decided that he didn't much care where he and McWhorter ate, as long as it wasn't the Champs Elysees. Saigon's restaurant and hotel owners were making a good thing out of the war. It could go on forever, as far as they were concerned. Because it wasn't air-conditioned, the My Canh was quiet at lunch time, and the food was edible. It would do.

The side streets were empty now except for military traffic, as Saigon lay panting under the oppressive blanket of noonday heat, the high French windows of the older houses shuttered against the sun. As the taxi bumped along beside the Saigon River, past the Club Nautique, a Sûreté Citroen, followed by two truckloads of riot police, roared by them, the claxon of the Citroen ringing in warning. The riot police, standing braced behind the rows of round, green wicker shields attached to the wooden sides of the truck bodies, swayed in the beds of the trucks, their helmets bobbing, their bamboo truncheons waving in the air as the vehicles took the corner, going fast.

"What's that all about?" Harry asked.

McWhorter grunted.

"You've been away. Goes on all the time."

"What does it mean?"

"Mean? It means Nhu's goons are off to beat up some students. The Buddhists will be next. Here we are. I'll get it."

The taxi had stopped in front of the barge-restaurant, which was securely mired in the mud of the river bottom, from which came an evil smell of rotting vegetables, excrement, and fuel oil.

"Peeeuu!" McWhorter exclaimed as the taxi drove away, "can you stand it?"

"Sure. I'm not very hungry."

"I'll remember my tide table next time," McWhorter said.

The two Americans walked up the narrow gangplank to the restaurant. The overhead fans turned slowly over a dining room empty except for three waiters sitting at a corner table, engrossed in the click of their mahjong pieces. Strange that the place, despite the heat, should be so empty, Harry thought. One of the waiters pulled himself away from the game with obvious reluctance and padded over to them on bare feet.

"This way, please," the waiter said, leading the way to a small table looking out over the steel-gray river to the green of the distant shore. An armed junk of the Pajama Navy, its motor coughing horribly, like an old man unable to clear his throat of phlegm, chugged slowly up the sad, gray river. The sailors had stripped off their black pajama uniforms and berets and, with the exception of the bored-looking machine-gunner in the bow, lay sleeping in their breechclouts. On the Quai de l'Argonne, beyond the Club Nautique, a crane toiled industriously, lifting snub-nosed fighter planes from the deck of a small escort carrier, lowering them to the dock. They are old planes, Harry thought, but dependable and slow enough for this sort of work. He felt good about seeing the old prop jobs. They were old friends from Korea. And he remembered the plane coming in low over the rim of the hills north of Wonju, its American markings and the word "NAVY," painted in huge white letters, glistening in the morning sun. The Marines standing in their green undershirts in the chow line, hatless in the Korean spring morning, rattling their mess gear in their hands in anticipation of breakfast, watching the plane without interest, first just a small black dot above the crest of the hills, gradually growing larger until they could recognize its markings and see the sway of its wings, coming on fast and low, its throttle roaring. The firing of the rockets momentarily had seemed to halt the plane's flight, to leave it hanging there above the dissolving green circle of Marines breaking for cover. Then the napalm bomb had detached itself from the plane's belly, a fat, ungainly turd, black against the sun, which fell lazily in a graceful parabola, sending a sheet of greasy flame and a wall of hot air rolling across the battery, as if someone had thrown open the door of a gigantic furnace. Standing at the door of the fire-control center, his own mess kit dangling from his hand, Harry thought he had seen the pilot turn to look down after he had dropped the napalm, and then he had poured on the gas, sweeping low over the valley, his wings waggling, until he disappeared behind Hill 702, already white with peach blossoms. He realized suddenly that McWhorter was talking to him.

"Pardon?"

"Where've you been? I was saying we ought to place our order before this guy gets back to his crap game. Otherwise we'll be here for hours."

"Sorry. I was thinking of something else."

Harry studied the menu, the left side in French, printed in a script tinted violet. In deference to South Vietnam's altered political orientation, a badly typed English version appeared on the right side of the page.

"Steak for me, I think," McWhorter said. "A bottle of wine?"

"Not for me. Too hot. I'll have a bottle of beer, an omelet, and an endive salad. I'm not very hungry."

McWhorter ordered, decided on beer, and the waiter took back the menus. Charlottesville seemed a very long time ago. The fact that McWhorter had gone prematurely bald made it seem even longer. But his face, Harry noticed, still had that young, alert appearance.

"You don't look so hot, Harry. How much can you tell me about this *moi* deal? I've got a pretty good idea."

"Not much, I'm afraid. And they don't like being called *moi*, you know."

Harry wondered how far he could trust McWhorter. The reporter knew the Saigon situation far better than he. He might have some idea as to what Diem's intentions were for the mountain people. He decided to give it a try.

"Tell me something, John. Have you any idea what Diem thinks about the montagnards, I mean about how they fit into the general political and social picture?"

"I shouldn't think he thinks about them very much at all. He's Annamese and you know what that means."

"Yes. But if he did make a commitment to them, would he keep it?"

"Hell, Harry, I don't know. What are you getting at, anyway?"

"Nothing. Just thinking. How's the war going here?"

"Badly. We can't win with this Catholic mandarin, Harry. He's nothing but a yellow Frenchman. Hell, he speaks French better than he does Annamese. Culturally, he's as French as Sartre. We need Asian leadership here. Somebody like

Magsaysay, who'll get out in a sports shirt and talk to the people."

"Can we win it without him?"

"That's a dumb question. We're spending two million bucks a day and sixteen thousand Americans are fighting here. For what? To keep in power an absolutist who's more at home on the Faubourg St. Honoré than on the Rue Catinat? Doesn't make sense to me."

"What's the alternative to Diem?"

"Don't ask me. But there's bound to be someone better. He's got thirty thousand political prisoners in the pokey. The Vietcong owns most of this real estate after dark. The Buddhists are sore as boils. Something big's going to happen this afternoon. The embassy put out an order this morning for all dependents to stay off the streets today."

That partially explains the emptiness of the streets, Harry thought, the lack of business here. The waiter brought their beer, good Dutch beer in green bottles, their necks wrapped in gold foil. The patrolling junk had disappeared around a bend, leaving the river empty and dead, breathless in the heat. Harry sipped the cold beer slowly, savoring its bitterness, wondering about Diem.

"I don't see how dumping Diem would change things," he said. "Sure, Diem is a tyrant. But the conditions which make him one would still obtain under any new regime. At least he's able."

"We don't know that a change wouldn't be for the better."

"No, we don't. But any government must act to ensure its own survival. And how the hell can you graft democracy onto a country with a three-thousand-year-old authoritarian tradition, no middle class, and no industrial base?"

"You've turned into quite the little fascist, haven't you, Harry? What would the good judge say?"

Harry was beginning to be irritated with McWhorter. Newspapermen always thought they knew all the answers.

" 'The good judge,' as you call him, always was more interested in people than in ideologies. He had more respect for realities than for theories. But you're right: he probably wouldn't agree with me."

"And what about your precious montagnards? I understand that you're pretty interested in their freedom?"

"Who told you that?"

"A Buddhist friend of mine, a bonze at the Xa Loi Pagoda.

I know him as Cao Van Thuan, but the name won't do you much good: he's probably got several others. You can't keep a secret in Saigon, Harry. Everybody at the Caravelle knows what you're up to."

"Your Buddhist friend seems to know entirely too much. And I'd regard it as a personal favor if you'd try to keep your mouth shut about this."

"Okay, okay. Don't get so bloody sore. I don't give a damn about your hillbillies."

The waiter, his white pajama suit limp in the heat, brought their food. Harry ate slowly and in silence, his thoughts in the hills where the Koho, all the cards stacked against them, waited for his answer. Yé would be sitting cross-legged in his longhouse lined with the colored mats, bronze gongs, and silver-studded buffalo-hide shields which were the wealth of a chief, dreaming of the hunts of his youth. Ilouha, what would she be doing? Drawing water from the stream, perhaps, or pounding manioc for the evening meal. Suddenly, fearful that the best for which he could hope for the Koho was official indifference, Harry felt heartily sick of Saigon, politics, and John McWhorter.

"When are you pulling out of here, John?" he asked.

"I dunno. I'll be here until Diem goes, unless they yank my visa. I'd like to see it through until then."

"And then?" Harry pushed his omelet away, half eaten. The endives were brown at their edges, sad in their greasy parody of a dressing. He did not want the food.

"Maybe Washington. I've been ten years in gook countries and I'm getting pretty fed up. You remember Alexander McDonald of the *Observer?*"

"The reporter who made it so big by writing pro-Castro stories when The Beard was still in the Sierra Maestra? The one who brought down Batista?"

"Yeah, that's the guy. Well, Diem can be my Batista. And then it's home for little Johnny McWhorter."

Home, Harry thought, as the ancient wall-phone at the other end of the dining room jangled impatiently, where is that? On a Leesburg porch reminiscing with a gray old man about a time long dead, a dream dissipated? In the hills with Ilouha and Yé, hunting men as if they were wild animals? In a cubbyhole of an office in McLean, digesting somebody else's reports? Home, he thought, is the place you go when you've been hurt, when the pain you have is so big you can take it no place else. He did not know where that place now was for him, sensing that he was not quite the same person he had been a few months before. We carry the same name, we look relatively the same, but always we are in the process of becoming different people. People and country and ideas become a part of us, like the soft growth on a deer's antlers. Will the real Harry Coltart please stand up? He did not know that person, any more than he had recognized the man in the mirror seen weeks before in the Koho country, or the knobby, naked man with the dead eyes lying on a bed at the Caravelle, peering at him over the rim of a beer glass. The waiter, he realized, was calling McWhorter's name.

"Mista Maquart," he was calling from the opposite end of the dining room, "Mista Maquart."

"I think he wants you," Harry said. "Telephone."

McWhorter shoved his plate aside, scrambled to his feet, and threw his soggy napkin on his chair.

"Get the bill will you, Harry?" he shouted over his shoulder, "this may be important."

Harry called for the bill and paid it, McWhorter leaning against the wall, his right hand pressing against his free ear, shutting out the sound of a siren wailing somewhere. He hung up suddenly, motioned to Harry to come, and ran for the street, shouting for a taxi. Harry clattered down the gangway, the planks swaying under his weight, to find McWhorter opening the door of a cab.

"What is it?" he demanded. "What's going on?"

"Get in. Tell you then."

Harry clambered into the cab, the weight of McWhorter's body forcing him against the opposite door. It was stiflingly hot, the street white with glare from the river.

"Chua Xa Loi," McWhorter shouted to the driver, "and step on it." The reporter threw himself back into the seat as the taxi lurched forward, the driver leaning on the horn. "It's about to happen," he said.

"What? What's happening?"

"The Buddhists. It's a helluva story."

"What are you talking about?" Harry asked.

"Wait and see."

Catinat, as the taxi approached the pagoda, was solid with bodies. Traffic was hopelessly snarled, horns blaring and hooting, and beyond them the imperative cry of the claxons. A truck tried to force its way through the mob but stalled. As the terrified driver tried to get out, the mob rocked the truck and finally turned it on its side. Somehow the mob got the driver up above their heads and passed him, bobbing like a beachball, from hand to hand, tearing at his clothes. Finally, naked and bloody, he disappeared from sight. Riot police, their wicker shields held high in front of their faces, their teeth clenched, flailed at the mob with their bamboo truncheons, trying to force a passage through the wall of human flesh. Those in front tried to give way before the blows, clawing at those behind them in their effort to escape. From the crowd came a low moan, the cry of an animal in pain. As they forced their way out of the cab, McWhorter tossing a handful of small bills over the driver's shoulder onto the front seat, a woman lost her footing and fell screaming under the feet of the mob, the cries of her agony eaten by the hoarse rumbling of the rabble. The police phalanx hacked its way toward them and hands tore at Harry's clothes, ripping his coat.

"Get . . . out of . . . here," he shouted at McWhorter.

"The wall," the reporter screamed, "get to the wall."

The two Americans fought their way onto the pavement and hurled themselves into a doorway. The police phalanx, unable to break through, changed directions, probing for a weak point, and pressed forward away from them and to the left, the truncheons whirling, the shields held high, the blows unheard in the din. Over the heads of the crowd, Harry could see tear gas cannisters shaped like ice cream containers wobbling in uncertain flight. And in answer, a rain of cobblestones rattled off the wicker shields of the police. They'll fire soon, Harry thought, soon the police will fire.

"This way," McWhorter shouted, "follow me."

He put his shoulder down and forced his way out onto the pavement again. "La presse," he bellowed, "j'suis journaliste Americain."

A squat Annamese in an open-necked shirt fought his way to McWhorter's side and shouted something in his ear. The reporter shouted back. Harry could hear nothing but the animal cries of the mob. There was no chance to go back. He followed McWhorter and the Annamese, using his elbows and knees, cursing himself for his stupidity. This had nothing to do with him.

Finally they broke through the mob. On the cobblestones in front of the pagoda, a triple circle of Buddhist bonzes, their monks' robes angry orange in the afternoon sun, stood with their arms linked. Within the circle, in the middle of the street, sat an old bonze, his sticklike legs crossed beneath him, his shaven head splotched with liver patches, his eyes vacant and fixed on something Harry could not see. The crowd surged backward and forward, against the triple chain of monks, giving off an odor strange to him. It had the richness of rancid butter mixed with something animal and sexual and, at the same time, pure and exalted. It was borne on the moans of the mob, was a part of it. Two monks tipped a container of liquid over the old bonze, turning his saffron robe to deep brown, and the pungent smell of gasoline pressed against Harry's nostrils, the odor growing with his dawning horror.

"No, no," he shouted, trying to force his way through the wall of orange robes, his hands slipping off bare, sweating shoulders, his fingernails gouging greasy flesh. But the wall would not yield and he found himself pinned breathlessly against the slippery shoulder of a young monk by the pressure of the crowd. The seated monk turned his head toward him and once more Harry saw the arc of the napalm bomb, young Burack running, his green undershirt and his hair on fire, the word "NAVY" mocking and clear.

Suddenly the old bonze erupted into a pillar of flame, the puff of flames and heat forcing back the crowd, from the throat of which came a new and greater moan that was half a shout of triumph, half a cry of fear, and with it came the terrible, sweet smell of burning flesh, the scent of madness. The old bonze did not move. No sound came from him. His mouth formed a black hole, as in a Goya sketch, frozen in surprise or exaltation. The flames licked thirstily around him, consuming his robe, eating the withered flesh, leaving only a charred scarecrow. Slowly, as if in resignation, the blackened shape tipped, the sticks of its legs still crossed, the palms of the hands together in the contemplative position, the black hole of the mouth frozen open, and the ruined body fell over onto its side in a flutter of ashes. The crowd howled in its frenzy and, far away, Harry could see the truncheons rising and falling rhythmically, flailing the living flesh, pressing toward the oily smoke which hung in a single wisp over the circle of monks.

"A camera, God if I only had a camera!" McWhorter shouted.

Harry was suddenly, explosively ill on the sweating

shoulder of the monk against whom he pressed. With all the
force left in his spent nervous system, Harry drove his doubled
first hard into the stomach of the bonze, pushing the surprised
eyes away from him with the heel of his other hand, his hand
sliding off a shoulder drenched in his own vomit.

CHAPTER NINE

As Loye the Rhadé plodded up the twisting red road, he was happy. Soon the command would be his. He had many plans. But his happiness was more than this. He was going home, back to his own country. Although he and Yan, his half-caste Koho guide, had climbed only a few hundred feet from the level of the plains, already the air seemed salted with a new freshness, the sparkling taste of the hills. After years in the lowlands, he had forgotten how good it was to walk in the hills, the soil soft and without rocks under your feet, the slope pulling gently at the calves of your legs. What portion of the hills had he not known as a boy? He had followed the roebuck in his own country and in that of the Koho, hunting with Cheo, his father, the chief of the southern Rhadé. There was none so accurate with crossbow or blow-gun, none so swift of foot as I, he boasted to himself. He had mastered all the praise-songs of his people, knew the secret springs where the elephant watered. Had the war not come, had Ilouha been given to him in accordance with the pledge, who could say that he would not one day have ruled over not only the Rhadé but the Koho, too, for Yé had no son. But the war had come and Cheo had sent him to serve with the French. He had seen much since the day the *Boc* officer had ordered him to stay behind and die in the T'ai country, that the others might cross the Black River and escape. He had accepted the staying behind and the dying because he was a soldier and he lived by the soldier's code, even as he lived now by the Party's law. He smiled as he recalled his naivete in those days. He had been, as Thuc had said, an unschooled puppy. He had not thought of the *Boc* officer as a colonialist. Nothing had been explained to him then. He had thought of the *Boc* only as a *Boc,* a man from across the bitter water, although this one had been a little different. This *Boc* had been born in the country and spoke the language of the hill tribes. He could not complain against the *Boc*. He had been

87

a good soldier, the *Boc,* not asking others to do that which he
could not or would not do himself. The *Boc* had been the
last to eat, the last to sleep, the first to rise. These were good
things. Now that he, Loye, was to lead, these were things to
remember. Loye remembered that, despite his weariness and
his desire to live that dark and terrible night, he had been
proud that the *Boc* had chosen him to lead the other two scouts
being left behind to cover the withdrawal, promoting him
corporal on the spot. He remembered with a smile how it had
seemed to him then no small thing, if one had to die, to die a
corporal. When the others had been killed and he had been
captured, he recalled the pang of regret which had shot
through him at the knowledge that he never would wear the
two small chevrons on his sleeve. Now that time was long
past and he was to be far more than a corporal. He was to
command his own people in the fight for liberation. How
proud Cheo will be, he thought.

They had been walking for two days from Nha Trang,
Loye making careful note of the guard posts and military
convoys which they passed. They traveled only by day,
sleeping in the forests, because they could not risk entering
the fortified villages. It was too dangerous to travel at night.
Both sides fired at those who moved by night. In their pockets
they carried passes identifying themselves as rubber tappers
working in the low foothills stolen long ago from the Koho.
Beyond the rubber plantations they would have no need of
passes. Beyond the plantations were only the forest and the
hills. Loye had read the passes, his lips moving silently, forming the unfamiliar French and Annamese words. They had
been on leave in Nha Trang, the passes said, and were authorized to return to their plantation within fifteen days, after
which time the passes were no longer valid. The passes were
signed by a *Boc* planter and countersigned by the local administrator. Loye did not know whether the signatures were
real or forged. This was something that did not concern him.
He only knew that the passes worked. At the first roadblock,
they had gone right through. Yan had explained later that
the soldier on duty had been one of them. There were many
such in Diem's army, he knew, men who, if they would not
fight for the Vietcong, at least were prepared to cooperate
with the Communists. At the last roadblock, they had been
forced to wait for more than an hour, while the guards studied
their papers and argued among themselves. Finally, Yan,
sucking on his broken pipe-stem, had given the soldiers a

little money. They had wanted more but Yan had told them they were poor men and had no more to give. Finally, the guards had grunted and let them go. Loye would have liked to lead the way but he recognized that Yan knew the area better than he and, until they reached the 301st Sector headquarters, technically was his superior. Loye satisfied himself with the thought that soon he would be chief in his own area, something Yan was not.

As they trudged on, climbing higher into the hills, the awareness slowly grew on Loye that he had been in this country before, although he had approached it from a different direction. He recognized no landmarks, but the tilt of the land, the general feel of it, was familiar to him. The image of it in his mind was not clear, probably because he had come that other time in a truck. It was difficult to recall the character of a piece of country when traveling in that fashion. It was not like walking, where a country stayed with you for a long time, until you had it fastened in your mind and could never forget it. In a truck you went too fast and the image of the country remained blurred and indistinct. He sensed, however, that they were close to the rubber plantation of his *Boc* officer, to which he had come with the officer when the *Boc* went on leave, and to the mission hospital where his wounded hand had been treated. Loye thought about the *Boc patjao* who had dressed his hand. The priest had a great name in the hills as a healer and the mission hospital always was crowded. It was a good hospital, far better than the government one where he had been taken in the early years of the fighting after stepping on a *punji*. At the government hospital you had to sleep on beds, high off the floor, so that if you fell you were sure to be injured. In the government hospital, a man was not allowed to spit. And the orderlies, men apparently without shame but with great authority, always were washing you with sponges. It was a shameful thing. Nor had he forgotten the business of the bedpans. Patients were not allowed to go outside to relieve themselves, as they were at the mission hospital. And the orderlies demanded money for the bedpans. Things were not this way at the hospital of the *Boc* priest. The fat one had been many years in the country and understood the people. The hospital's main ward was built like a longhouse, set on pilings a few feet above the ground, so that it was both cool and dry. The walls were of split bamboo, which admitted air and light. Only with the roof would Loye quarrel. The roof was of corrugated

iron and the smoke from the communal cooking fire could
not burrow through it. Still, it was an advantage during the
rains, when a thatched roof would have leaked. A man's
relatives were allowed to come to his side, to cook his food
for him, to sleep next to him. It was a good place, this mission
hospital the *Bocs* called Notre Dame des Bois, and the fat little
Boc priest with the iron-gray beard was a famous *patjao*.
Comrade Tran had insisted that the *Boc patjao* was an evil
man, that the French used Christianity to keep the people
subservient. Yet Loye was not sure of this. He knew the
hospital was the only one close to the Koho country. Surely
it was good to have a hospital? Christianity had nothing to
do with him. He followed the faith of his people. The *Boc*
priest had said nothing to him of these things.

Loye and Yan walked slowly, wordlessly, up the twisting
road, the great, green plains spreading out beneath them to the
distant, hazy blue of the sea. The plains were cut into great,
shimmering squares by the bunds which framed the rice
paddies. A river wormed its way through the plains toward
the sea, its waters glistening like dull silver in the morning
sun. Beyond the river, planes without wings churned their
way across the white sky. There had been none of this type
of plane during the time of the French war against Ho Chi
Minh. Comrade Tran had explained that the *Bocs* called
them helicopters. They came always in twos and threes.
Sometimes there were many more of them, numberless and
black against the sun, like fat dung-beetles. Loye knew that
these carried Diem's soldiers and that a big attack was on.
He had seen it in the delta. But always, he thought, we had
word of their coming from the comrades wearing the uniform
of Diem's troops. The VPA battalions would hide their arms
and uniforms, burying them in the ground and in the thatch
of the village roofs, and go out in small groups to work beside
the peasants in the paddies. Diem's troops knew this. Sometimes they shot the peasants, lining up the dead in long rows
for the Americans to count, and in this fashion some of the
comrades were killed. When the next raid came, the VPA
no longer had to threaten the peasants not to betray them.
Then the people understood that the Vietcong fought for
them, that Diem was their enemy. So Loye did not fear the
helicopters. The *Bocs* might own the sky, but you could
grow no rice in the sky. The land belonged to the Vietcong,
particularly after dark. During the day, part of the country
was Diem's. But after dark that country shrunk to the tips

of the bayonets of Diem's soldiers cowering in their sand-bagged forts. In the end, because of this, Loye thought, we will win.

The rough scrub growth of the low hills gave way to trees marching in leafy regiments as far as the eye could see, their bark, to a height of four feet off the ground, slashed in parallel diagonal chevrons, like the tribal markings Loye had seen on the faces of the black soldiers the *Bocs* had brought to fight the Vietminh, big, heavy-set men with flashing teeth, a sad, soft laughter in their unintelligible tongue. Loye had met many of these, after the great battle of Dienbienphu, at the re-education camps in the north. The black soldiers always were treated well, he remembered, and the Vietminh had a black man of their own, who seemed to be of the same people as the prisoners, who spoke to them in their own language. Later, after the French had given up and that stage of the war had ended, all of the black men, unlike the Anna-mese prisoners, many of whom had been bayoneted, were allowed to go to Haiphong for evacuation. Loye had won-dered about that and Comrade Tran had explained it to him. The countries of the black men still were ruled by France, as Vietnam had been. The black men would return to their own countries bearing news of what they had seen and done. Later some of them would become leaders in their own struggle for liberation. Truly, the Party had great wisdom.

As he and Yan walked beside the rubber trees, Loye noted that at the undermost end of the lowest gash cut into the bark of the trees, tin cups were attached. Into these flowed the milky white blood of the trees. These were old trees: each had as many chevrons as a regimental sergeant-major. To Loye as a boy it had seemed dangerous to treat a tree in this fashion. The Rhadé knew that spirits lived in trees, as they did in rocks and waterfalls, and he had felt sure that to bleed a spirit was a very wrong thing. Still, he had known even then that the *Bocs* did not believe this and perhaps, being alien, were immune from such misfortunes as might spring from the crime. In any case, he had known that the trees were strangers in the land, brought by the *Bocs* many years before from some other place. So perhaps wandering spirits spurned them. He laughed now at his boyish superstition, watching the tappers, each carrying two buckets slung from the oppo-site ends of a bamboo yoke, collecting the blood of the trees, calling to each other as they emptied the tin cups into their buckets. He knew from his visit to the plantation of the *Boc* officer many years before that the tappers normally went out very early, before it was light, to collect the sap. He thought this was because the sap flowed more easily when it was cool, but he did not know this. Now the tappers went late to the trees. Perhaps, he thought, it is because of the war. They are afraid.

Loye and Yan stopped to rest beside the road when the sun was high. The tappers came trudging up the road past them, strung out in a long column, their bare shoulders shaded from the sun by their wide-brimmed coolie hats, the buckets of sap bobbing on their yokes, the tappers' breath coming hard, in short gasps, the muscles of their thin calves bunched under their loads. One stopped to rest and gave them water from a gourd in exchange for a cigarette.

"What is the news?" Yan asked the tapper. He was a very thin man and old, his chest muscles beginning to sag.

"How are you called?" the tapper asked. "I have seen your face but you are not of this place."

"I am called Yan. Often I have come to visit in the hut of Mi Tang, the three-fingered one. I am of the people. And you?"

"I have no politics. But as you can see, I am a worker," the tapper added.

Yan nodded, satisfied.

"Any trucks, Father?" he asked.

"Five earlier this morning, heading south. With soldiers," the tapper replied.

"They passed us on the road earlier this morning," Loye interjected. He, after all, was the man of importance. Yan was only a guide.

"Where are you going?" the tapper inquired.

"To the mission hospital of the *Boc patjao*," Yan replied, "the place which they call Notre Dame des Bois."

"It is better to go through the rubber trees. It is not far that way and there were troops on the road when we came down from the plantation house this morning. You know the way?"

Yan nodded.

"I know it. Go in peace, Father."

The tapper struggled to his feet, balancing the yoke on his shoulder, the milky liquid swaying in the buckets, grunted a farewell and hurried off to catch up with the other workers. Yan motioned to Loye to follow him and left the road, cutting through the trees. The underbrush had been cut back under the trees and the walking was easy and cool. Loye knew now, from Yan's words and from his own instinct, that they were among the rubber trees of his *Boc* officer, heading for the mission hospital where his hand had been treated. But he did not reflect long on this. He had much else of more importance to think about. He had to work out his strategy for dealing with Erohé and Yé's Kohos. But it would be better, he decided, to wait until he reached his sector headquarters before making any definite plans. Comrade Mao, the great leader of the Chinese, had laid down the principles. All he had to do was to discover the secret of their local application and then to execute his plan. Comrade Tran had read to him all of Comrade Mao's writings on guerrilla warfare. One section in particular had stuck in his mind:

". . . seem to come from the east and attack from the west; avoid the solid, attack the hollow; attack, withdraw; deliver a lightning blow, seek a lightning decision. Withdraw when the enemy advances; harass him when he stops; strike him when he is weary; pursue him when he withdraws."

These were wise words. He knew this both as a hunter and a soldier. I have only to avoid the solid and strike the hollow, he thought to himself, and Yé will give up the *Boc*. Thinking of Yé brought Ilouha to his mind. She would come to him when Erohé was dead, he was sure of that. He quickened his pace until he was abreast of Yan.

There was more sunlight in the trees ahead and Loye sensed that they were coming to the end of the forest. Soon, through the last rows of trees, he could see a longhouse with a corrugated iron roof, set a few feet above the ground and surrounded by flower beds. It was, as he had suspected, Notre Dame des Bois, the mission hospital of the fat little priest, he who had treated his wounded hand. The plantation house of the *Boc* officer, then, was no more than three miles away.

The rubber trees backed into the huts where the hospital workers lived. Loye and Yan stepped casually from the forest and walked among the huts, the latter leading the way. As they mixed with the workers, Loye saw the priest who had treated his hand standing on the steps of the hospital, joking with a group of Annamese. It was the same man. He had grown fatter. His belly swelled over the belt which held his dirty white cassock. And his beard was much grayer than Loye remembered it. But the brown eyes were just as bright and shrewd, the flesh around the eyes much lined from laughing. The square, white hands looked just as rough and capable. It was the same man. As they passed, Loye sensed the priest studying him closely, but the *Boc* never stopped talking. Loye walked on, his pace unchanged, following Yan.

The man Yan sought was not in his hut. But his woman was there and she told Yan that Mi Tang would return later in the day. She seemed to know Yan.

"Where has he gone?" Yan asked.

"Far. But he will return," she said.

"Go, then, some distance from here and guard while we sleep, for I noticed the *Boc* priest studying us when we came. If anyone comes, call out as if you had stepped on a live coal. We will wait for Mi Tang."

In the evening, Mi Tang had come. He was a tall man, thin, with the few long hairs at the end of his chin gathered into a small goatee. Loye noticed that the last two fingers of his left hand were missing to the knuckle, the flesh there padded into a heavy callous. Mi Tang and Yan talked quietly in one corner of the hut while Loye squatted before the fire, his mind dreaming in its glowing coals. He lacked the gift of prophecy, which his father had, but in the coals, as he stared at them unblinking, his gaze fixed, there danced a vision. He saw buildings burning and men running; he saw himself and he saw a *Boc*. One of the figures doubled over and fell. He could not see which man it was and the vision dissolved when he realized Yan was speaking to him.

"I had thought it would be good to spend some days here," Yan was saying, "so that you could know this country, which lies just beyond the southern tip of your sector. But we cannot do that. We must leave for the Rhadé hills tomorrow."

"Why?" Loye asked. "What has happened?"

"Mi Tang," Yan said, pointing to the three-fingered one, "has come this day from your sector headquarters. There are orders waiting for you there. Important orders from Comrade Thuc in Saigon."

CHAPTER TEN

"I'M GLAD YOU CAME, Harry," Marc Michaud said in his slightly lisping St. Cyr English. "It's been a long time and the occasion demands a special drink. You'll like it, I hope."

Marc stood beside the round, rattan table which served as a bar, his weight on his good leg, slowly stirring an iced pitcher of opaque liquid. From the wide veranda of the plantation house, its walls and roof frothing with vivid, purple bougainvillaea, almost black in the failing light, Harry looked out over a neatly manicured lawn fringed with trac trees to a rolling, slate-gray forest and, far beneath the forest, the golden sweep of a river, its waters burnished like copper by the rays of the dying sun. From the veranda you could not recognize the regular pattern of the trees, or see the slash marks on their trunks. The rubber plantation appeared to be the work of nature, not man. The air was soft and scented, sweet with the heavy perfume of honeysuckle, over the blossoms of which hovered on invisible wings a pair of purple sunbirds. Harry breathed deeply, contented, at peace. The past four days, in the rambling old house with its high ceilings and thick, cool walls, had been good ones. He and Marc had not done much. They had visited the nearby mission hospital of Notre Dame des Bois, run by Marc's friend, old Father Dupleix, and shot teal down by the river. Usually Harry slept late, until the sun came filtering through the high, louvered doors, the hard, elongated, French pillow damp under his head, the mosquito net gathered above him like a cumulus cloud. Finally the Annamese servant would come on bare feet to bring fruit juice and Perrier, and cool water for the basin. Once, when he could not sleep, he had left his bedroom early, when dawn was breaking, to find Marc clumping up and down the veranda, his hands clasped behind him. The two of them had walked, then, among the rubber trees, the tappers flitting between the rows like ghosts, down to a forest pool where they had swum naked in water cold beyond believing, the

95

Ko-el birds cooing in the underbrush in shocked surprise. In Marc's old Deux Chevaux they had driven to the limits of the plantation, and walked much, the crippled Frenchman stomping through the forest, knowing it, loving it, a part of it. Late in the mornings, when the sun hung heavy and hot above the rubber trees, they returned always to the coolness of the house. After lunch Harry would go to his room to sleep, a strip of cloth around his middle, the overhead fan turning slowly and hypnotically, creating its own turgid rhythm of life. Usually in the late afternoon he read and then, as evening drew near, went to join Marc on the veranda for cocktails and conversation. They had talked of women, of books, of the price of rubber, but never of the war. Now Harry wanted to know. He was ready to talk about it in the quiet peace of the fading light. From the direction of the river, in the hush of the gathering dusk, came thin voices singing in French. Harry thought he had never heard anything more beautiful.

"The tappers' children coming home from school," Marc said, his head cocked to one side, leaving the ice to swirl slowly, clinking softly against the glass of the pitcher. "Nice, isn't it?"

"Very nice," Harry replied. "You've a wonderful place here, Marc. It's hard to believe there's a war out there."

The Frenchman made a wry face and returned to his stirring.

"Always there's a war in Indochina, mon ami, always. Or so it seems. Perhaps we would miss it if there were none."

"You don't believe that, Marc."

"No, I don't believe it. It's just a thing one says. Try this." He poured the milky liquid into a tall tumbler fashioned of very thin polished wood and handed it to Harry.

"No more martinis?"

"Never since Korea. I don't know why."

"We had some good times there. And in Japan."

"Yes." Marc raised his tumbler. "To those good times."

"To our friends who are in the sands," Harry replied, sipping the cool, sweet drink.

Michaud laughed, throwing his lean, whippet's body into a rattan chair, facing Harry squarely, not trying to hide the ruined left side of his face.

"So now you are a Legionnaire, eh? Who taught you that toast?"

"You did, in Saigon. It's right, isn't it?"

"Yes, it's right. Legio patria nostra."

But the Legion, Harry thought to himself, was more than a home for many. For many it was a grave, and now the Legion was disgraced by the Algerian mutiny. "Tiens voila du boudin . . ." seldom would the old marching song be heard. And perhaps it was just as well.

"Was it very bad, Marc?" he asked.

"Bad? What?"

"The Legion. Algeria."

"No, it was not so bad. Nothing like the Groupement Mobile here. In five days of fighting on Route 19, the First Korea Battalion lost more men than in two years in Korea."

"Where was that?"

"Near Pleiku, north of where you're working, at a place called Chu-Dreh Pass. They cut us to pieces with mortars and recoilless rifles. There were no drainage ditches at the top of the pass and we had to lie there and take it. They were behind us, so we couldn't go back. And the road ahead was blocked by disabled trucks. We'd been mauled at Ankhé and Kilometer 15 and it was just too much. I kept waiting for helicopters to come to evacuate the wounded, forgetting that this was not Korea. The French are a parsimonious people, Harry. Our wounded must walk. Only 107 of us came out and the First Korea ceased to exist as a unit."

The light was almost gone. Harry could barely see Marc's intent, ravaged face as the Frenchman toyed with his glass.

"After that?" Harry asked.

"For me, a Groupement Mixte. Being born here, I could speak some of the hill dialects. I was with the T'ai."

"How did you get out after Geneva?"

The Frenchman laughed sardonically.

"It was a very long walk. Through Laos. Many did not make it. Some still are trapped up there, I suppose, unless they are dead by now."

Harry nodded. One such Frenchman was known to have lived with a small group of partisans for three years behind the Communist lines. Then his radio had gone dead.

"A helluva deal," Harry said. "You know how things are now with the T'ai?"

"One hears rumors. It is a hard thing to persuade a people to destroy itself, Harry."

"Was there a choice?"

"Always there's a choice. Had we not raised the T'ais

against the Vietminh, the northern montagnards might have made their peace with Ho Chi Minh. Now he's destroying them, their way of life, everything."

"Sometimes, perhaps, it's better to die."

"Balls, mon ami, pure balls. Look at me. Would I be better dead?"

"Don't talk rot, Marc."

"Take a closer look." The Frenchman leaned back and flipped a wall switch, the harsh light of the big bulb glancing off the sheet of tight, smooth scar tissue which ran from his left eyebrow down to his jaw, pulling the left corner of his mouth down into a perpetual snarl. "An SKAZ shell fragment. Pretty? Plastic surgery is not a T'ai strongpoint."

"Marc, I wish . . ."

"Don't wish, Harry, unless you can still wish for a clean conscience. What a trade we apprenticed ourselves to! Clausewitz and Jomini say nothing about what it is like to betray a simple people. Nor are they informative as to what one should do with one's life after acquiring a stiff knee and a shot-away face. But there, I'm sorry; you are on leave and this is not amusing. How do you like your drink?"

"Fine. Great. What is it?"

"Gin and the juice of the passion fruit. From the garden. Not the gin, I'm happy to say. That's from London."

"Sans Souci's a beautiful place, Marc." It had been a mistake to talk about the war. Harry couldn't stand to see Marc eaten with bitterness, detesting his broken body. He remembered that there had been a girl, that the engagement had been broken at Marc's insistence when they found it was too late to do anything for his face. It was better to talk about something, anything else. Through the open windows, he could hear the soft shuffle of bare feet on wooden floors as the servants set the table for dinner.

"Yes, beautiful. I was born here, you know, in the room you're sleeping in. I'm the last of my family and I hope to die here. If you'll give me the chance."

"Me? What do you mean by that?"

"This damned war. It's got to stop. It can't go on. The country can't take any more. The Vietnamese have been fighting for twenty years. A whole generation has grown up which has never known peace."

"You know we've got to keep fighting."

"Do you really think you can succeed where we have

failed? You, with your sixteen thousand men, where we had a quarter of a million?"

"It's different now, Marc. The Vietnamese are fighting for their freedom."

The Frenchman vaulted to his feet and paced up and down the veranda, shaking his head.

"Harry, Harry! You're not a schoolboy! The Vietnamese are fighting because they are forced to fight! Do you really believe you can wave your fluorescent wizard's wand and overnight turn fourteen million Asian peasants into homogenized, super Grade-A democrats? This is not how the world is, Harry."

"You're wrong, Marc."

"Unfortunately, I'm not. Already we have two administrations in Vietnam, Diem's and the Vietcong. How do you think I'm able to operate here at Sans Souci? Why are there no Vietcong attacks? I'll tell you: because I pay taxes to the Vietcong as well as to the republic; because if I see strange men among my rubber trees, I look the other way. How do you think a Vietnamese administrator avoids assassination? By reaching a modus vivendi with the local Vietcong leader. Why is it that when the Vietcong attack a fort, the gate always is found unlocked? Why do they always know when and where Diem's troops are going to attack? Because the Vietcong are everywhere, that's why. They're already running this country! The war is lost!"

"And how long do you think you'd survive under a Communist administration?"

"You're oversimplifying again, Harry. All the elements which oppose Diem aren't Communist."

"No, only the effective ones. How long would a popular front neutralist government last in Saigon? One year? Two? Ultimately, the Communists would capture it. It's happening now in Laos. Cambodia will be next."

"Cambodia is a good thermometer," Marc retorted. "Sihanouk is a perceptive man. When he begins to curse you, you may be sure you're losing Southeast Asia."

"And where will a neutralist Vietnam leave an ex-Foreign Legion officer?"

Marc stood silently for a moment, chewing his under lip.

"I don't deceive myself into thinking I have much future here. I only know I have no future anywhere else. France is finished for me, Harry. I don't belong there. A European France, shorn of its overseas limbs, has no meaning for me.

Nor have I anything to contribute to it. I belong to another tradition, another time, another France. I recognize this."

"Then what do you want? I don't follow you."

"Only a few years more, in peace, in the land where I was born. Even under a Communist regime they'll need people like me for a transition period. I can grow rubber."

"And you'd help them?" Marc's words shocked Harry. He couldn't believe that he meant what he was saying.

"Harry, this is not my war. Korea, Vietnam, Algeria: three is enough. I've seen too much killing. I would trade a lot to see Indochina at peace again, as it was in 1940 when I was growing up here. Is that asking too much?"

"I'm afraid it is, Marc. We've got to fight here and you know it."

"Well, that's that. Perhaps you're right. Let's talk about something else. What have you enjoyed most in your visit here? I want to know so that we can do it again when you come back."

Marc refilled his glass.

"It's all been good, Marc: the duck shooting, the swimming, the tramping around the place. I really enjoyed looking around Notre Dame des Bois; I'm only sorry that Father Dupleix wasn't there."

"Yes, the mission is quite a place. He built the hospital virtually with his bare hands. And the little school, too."

"The school? I didn't see that."

"Didn't you? Father Dupleix wouldn't have let you off so easily. It's the double longhouse between the hospital and the leper colony. It's an orphanage as well."

"An orphanage?"

"He started it in 1948. Most of them are children whose relatives were killed either in Vietcong raids or in government attacks on Vietcong villages. The human flotsam of war."

"That's quite a thing," Harry said.

"It is, indeed. It's made a big difference to us here at Sans Souci having a hospital a couple of miles down the road, and to the montagnards. Notre Dame des Bois is the only hospital or school within walking distance of the hills."

"How long will he be able to keep going, with the Vietcong, I mean?"

"So far they've left him alone, perhaps because he never asks a sick man or an orphan about his politics. He's very good with the Vietnamese. Not that he's a sentimentalist. He knows all their warts and wens and can be damned tough with them. But he understands them, treats them fairly, and he likes most of them. He has that rare capacity to love without being sloppy about it. Notre Dame is his whole life."

"I'm sorry I didn't get a chance to meet him."

"You will. I've asked him to dinner." Marc paused. "Unless I'm mistaken, that's his motorcycle I hear now."

In the distance, Harry could hear the faint noise of a small motor pulling up a slope. Marc slapped his hands softly and an Annamese servant brought more ice and clean ashtrays. Harry was glad Father Dupleix was joining them. He did not want to talk about the war any more. Even when he and Marc had talked of other things, always the war was there, just outside their range of vision and conversation, mute and terrible, crouching like an animal in the darkness. Marc has changed, Harry thought, he has changed a great deal even in the three months since last I saw him. Perhaps it was the wound. There would be bad days when such things could become unbearable, when the dead flesh would throb with all the pain not only of what had happened to you but of what you had seen happen to others.

Marc was mixing another round when the priest arrived on his motorcycle, his beret tucked under his goggles, his white cassock hiked up. He rode low on the machine, leaning forward despite his girth, and came up the red clay driveway very fast, the throttle roaring, his headlight dancing as he took the bumps.

"Father Dupleix!" Marc shouted, "it's kind of you to come but you'll murder yourself one day if you don't slow down."

The priest killed the engine, leaned the ancient motorcycle against a trac tree, and stomped up the stairs of the veranda, the old wood creaking under his boots. Like many small, round men, he held himself very erect, his shoulders back, in an attempt, Harry guessed, to give himself height. The priest's beard was very dusty and there was an elliptical line across his forehead where the beret had protected his head from the dirt. A broad smile revealed uneven, tobacco-stained teeth. Not a man to mortify the flesh, Harry thought.

"Kind," he bellowed. "It's you who are kind, Marc, to give me an excuse to get away from that cursed hospital. As for my driving, kindly show a bit more respect for the cloth. This will be your friend Mr. Coltart?"

Harry nodded and offered his hand.

"Please call me Harry, Father," he said, as the priest took his hand in his own outsized paw and squeezed it hard.

"Eh, bien. Harry it is. Everything comes easily to you Americans." The priest threw his leather driving gauntlets and his goggles into an empty chair, and fell into another with a groan.

"A drink, Father?" Marc asked.

"For God's sake, yes. I'm choked with dust from that miserable road. Beer, please."

The priest turned to Harry, brushing the dust from his cassock.

"It's good you've come. One has so little opportunity to use one's English. Now, why are you in Vietnam," he asked, his eyes twinkling mischievously, "to teach us how to live or to show us how to die?"

"Neither, Father. Just to help."

"Harry is working in the Koho country," Marc interjected, "a project involving rural water supplies." There was no trace of irony in his voice but his eyes mocked Harry.

"Good. We can use all the help we can get. And what is your impression?"

"Of the war?" Harry asked. It was a subject which could not be avoided.

"Yes, of the war, because that is all Vietnam is nowadays. It used to be a place where people lived. Now it is just a place where people die." Father Dupleix ran a chunky hand through his uncut, gray hair and accepted the glass of beer from Marc, leaning back, the chair protesting under his weight.

"Not too badly except in the delta. Saigon is another matter," Harry said.

"Yes. You've heard about the bonze?"

"He saw it, Father," Marc said, returning to his seat.

"Not a pretty thing," the priest said, turning his glass slowly in his hand, studying the refraction of the light through the beer.

"How can they do such a thing?" Harry asked.

The priest shrugged his square shoulders.

"Self-immolation is a custom of long standing. But I think this was done with two purposes: to attempt to turn the Buddhists against the Catholics and to widen the split between Diem and the Americans."

"Will it work?" Harry asked.

"As for the Americans, you are a better judge than I.

Probably there will be other burnings. There is plenty of opposition to Diem: Communists, neo-Communists, students, trade unionists, disaffected officers, the sects, liberals. Every one out of power would like to have it, although in this country God knows why."

"What about the religious issue?" Harry asked. "Having a Catholic president in a Buddhist country?"

The priest snorted.

"You've got a Catholic president in a Protestant country. Diem was a Catholic when he opposed the French. He was a Catholic in the years when he saved this country. He's still a Catholic. But he came to power not because he was a Catholic but because he was able; he holds it because he is strong. If Diem is a tyrant, he is one not because of his Catholicism but in spite of it."

"And the Church, Father?" Marc asked. "Where does the Church stand?"

"Bah, don't ask me. I'm just a simple priest. For answers to questions such as these, you must go to Rome. But the Church is like communism in that it thinks in historical terms. It will support Diem as far as it can, remembering what has happened to the Church in China and North Vietnam. If it becomes clear that Diem has lost, then the Church must think in terms of the survival of the faith in this part of Asia. It must, to use an American term, make the best deal possible for itself."

"And what about your work, Father?" Harry asked, settling back into his chair, shading his eyes against the light, around which hummed a cloud of insects. Marc got to his feet and flicked it off, leaving them in darkness.

"My work? You've seen the hospital, I understand. It's rough but we do our best. We also have a small leper colony and I try to teach a few squalling brats a knowledge which probably will be of little use to them."

"Father Dupleix has been here for thirty years," Marc said. "Sans Souci and Notre Dame des Bois were virgin forest when he and my father came here."

"Those were good days," the priest said slowly. "The people trusted us then. Trust is a wonderful thing to experience. All things seemed possible then. Yet somehow we failed, we failed the Vietnamese. How I'm not sure, but somehow we betrayed them and that trust disappeared."

"You're too hard on yourself, Father," Marc said. "They still trust you."

"No, Marc, they don't. Oh, they're vaguely fond of me, some of them. They're used to me. I'm part of the scene. But now they see me as a white man. They didn't before and that's what trust means out here."

"Perhaps your failure was that you refused to let the Vietnamese rule themselves," Harry said. "Until it was too late."

"You Americans," the priest chided gently, "with your simple answers to complex situations. You're too impatient. You lack a sense of limits, of proportion. Perhaps it comes from living in a big country. Tossing carbon copies of the American constitution around Asia will solve no more problems than it has in South America or Africa."

"Still, Harry is not entirely wrong, Father," Marc said.

"Of course politics had something to do with it, but the betrayal was far deeper than that. Perhaps it was that we lost faith in ourselves. We taught the Vietnamese to believe in us and in what we stood for. We made men like Diem into social and political Eurasians. And then we stopped believing in ourselves. We destroyed what they had, replaced it with our own system and then said 'sorry, fellows, we were wrong.' There could be no greater betrayal than this."

Harry said nothing. Dammit, he thought, this war can be won if we're willing to pay the price. The U.S. wanted Vietnam cheaply in terms of American lives. It was all right for the Vietnamese to die and America was willing to finance the thing. But American lives were another thing. How much American blood was Vietnam worth in Ft. Wayne or Spartanburg? Not much he suspected.

Father Dupleix and Marc were speaking in French. Marc switched back to English when he noticed that Harry was back with them again.

"This may interest you, Harry," he said. "Two Rhadé passed through Notre Dame des Bois last night. Father Dupleix thinks they were Vietcong soldiers. They're headed for the Koho country, according to his servant."

"Does he know anything about either of them?"

"One he did not recognize. The other he believes was a scout for my Groupement Mixte. Ten years ago I left him and two others behind to cover our retreat across the Black River. I haven't seen him since and I'd assumed he was dead."

"How did you know him, Father?" Harry asked.

"Marc brought him to me once with a wounded hand, when he was home on leave."

Two men more or less would not make much difference,

Harry thought, unless they were very good men. Still, it could be important.

"What kind of a fellow was the one you know, Marc?" Harry asked.

"A good soldier, I'm afraid. Which is why I left him behind. I made him a corporal on the spot, although he was very young. In the old days he was the type of person who, if he stayed in, would make sergeant-major."

"Why are you so sure he's with the Vietcong?"

"As a Rhadé, he would have been too valuable to them. They wouldn't have let him come south until he'd gone through the re-education process."

"I wonder if . . ."

The jangling of the ancient telephone in the hallway interrupted Harry's question. Marc limped off the veranda and Harry could hear him shouting over the phone in French.

"It's for you, Harry," he called. "The A.I.D. mission in Saigon."

CHAPTER ELEVEN

"WEEE GONAH TWEEST tonigh'," squealed the little Annamese vocalist, "yis, daddee, yis, daddee, yis, tweest," shouting into the microphone, her fragile voice cutting thinly through the wailing saxophones of Pink Mareel's combo. The bass, a stubby Filipino much smaller than his instrument, spun the big fiddle, slapping at it with his little hands, trying to duplicate a skill he could only mimic. At the circular bar stood crew-cut Americans in white athletic socks, loafers, khaki trousers, and sports shirts, their feet firmly anchored, the rest of their bodies gyrating, swaying to the music. On the other side of the narrow strip of polished wood, hostesses teetering on spiked heels and wearing western clothes, joyless smiles frozen on their secret, Oriental faces, swung their thin hips to complete the parody of the dance, their delicate, snapping fingers fluttering like small birds over the hairy hands of the drinkers. An American reached across the bar, cupping his hand over the small, pointed breast of the hostess opposite him. She squealed and slapped the man playfully, her anger false. Her eyes, Harry Coltart noted, revealed no emotion. They were in another place. He tried to go with her to that place, to imagine what her real thoughts and emotions might be, but he could not do it. There was too much he didn't know. "Tweest, bebee, tweest," howled the little singer and the writhing men at the bar, their eyes flashing with a false joy, trying to deny the soldier's loneliness in an alien and ravaged land, roared back a chorus of meaningless words. The band came back on the up-beat, cramming the dark and smoky cave of the Capriccio with noise, the faces of the players blank, the revolving pink lights behind the bar glittering on the brass of their instruments. At tables the size of generous pancakes, which lined the walls and faded into the gloom of recessed nooks, sat more Americans with their Vietnamese girl friends, the men tapping out a sharp, staccato tattoo with swizzle sticks on their tables and glasses, in time

106

with the music, the girls giggling behind screening fingers, sipping their dollar-fifty glasses of fruit juice. In one corner, behind two pails of ice from which protruded bottles of champagne, sat three fat Vietnamese men in sun glasses and tight, dark blue suits. The men sat in silence, their faces empty behind the sun glasses. Their women, French, very thin, and too heavily made up, their mouths scarlet slashes against the white powder on their faces, chattered stridently.

The table was too small and fragile to give him support so, although he was tired after the drive from Sans Souci, Harry Coltart sat very straight in his chair, aware of his unseemly aloneness. Watching the crippled gyrations of the Americans at the bar and the burlesque of their partners, it seemed to him a thing sad and wrong that the government should have prohibited dancing as unseemly for a people at war. Harry was not concerned with whether or not this puritanism, by most people attributed to Madame Nhu, was genuine or assumed. He knew only that what it produced was deformed and ridiculous. He knew there were "twist-easies" where the better-heeled Americans went, contrary to army orders. But these were places primarily for officers and civilians, because the risk for the hostesses was great and the prices, accordingly, were high. The edict, he knew, was aimed primarily at Americans. Most Vietnamese looked and, he sensed, felt slightly ridiculous when dancing in the western fashion. Perhaps, as some said, the order really was an attempt to slow what Marc had termed the "coca-cola-ization" of Vietnam. We have a wonderful talent, Harry thought to himself, for deforming other societies. And for destruction. The disposal and the incinerator are the real symbols of our culture.

It was an odd place, he thought, for Englehardt to arrange a meeting. A quiet dinner at the Guillaume Tell would have seemed more appropriate. But Englehardt had rejected the suggestion and fixed on the Capriccio. Perhaps it was because no observer could believe that a discussion of any importance could take place in such a setting. That was the way Englehardt's mind worked. Harry had eaten alone and early at Cheap Charlie's, down by the Quai de l'Argonne. After his time in the hills, he found western food heavy and rich while the Cantonese food of the Chinese restaurant sat well on his stomach.

The band lapsed into silence and Harry sat, moodily twirling the glass of cut whisky, studying the faces of the three Vietnamese in the corner. Profiteers paying homage to their ruined success, for profiteers were the only Vietnamese who could afford French whores and champagne. There was much money to be made in Vietnam now, as there was in any war. He had seen those same bland faces in Korea, faces which could get you whisky by the case, new jeeps, penicillin, or a fine piece of jade. Harry neither resented the profiteers nor hated them. He saw them only as a part of the human conditions accompanying war, like syphilis or frostbite. The profiteers were the human manifestation of the evil, not the evil itself. It did no good to draft profiteers and send them to the front. You could not draft syphilis. The times demanded the evil and always there were men to fill the needs of the times. In war the many suffered and the few grew fat, feeding on the suffering of the many, licking at the foulness of dead hopes, like a bitch devouring the afterbirth of her pups. In the end, right did not triumph. The shattered dreams and the wrecked bodies could not be made whole again, although America was good at the latter. Ruined bodies were something America could not bear. You looked away, embarrassed, knowing that what you had seen was an abomination. Plastic surgery for the ravaged flesh. Shut the old away, discreetly out of sight in retirement homes for senior citizens. Shield the children from a knowledge of death. Hide the congenitally deformed in special institutions where they'll be kindly cared for. But never, never allow the ugly to become a part of the American scene. No, this was not our style. Nor did the profiteers and the con men and the soldiers who always managed to find essential jobs to perform in the rear get what my father's generation so self-righteously termed "their just deserts." The killing just stopped for a while. That was the meaning of peace. And the broken little people picked up again the threads of their insignificant lives and the profiteers found something else to do.

Cut it out, Harry said to himself. He knew there was more to it than that, a meaningful pattern to the tapestry of life. He guessed that he was gloomy and depressed in anticipation of what Englehardt would have to tell him. Harry could not believe that Diem would agree to grant any real measure of self-rule to the montagnards. The montagnard problem was one with which every Vietnamese ruler had been faced and with which none had come to grips. There was no reason to believe that Diem would be the man to do so, not at least at this time in the current situation. It would take a very big man, Harry reflected, to make a decision which could and would be interpreted in some quarters as weakness. Faced with riots in the streets of Saigon, rumblings within the army, restiveness among the religious sects, and increased military pressure from the Vietcong, it was hard to believe that he could give in to what essentially was a divisive pressure without igniting similar pressures among other dissident groups. It wouldn't make sense, unless Diem valued the participation of the montagnards in the war far more highly than Harry thought.

Yet there was the business of the telephone call to Sans Souci. The call, because of the security aspect, had revealed nothing. The voice at the other end of the line had said only that Englehardt, using one of his code designations, would appreciate his return to Saigon at his earliest convenience. Nor had Englehardt made any reference to the situation when they'd talked on the phone earlier today. Again, that was to be expected. It was assumed in Saigon that all telephones were tapped, either by Nhu's police or by the Vietcong, or by both. Yet there could be no logical reason for his premature recall to Saigon if Diem's answer were negative.

Harry was dissecting this fragile hope, subjecting it to scrutiny from every angle, studying his half-empty glass of whisky with great seriousness as if he hoped to find the answer there, when he saw Englehardt's head and chest floating toward him, his body cut off at the arm pits by the haze of smoke which filled the Capriccio. Harry stood up, motioning to his chief, and the round, flaccid face bobbed in recognition, changing course through the babble of voices, the squealing of the hostesses.

"Evening," Harry said.

"Hi. Good crowd tonight," Englehardt commented as he slid into a chair.

"Yes. What'll it be?"

"Beer, I guess. Safer in these joints."

Harry attracted a waiter's attention and ordered an Amstel and another whisky while Englehardt settled into his chair, glancing around the bar, getting his bearings like an old dog in an unfamiliar room. Satisfied, he pulled his pipe out of his pocket, filled it, lit a match and then another, making sucking noises, the flame from the matches playing on the broken blood vessels in his pudgy cheeks, illuminating the deep crows' feet at the corners of his eyes.

"How," he asked between the sucking noises, "was Michaud's?"

"Great. I had a good time."

"Good. He's quite a boy. You know about his record. He was helpful to us at first, when the Agency was just getting started here, but he seems to have lost interest."

"He's been through a lot," Harry said.

"Yes, that's right. There always comes a time when you want out, when you've had enough. It's best for everybody concerned if you do get out when that time comes."

"I suppose so."

"You haven't reached that point, have you, Harry?" Englehardt asked quietly.

Harry felt himself flushing. The question irritated him. Despite the two abortive attacks, the Koho operation had, he thought, been going well.

"Of course not. What are you getting at?"

"Nothing. Just wondered. You've seemed a bit preoccupied lately, depressed. I'd been afraid you might be getting yourself too involved emotionally in this job."

"Well, quit worrying about that," Harry snapped. "I'm okay."

"Right. Well, let's get down to business: the man has given the green light to what you wanted. He says yes."

Harry's irritation with Englehardt evaporated as the words sunk in.

"You don't mean it! He agrees to everything?"

"Everything. It wasn't easy, Harry. There are a lot of reasons, many of which I know you understand, why our friend should resist change just now."

"And why did he agree?" This was a thing Harry wanted to be very sure about. He was prepared to try to keep the Koho in the war without a pledge but he was not willing to lie to them.

"He didn't like it. He bought it for only one reason: I was able to convince him, on the basis of your statements, reinforced by McPherson and Eisenberg's reports, that the alternative would be worse."

"What do you mean?" Harry asked.

"Tweest aull nigh', tweest roun' klok, tweest righ' now whi dutha sqayas rock," groaned the little singer as Pink Mareel's combo surged into raucous life. The Americans at the bar, in response to the music, began to shift their weight from foot to foot, their bottoms wagging, their arms held high, bent at the elbows, their fingers snapping.

"Just this," said Englehardt, leaning toward Harry until their faces almost touched, "that he couldn't afford to have your Hatfields and McCoys going over to the opposition firm with everything else hotting up. He figures he can handle his other problems."

"But won't this stir up trouble for him with the Buddhists and other groups which want more freedom?" Harry asked, forgetting to employ the code they had followed in their discussion.

Englehardt waggled a finger at him in admonition for his lapse.

"He's banking on it causing no new troubles he can't handle. He's got to have that autobahn cut."

It made sense, but somehow Harry didn't believe it. He didn't know enough about Diem to be sure. Only Englehardt was in a position to tell.

"Does he mean it?" Harry asked, looking straight at Englehardt's eyes. "Can I trust him? I've got to have the truth, Ramsey." Harry noticed that he had called Englehardt by his first name, as if through this intimacy to force from him the truth. The familiar blue eyes did not falter.

"I've known our friend a long time, Harry. He's a tough, complex man, but he's fair. I say you've got to trust him on this one."

Harry was silent, pulling deeply on his cigarette, studying Englehardt's face. The atmosphere of the bistro was close and oppressive, stinking of cigarettes and sweat, of fat long congealed in cold frying pans. It was hard in that place to feel the cool dawns of the hills, to visualize Ilouha bending bare-breasted over the cooking stones, her hair caught back behind her ear with a flower. Nor could he conjure up in his mind's eye the gnarled, wise face of Yé, full of years and many hunts. Both they and the mountains seemed a blurred dream, far away. He wanted that place where they were with a sudden urgency, wanted it for himself and for them. But he was not yet sure it could be. He had only Diem's word which, despite Englehardt's protestations, might not be good. Even if Diem were acting in good faith, the pledge would be without value if, as McWhorter had suggested, he were overthrown. Yet if the Vietcong should win, would the situation of the montagnards be any better, even if they had a record of neutrality behind them? Marc had suggested that such a record might have done the T'ai some good. But Harry wasn't convinced of this. The hill tribes were too backward to prosper under any form of government. In a sense they had been a doomed people ever since the Chams had forced them out of the plains and into their barren hills a thousand years ago. At least if Diem won, and a montagnard commitment certainly would contribute to that end, there could be American leverage. If the montagnards came out against the Vietcong, it might be possible to force Diem at least into partially honoring his pledge, even if he now had no intention of so doing. There remained, for Harry one final question to be asked.

"What about you, Ramsey," he inquired, "will you give me your word that, to the best of your knowledge, our friend is acting in good faith?"

The older man gazed steadily at Harry, his blue eyes unwinking, the pink light from the bar playing on his fleshy, tired face.

"Have I ever let you down, Harry?" he asked. "You asked for a commitment. I've gotten you one."

He resented that question, Harry thought, as Englehardt banged his pipe on the edge of the ashtray. And maybe he's got a right to do so. Englehardt had no need to prove either his honesty or his humanity. Harry had been witness to both at Dos Lobos and in the Kiernan affair. The man's name stood for something. Suddenly, Harry was ashamed that he had asked the question.

"What do you want me to do?" Harry inquired, the saxophones wailing, the vocalist, her thin arms outstretched, her mouth contorted, pinned against the pink coated tapestry of Pink Mareel's band by the purple shaft of the spotlight.

"Get back up there and get this thing moving. We need victories in this town, Harry, we need them bad. Washington needs them. You've got to do a job for us, Harry."

"I'll do my best. And thanks."

"Good for you, boy. I'll have a jeep and helicopter for you at six tomorrow morning."

"I'll need some stuff."

"Already done. That chopper is jammed with enough hardware and gold to make your hillbillies jump for joy. Now let's get out of this flea-trap."

Harry followed Englehardt out into the soft, decaying night, the older man's back straight in the haze of smoke, leaving behind him the soldiers writhing at the bar in front of the fluttering hands and frozen smiles of the hostesses, the faces

of the Vietnamese profiteers in the corner expressionless and
all-knowing, the saxophones calling wildly to a people who
could not hear.

Odd, Harry thought to himself as he taxied back to the
hotel, that he was confident enough to order that chopper
before he'd heard my answer.

CHAPTER TWELVE

JOHN MCWHORTER was sleepy but he tasted the edge of excitement as the jeep trundled down the runway of Saigon's Tan Son Nhut airport, its headlights pinning the banana-shaped Piaseckis to the wall of the night like strange insects to black paper. A long row of twin-engined transport planes stood parked behind the helicopters, their crews busily preparing for another day at war, flashlights shimmering, metal banging against metal. McWhorter wanted coffee badly to chase the sleep from his mind; he wanted to savor the moment, knowing it to be good. There was something about being in the company of armed men, men going out to kill, which stirred an ancient emotion, bred in the bones of men. He had experienced it before in Korea, in the flinty hills of the Algerian Kabilya, among the myth-haunted olive groves of Cyprus, and now it came back to him with all the old urgency and he welcomed it, inhaling deeply, cocking his foot outside the body of the jeep, on the battered, gray fender. When first he had tasted that excitement, on the pitching landing craft boring in through the night toward Inchon, it had taken him by surprise and he remembered being a little shocked, as if he had discovered something shameful about himself. Later he had recognized it for what it was, accepted it, and been grateful that it had been this rather than fear.

He found that after a few weeks life in the capitals of countries at war became unreal, stifling, insupportable. The capital was a clouded glass which concealed the real events taking place in the countryside. When you began to feel that way, it was good to pull on a pair of boondockers and a set of army dungarees with your surname printed above your left breast pocket and go out to the war. Almost always you came back a little changed, feeling that you had seen something of importance, and your writing assumed a new force and vigor. You lost it after a while, when you had sat too long in the Caravelle bar and attended too many press conferences, and

114

then you went out again, seeing it all again, but always from a new perspective, as if your eyes were borrowed, and it gave you something you had not had before.

"Here we are," said the pilot, turning off the runway beside an H-21, *"Little Miss Linda."*

The gunner climbed out of the back of the jeep and began handing gear up to the young crew chief. McWhorter had shaken hands with the pilot and the gunner in the briefing room but had carried with him no impression of them except that they were young, clean shaven, and very serious. It was still too dark to make out their features.

"Give you a hand," volunteered McWhorter, helping to pass the two .30 caliber air-cooled machine guns, the olive-green metal boxes of ammunition, the two M-14 7.62 millimeter rifles, and the case of C-rations into the doorless rear opening, aware of his clumsiness and irritated by it. The gunner clambered aboard and began to mount the two machine guns, his own at the forward right aperture and the crew chief's at the left rear door.

"Goin' t' get me a transfer to a line outfit," complained the crew chief, a moon-faced youngster not more than twenty.

"You crazy or somethin'?" the gunner replied.

"No place to duck in these mothah-fuckahs. Lost two yesterday up by Ben Cat."

The gunner grunted noncommittally.

"Got any coffee?" McWhorter asked. He didn't much like the idea of spending the day in an H-21. He had hoped he would draw an HU-1B. The Hueys were armed with 2.75 inch rockets and carried a little armor. "Flying coffins" was another name for the old Piaseckis.

"Yeah. Thermos in the back. Just a minute," said the crew chief, busy with the ammunition boxes. McWhorter felt the loneliness of having no part to play among a group of men each with a specific, well-defined task. He slumped down onto one of the canvas ledges which faced each other across the body of the chopper, watching jealously as the gunner completed the fixing of the machine gun into its firing socket, threading through the feed slide the long belt of bullets, shining dully in the gray, dawn light.

"Mornin'," said a small, compact man with a hard, pockmarked face, as he shouldered his way past McWhorter up to the bubble in *Little Miss Linda's* nose, seating himself beside the pilot in the cockpit, joining in the monotonous litany of the pre-flight checkoff. The new arrival twisted around in his seat and McWhorter saw that he wore the red and gold single bar of a warrant officer.

"Got that fuel pump fixed, Anderson?" the warrant officer shouted.

"Yeah," the crew chief replied, "it's okay."

"Last time I flew this mothaw there was oil spurting all over the fucking place."

"It's fixed."

"Better be," the older man said. The pilot said something to the warrant officer and received a nod in reply. The four soldiers struggled into their bulky, bulletproof vests and plastic helmets. The helmets looked like those worn by football players, except for the fact that they had plastic visors and were wired for the intercom. The gunner and the crew chief clipped to the webbed harnesses around their bodies eight-foot safety belts secured to the interior of the helicopter. The pilot turned around and jerked his thumb into the air and the gunner and the crew chief, standing at their machine guns in the open hatches, repeated the signal. McWhorter braced himself as the forward engine coughed once and roared into life, the Piasecki shuddering under the thrust of the whirling blades. Then the rear engine caught and the helicopter was full of the arrogant roaring of the engines and the whistle of trapped air. The helicopter lurched vertically into the air and McWhorter felt his stomach drop and then it caught up with him and the chopper was whirling off into the dawn, still rising but gaining forward impetus and beneath him, between the crew chief's legs, he saw the airfield shrinking in size, the long row of twin-engined transport planes, their engines slowly turning over, dwindling to children's toys. McWhorter staggered to his feet and made his way unsteadily back to the doorless rear opening, his hands braced against the helicopter's roof. He tapped the crew chief on the shoulder and pointed at another helicopter flying just behind and beneath them.

"Why the shadow?" he asked. The crew chief shook his head, pointed at his helmet, and then took it off, steadying himself by one hand on the machine gun mount.

"What?" he asked.

"Why the other chopper?" McWhorter asked.

"Never go out in less than pairs no more," the boy replied. "Somebody to pick you up if you get a lead breakfast." Mc-

Whorter nodded, returned to his seat, and began jotting notes on a folded piece of paper.

He had barely finished his notes when the helicopter fell away in a slanting dive, slicing through the thin morning air to land at Bien Hoa, the big military airfield and operations center northeast of Saigon. An American Army captain in green fatigues drove out to the helicopter in a jeep and shouted up to the pilot between his cupped hands:

"Beria and Xuyen Moc this morning, Ben Cat this afternoon. Milk-run stuff. Major'll be along with your passengers."

"Shee-it," moaned the crew chief, slapping his machine gun with his open palm, "had a feeling we'd draw Ben Cat when I got up this mornin'. Just had a feeling. Get shot up every damned time we go in there."

McWhorter said nothing, smiling faintly at the boy, feeling the small fear worrying daintily at his stomach, like a mouse nibbling a cracker. He would give the boy no satisfaction. He lit a cigarette and kept silent. A group of American artillery officers accompanied by an equal number of Vietnamese strode out of the operations shack and climbed aboard the two helicopters. The Vietnamese officers wore the same high-laced, black, combat boots, starched, olive-green dungarees, and round-topped fatigue caps as the Americans. Only their insignia of rank was different. They seemed frail and boyish among the Americans. Two of the Americans dragged aboard a pair of 4.2 inch mortar standards, the piece of equipment which supports the tube and absorbs the shock of the explosion. The officers nodded to McWhorter and crowded onto the canvas ledges facing each other, conversation impossible as the two triple-bladed rotors drew the chopper rapidly upward. Between the muscular calves of the crew chief, McWhorter could see the shrinking earth moving by at ninety miles an hour, a succession of palm-fringed rice paddies varying in color from muddy brown to emerald green, over which whirred a cloud of pintail snipe. A pair of slate-gray water buffaloes, lethargically tossing their great scimitar horns, wallowed happily in a mudhole, three naked boys astride their patient backs. The wet skins of the boys glistened in the morning light as they waved at the helicopters, laughing, white-toothed. The crew chief's solemn, empty, young face softened behind his plastic visor and he waved slowly to the boys. McWhorter jotted notes furiously on his folded piece of paper as the land slid by beneath him, the rice paddies

giving way to banana plantations and then to jungle laced with
secret creeks snaking their way down to a river of slow-
flowing silver upon which floated a single junk, its prow
forcing a wide V of ripples on the placid water. McWhorter
breathed deeply, sucking in the remembered odor of war, an
amalgam of vomit, cosmoline, hot oil, sweat, leather, and
tobacco, marbled by thin streaks of fear and excitement.

The slender Vietnamese officer next to McWhorter sat with
a plastic map case balanced on his knees. His eyes, nervous and
beady as a ferret's, shifted from the map case to the door as
he searched for terrain features which he could identify on the
map. The American major on the other side of the Vietnamese
officer pulled a crumpled sweat-stained notebook from his
pocket, scribbled something on it, tore out the sheet, and
handed it to the Vietnamese officer with a smile. The Vietnamese held the note, badly scrawled because of the vibration
of the chopper, close to his face. McWhorter leaned over his
shoulder and looked at the note. It read: "I've been selected
for Lt. Colonel." The Vietnamese officer flashed a toothy
smile, bobbed his head vigorously, and wrung the major's
hand.

A few minutes later the chopper dropped down on Beria, a
quiet-looking town with sedate, tree-lined streets, whitewashed churches and a soccer field edged with bright pink
landing panels. All the officers, except for a big, cigar-
smoking captain from Texas and one of the Vietnamese, left
Little Miss Linda. The pilots kept the big rotors of their
choppers revolving slowly while the officers jumped to the
ground, then climbed quickly into the air again.

McWhorter was uncertain of the chopper's position, but
it seemed obvious that they were over a quiet area. The crew
chief locked his machine gun into its stationary mount and sat
on the floor, the M-14 in his lap, his legs dangling out the
doorway above the placid, green face of Vietnam. The gentle
sunlight glancing off the flooded rice paddies gave the land
the appearance of being jellied in an aspic over which the
two misshaped helicopters chased their shadows in fruitless
pursuit. The crew chief was worrying a pimple on his chin,
his legs locked around the rifle, his brow knit in concentration.
Finally he gave up on the pimple. From time to time, he
pulled a small Kodak from inside his bulletproof vest and
snapped pictures of the countryside.

Somewhere down beneath them, McWhorter thought, but
further to the north, in the hills, is Harry Coltart. How long

it seemed, the time when he and Harry had met at the University of Virginia's Woodrow Wilson School. Coltart was an odd one, a man whose motivations seemed obscure. Yet his origins were clear enough: small-town Virginia, middle class, although nurturing a familial memory of better times. Noblesse oblige right up to the ears. He liked Harry Coltart, but in a curious way the Virginian's world and the real one seemed to mesh only at certain points. Coltart, he mused, clings to many concepts, God, honor with a capital H, a mystical attachment to the soil, concepts which are fine in themselves but no longer have much relevance; Harry made trouble for himself by insisting upon them. McWhorter remembered driving through the rolling countryside of northern Virginia, along a curving black-topped road beside neatly whitewashed fences. Fat brown and white cattle grazed in the stubble of cornfields, the autumn air was sharp and clean with the smell of wood smoke and dying leaves and Harry Coltart was talking about "the family place" as if it still belonged to the old judge. The farm had, McWhorter knew, been sold to wealthy New Yorkers years before, people who used it as a casual hobby, a plaything, a tax write-off. Yet Harry had talked of the smoke-filled woods and the red, greasy soil as if they still were his, as if New Yorkers had nothing to do with it, as if the land and the ruined Coltart family shared a collective character, a being which could not be altered by the accident of legal ownership. That had been the last he'd seen of Harry until several months before, quite by accident, he'd come upon him talking in the bar of the Caravelle with the fat man they called Englehardt. It had been quite a surprise. Yes, Harry Coltart was a decent person: that was his principal problem.

The crew chief scrambled to his feet, unlocking his machine gun, and beneath them McWhorter saw what he took to be Xuyen Moc, an untidy little market town floating on the edge of a soggy plain. The choppers circled the field twice, the pilots studying the forest which crept up to the borders of the pink panels which lined the landing strip.

"Why all this?" McWhorter asked.

"Dunno," the big Texan replied. "Maybe neither of these pilots have been here before and they want to be sure the field is secure. Everybody's a bit edgy nowadays."

McWhorter nodded.

"We'll be here about an hour," the captain continued, chewing on his cold cigar butt, "come along, if you like."

The chopper dropped down fast, hitting the ground with a bump, and the two officers, followed by McWhorter, made the four-foot, ankle-jarring jump to the ground. Xuyen Moc's garrison, a reinforced mortar platoon, huddled in a stockade of sharpened stakes set in chest-high earthworks topped off by soggy sandbags. There was a little barbed wire around the position, McWhorter noted, but it was carelessly laid and would have presented no real obstacle to a determined attacker. Grass four feet high grew right up to the edge of the earthworks, affording good concealment for infiltrators. The Texan inspected the four mortar positions set in the angles of the decrepit fort, checking the lie of their aiming stakes and the condition of the rounds in each sandbagged, underground ammunition room. Mud was everywhere. In the subterranean fire-center, the battery commander showed the Texan his fire-chart encased in a moldy plastic cover. The battery had not fired a mission in two weeks.

"How many hamlets in your area?" the Texan asked.

"Fourteen," replied the slender Vietnamese battery commander. "Two I support from this position. When others are attacked, we sometimes go out." McWhorter thought the Vietnamese looked slightly bored with the whole affair.

"Isn't there a better position?" McWhorter asked. "One from which you could cover more hamlets?"

The battery commander nodded.

"Xuyen Moc is headquarters of the district chief," the Vietnamese added. "We must be here to protect him."

"It's a problem," the Texan interjected. "If the army didn't spend half its time protecting the local administrators, the Vietcong would assassinate them all. But it's a helluva way to try to fight a war."

"Can't the police or the territorial militia handle that?" McWhorter asked.

The Texan shook his head and made a face.

"Not reliable. Honeycombed with Vietcong."

"How's the war look to you, Captain?" McWhorter asked.

The Texan smiled wryly.

"Some of the units," he answered, "aren't too bad. All depends on the officers. None of them are up to ROK standards, and that's low enough. Got me a two-year-old boy back in Houston. He'll be advising these fellows before this war is won."

"We're losing then?"

"Wouldn't say that. But we sure aren't winning."

The Texan thanked the battery commander and turned to the English-speaking officer who had come in the helicopter. "Tell the garrison commander that I'm having a look at his men's quarters. I'll join him in his command post in five minutes."

McWhorter followed the Texan into the first cantonment, a long, single-roomed shelter with a dirt floor, wooden half-sides, and a thatched roof. The captain tested the thatch for dampness and shook his head in dismay. Rows of cots lined the dimly lit room. Cardboard boxes, perhaps containing the soldiers' possessions, were stacked in the corners, and a row of carbines leaned against the wall. From the rough-hewn rafters hung blankets and torn mosquito nets. A puppy chased a scrawny chicken among the cots. A Vietnamese woman was cooking rice over a small fire next to the wall. She looked up from her task and then returned to it. The captain sniffed noncommittally.

"Let's get back to the command post. Chopper pilots will be getting fidgety," he said.

The command post was underground, very dark and cool. At a large, wooden table sat the garrison commander, a slender, middle-aged man with a delicate, dissolute face. He rose to his feet, smiled and shook hands first with the Texan, then with McWhorter. On the sandbagged wall hung a commerical calendar showing a big-breasted blond in a red bathing suit. Some of the dates on the calendar were circled and McWhorter wondered what their significance might be. His busy pencil stabbed at the piece of copy paper folded in his hand. He noticed that the garrison commander wore an enormous gentian violet ring on his left hand, the little finger of which bore a nail at least a half an inch long. Not many rifle bolts, he thought, had been worked by those delicate hands.

A soldier brought five bottles of warm root beer, removed the caps with his teeth, and poured the liquid into tin canteen cups. McWhorter and the Texan sipped their drinks in silence while the English-speaking officer chattered with the garrison commander and the battery commander.

"The garrison commander's generator is broken," the English-speaking officer said to the Texan. "He apologizes for the lack of ice and wonders if you could take the generator back to Bien Hoa to be fixed."

"Suppose so. Have him get it aboard right away. And tell

him I'd suggest he have that high grass cut back. And get some drainage ditches in, or his ammo will go bad on him."

The English-speaking officer translated the Texan's words and nodded his head while the garrison commander replied.

"He's been meaning to," he said, "and the generator's already aboard."

The day wore on with a succession of short hops, and McWhorter began to suspect that the scent of the war for which he had come was evading him, that the freshness, the new perspective, was not to be. His head ached and he felt vaguely cheated. Then it happened at Ben Cat. The quick, corkscrew drop into the beleaguered post on bloody Highway 13, undertaken to deliver four wooden bureaus and a case of whisky to the advisor to the Vietnamese Seventh Regiment, provoked a desultory burst of small arms fire from far away in the jungle. There a Vietnamese medical officer dashed out to the helicopters.

"Please, sirs," he said breathlessly to the pilots of the two helicopters, "an officer is badly wounded near the river. Can you pick him up?"

Little Miss Linda's pilot's young face turned slightly gray and he suddenly looked much older.

"We're not supposed to go in there without an escort of Hueys. You know that," he replied to the medical officer.

"Why not jeep him out?" asked the warrant officer with the pock-marked face.

The doctor shook his head.

"The road's mined and he's too badly hurt to stand the ride, anyway."

"What about it, Carlson?" the warrant officer said to the pilot.

"Yeah. We'll get him for you, Doc. Climb aboard." The pilot, McWhorter thought, did not look at all happy.

McWhorter scribbled a description of the Vietnamese doctor on his folded piece of copy paper as the rotors turned over slowly, gaining power, and the two choppers shot into the air, climbing out of range of the crackling ground fire from the jungle around Ben Cat. McWhorter had not put on the bulletproof vest handed him by the crew chief at Tan Son Nhut. Now he slipped it under him surreptitiously, sitting on it. Beneath the chopper, between the crew chief's legs, he saw the great, gray snake of the river, crawling hesitantly through the jungle's rough pelt toward mountains distant and blue. The pilot, flying high and well out of small-arms range, followed the course of the river for fifteen minutes before banking the chopper sharply, stretching tight the safety harness of the crew chief, and McWhorter saw a clearing filled with green tents and thatched shelters, and the tiny dots of men running among them. The helicopter spiraled down dizzily in a fast, sickening corkscrew, bumping hard twice and then settling uneasily to the earth among the green tents, the rotors sucking up dust in a choking cloud. The pilot kept the rotors turning over and the Vietnamese doctor jumped from the shivering helicopter to meet four men running hard toward the clearing, a stretcher between them. The doctor and the stretcher-bearers shoved the litter up to the door, the crew chief and the gunner pulling it in, the wounded man rolling from side to side, whimpering softly.

The man on the stretcher, although he wore the insignia of an officer, was barefoot. War has not changed very much, McWhorter thought. They still rob the wounded in every army. He wondered if the man still had his wallet. The officer's beltless trousers were undone, revealing white undershorts marked with red polka dots. His head was wrapped in a bloody bandage and his bruised face was splotched with iodine stains which covered small cuts. Other bandages had been wrapped hastily around an elbow, a finger, and a toe. Must have been a grenade, McWhorter thought to himself, or a mine. The wounded man's eyes opened and closed spasmodically, as if he were having trouble focusing them. A cardboard medical tag was tied to the buttonhole of his dungaree jacket pocket.

The Vietnamese doctor ran up the landing strip to the helicopter's nose, cupped his hands and shouted to the pilot. McWhorter could hear the words only indistinctly over the impatient roaring of the motors:

"One more . . . wounded badly . . . coming now . . . wait, please wait . . ."

The pilot slapped his forehead with his open palm and slumped down into his seat, muttering to himself. It was very hot and beads of sweat stood out on the brow of the wounded officer, his hands shaking spasmodically by his sides. Four more soldiers ran forward with another stretcher. Other Vietnamese clad only in undershorts or breechclouts stood watching the helicopter from the lips of their gun emplacements, their hands on their narrow hips. McWhorter gave them the thumbs-up signal, but they only stared at him curiously. On the stretcher was what appeared to be a rough bag made of pieces of burlap and patches of blankets sewn together. The bag rolled from side to side as the soldiers carried it toward the helicopter. Whatever was in the bag was very small. The soldiers handed the stretcher up to the crew chief and the gunner, and McWhorter noticed that the litter was sticky with blood. The doctor clambered in after the stretcher and gave the thumbs-up signal to the pilot. He did not need to repeat it. The engines roared as Carlson jerked the stick back sharply, clawing for altitude, the stretchers sliding back toward the rear of the chopper until the doctor braced them with his feet, the crew chief firing a single burst of his machine gun into the jungle in response to a hail of small-arms fire, and then they were up and out of range, the jungle gray beneath them.

McWhorter relaxed and handed the doctor a pack of cigarettes, motioning toward the wounded man. The doctor took a cigarette from the pack and held it in front of the wounded man's face, his eyebrows raised in interrogation. The wounded man nodded his head slightly.

The doctor braced himself, lit the cigarette, placed it between the wounded man's lips, and handed the pack back to McWhorter with a smile. McWhorter shook his head, unbuttoned the wounded man's other breast pocket, put the pack in, and buttoned it up again. The wounded man drew on the cigarette but his eyelids continued to flutter.

The doctor made his way back to the second stretcher, balancing himself by pressing his hands against the roof of the chopper. He pulled back the burlap and making a face knelt next to the stretcher. He shook his head, replaced the burlap, and walked back to the wounded officer, busying himself with the head dressing. The pilot left the warrant officer at the controls and swayed back into the main cabin.

"Land mine," said the doctor, looking up at the pilot and pointing at the burlap sack on the second stretcher. "Died on the way in. This one is okay. Thanks."

Carlson slumped down beside McWhorter and shook his head in disgust.

"No point keeping this chopper on the ground for a d.o.a. but you can't teach these guys anything. Once Dutch and me had to cart back nineteen dead ones that had been lying in a rice paddy three days. Puked all the way until we soaked handkerchiefs in gasoline and tied them over our mouths. Since then I don't carry no bodies unless they're bagged or fresh."

Through the open door McWhorter could see the dolls'
houses on the outskirts of Saigon. Soon, he knew, they would
be back at Tan Son Nhut. He glanced at his almost illegible
notes. It had not been a bad day after all. He would catch a
jeep to the modernistic pile of St. Gobain glass and Italian
marble which was the Caravelle and go directly to the bar.
He would talk about the war with the cluster of reporters at
the bar, their envious eyes hating his dungarees. Then he
would go to his room and knock out the story about the
wounded officer whose boots had been stolen and the dead
man in the burlap sack. Ben Cat was a very good dateline
and he sensed he would write with a new vigor and percep-
tion. It could be a very nice little story.

Part Three

THE BUFFALO

CHAPTER THIRTEEN

LOYE LAY ON HIS BELLY in the reeds, studying the mission buildings bathed in moonlight beneath him. The grounds of Notre Dame des Bois were washed with the pale white light and he knew, although he wore no watch, that he had four hours until dawn. Soon the moon would sink into the hills and darkness would fill the land. Already it was happening; the outlines of the long, low hospital building, of the church with its bamboo spire and cross, of the houses of the priest and his staff, were becoming smudged and indistinct. It was almost time. In the few minutes left to him, Loye went over his plan. He was a little nervous because it was the first time he had commanded in action. Still, the plan was good because it was simple. Nothing could go wrong and there should be little resistance. He had ambushes set up on the road two miles to either side of Notre Dame des Bois. If government troops answered the attack, his ambush teams would delay them long enough for him to withdraw with the main body of his men into the rubber plantation, falling back upon the hills. Diem's troops would not follow him into the hills. Not at night. Night and the hills fight with us, he thought. "Avoid the solid; attack the hollow," Comrade Mao had written and the operation certainly was in accord with this maxim. A lone *Boc* priest and a handful of hospital orderlies hardly could offer much resistance.

He had been a little surprised on reaching his sector headquarters to find the orders for the attack waiting for him. At first he had not understood what was to be gained by destroying the mission. The hospital, he knew, was the only one within reach of the southern montagnards. Then the political *can-bo* had explained to him that the *Boc* priest and the nearby French planter, he who had been Loye's own officer, were friends of Erohé, that it was hoped that the attack would lure Erohé down out of the hills where he could be ambushed and destroyed. Aside from the fact that the montagnards would

miss the hospital, Loye saw nothing wrong in attacking it;
Notre Dame des Bois was, after all, a part of the society the
Vietcong intended to destroy. The mission was not whole-
heartedly with the people, for medical care was given indiscriminately, to wounded government soldiers, to those wholly
without politics, and to sick Diemist administrators, as well as
to members of the Vietcong. Yet, he thought to himself, when
I wore the uniform of the French, we did not attack hospitals.
It occurred to him then that the Vietminh had possessed no
hospitals to be attacked, even as his men today had none. You
did what you could for a wounded man and he either lived
or he died. There was no such thing as a noncombatant in
this war. There were only known friends. Everyone else,
man, woman, and child, priest and doctor, was to be regarded
as an enemy. He was a little sorry about the business of having
to kill the priest, but he was a *Boc* and undoubtedly an enemy
of the people.

As he watched the slow digestion of the mission buildings
by the darkness, the soft moonlight melting in the crisp, night
air, Loye felt rested and ready, the monkey meat and rice
warm in his stomach. It had been a long march from the
forest clearing which was his headquarters, its approaches
studded with *punjis* dipped in human excrement. The men,
particularly those carrying the heavy mortar, had been very
tired by the time they had passed through the rubber and into
the bush at the outskirts of the mission. They had lain up
in the bush for two days, recovering their strength, spying out
the land, erecting the aiming stakes for the mortar, waiting for
the moon to be right. There was no reason to hurry. The
fattest roebuck, Loye knew, fell not to the quickest hunter,
but the surest. Besides, the wait had given him a chance to get
to know his men. Most of them were Annamese or half-caste
Annamese-montagnards, although he had a sprinkling of hill
men. This would change, he knew, once the news reached the
Rhadé that he was leading the Vietcong. Many Rhadé would
come then; Cheo would send them. Until then, his men were
not too bad, although few had seen much serious fighting.
Only the mortar crew was from a Chu Luc division, but he
was glad to have even these few regulars. Loye reckoned he
had drawn his net around Notre Dame des Bois with care.
He had visited both the nearby government forts and talked
with the soldiers. Most of them were not enthusiastic about
the war. He did not think they would come out in the night
to defend the mission. And if they did, they would come too

late. They would find trees felled across the road and, at the ambushes, the grenades of his blocking teams. He would like to have arranged with the guards to put a little sugar into the gas tanks of the trucks, but he was not sure enough of them to attempt that. Still, there would be plenty of time. The moment was at hand.

Loye inhaled deeply, filling his lungs with the cool, night air, raised the whistle to his lips and blew one long, insistent note. Almost before the noise of his whistle had died, he heard the pop of the mortar off to his right, the compelling sigh of the shell as it reached the height of its arc and dropped toward the mission, slicing through the night. His muscles tightened in anticipation of the explosion. The projectile hit the rusty corrugated iron roof of the hospital with the clang of a metal bar striking a gong, illuminating the grounds of Notre Dame des Bois for a brief instant, showering the darkness with sparks, filling it with the eerie shrieking of wounded metal. For a full fifteen seconds the night was bloated with an immense silence, broken only by the sputtering of a small flame in the thatched wall of the hospital near where the shell had hit. The silence was so consummate, so complete and rounded, that for a moment Loye feared that he had been betrayed, that the bearded priest they called Father Dupleix had fled, taking with him his patients. Then the silence gave way to the thin sound of wailing, as of that of threatened children, and this cry swelled until it gained weight and dimensions, a great whimper of terror punctuated by shouts and howls and the sound as of tearing silk as the thatched walls gave way under pressure, and of many bare feet pounding on a wooden floor set above the ground, like rapid beating on a tightly-stretched drum. The second shell exploded in a brilliant flash high above the mission, flooding the grounds with a wavering light, the shadows jumping from side to side, the glare growing more luminous and unreal as the sputtering flare began its slow, undulating fall toward the earth. Now, Loye thought to himself, the Chu Luc mortar crew will be breaking down their weapon, one man taking the heavy base plate, another the tube and bipod, the third the ammunition, all of them running hard for the road and the shelter of the rubber trees. Their work was done, their shells too precious to be expended on such a target as the hospital, their weapon too valuable to remain long in action.

In the brilliant, unreal radiance of the flare, Loye saw a swirling mass of men and women burst from the door of the

hospital, exploding onto the veranda. Then the machine gun
began to chatter in long, voluptuous, rippling bursts and the
knot of bodies disintegrated into individual black clots which
tumbled forward onto the floor of the veranda, spilling down
the steps and into the dust. One man, his face distorted by
an expression of enraged embarrassment, as if he had been
surprised by a stranger while relieving himself, pitched forward against the railing, hung there for an instant until the
split bamboo gave way under his wounded weight, and then
tumbled awkwardly into the flower bed, dragging the railing
with him, crushing the blossoms. The patients not hit by the
fire of the machine gun scrambled back toward the door,
struggling to re-enter the building. As the flare drifted closer
to the ground, Loye could see a man dressed in a black cotton
pajama suit, apparently hit in the spine, flopping across the
veranda, unable to rise, one hand held up in supplication for
an assistance which did not come. In the flare's dying light,
which set huge, unearthly shadows to cavorting on the
powdered dust of the hospital grounds, Loye watched as
one of his men broke from cover with a flaming torch in
his hand, raced toward the building, stopped and lofted the
brand toward the hospital. The torch, in the darkness left
by the flare sputtering on the ground, sailed end over end in
a lazy parabola, sparks trailing out behind it, like a shooting
star in a summer sky. The torch stuck in the thatch and then
the wall burst into flames with a gentle *pouff*. The other wall,
ablaze near the spot where the mortar had caved in the roof,
already gave off a flickering light which the new fire strengthened, flooding the clearing of Notre Dame des Bois with a
gentle, festive halo against which reverberated the swelling
howls of the wounded, trapped in the burning building. Once
more the patients tried to rush the door and were driven back
by the barking of the machine gun. Others forced their way
through the yielding walls and jumped from the windows,
some to fall under the fire of his riflemen, others to stumble
away into the shadows. Another of his men, Toa he thought
it was, raced into the firelight and stopped short to pull a pin
from a grenade, his body caught and silhouetted against the
fire, the light playing on the bunched muscles of his bent
body, as if in some ritualistic pose. Toa hurled the grenade
with a stiff-armed motion and the momentum of his throw
sent him sprawling on the ground. The grenade rattled on
the wooden floor of the veranda and bounced into the black

maw of the door, from which came a sharp, bright flash, a dull
explosion, and new, wilder shrieking.

Loye uttered a whoop of triumph and leaped to his feet,
racing his huge and distorted shadow through the guttering
light cast by the burning building, the howls of the dying
clamorous in his ears, his nostrils tickled by the sweet smell of
charring flesh, dodging from side to side, as if he were avoiding holes in the hospital's ground.

As he reached his objective, the small house behind and to
the left of the hospital, the door swung open and the bearded
priest stepped onto the veranda, naked except for a strip of
brightly colored cotton around his loins, folds of fat bulging
over the top of the material, his feet bare. In one hand the
Boc patjao carried a heavy walking stick which was almost
a cudgel; in the other he grasped a crucifix. Loye skidded
to a stop, the toes of his bare feet gripping the ground and,
for an instant, the two men stood facing each other, Loye
covering the *Boc* with his machine pistol.

"You!" the priest shouted in accusation, his head low, his
eyes glowering, his legs set wide apart, like an old *serow*
brought to bay by a pack of hunting dogs.

Loye saw the priest's eyes flick away from him, over his
head the light from the burning building flashing in the whites
of his eyes, his jaw working as he listened to the crackling of
the flames and the screams of the dying. An oath Loye could
not understand broke not from the lips of the *patjao* but from
deep down inside him, so terrible was it in its anger and
pain, as the *Boc* hurled his cudgel and charged down the steps,
the crucifix trailing from his left hand. Loye dropped to one
knee as the stick sailed over his shoulder and pressed the
trigger of the machine pistol. The impact of the bullets
doubled up the priest and halted his charge. Then the *Boc*
straightened up, blood spurting from the wounds tattooing
his belly, and came on again.

"Notre Dame des Bois," he shouted, lurching forward.

Loye rose to his feet, balancing easily upon them, ready to
step aside, and clubbed the machine pistol. But the priest
collapsed at his feet, face down in the dust, his cloth trailing
out behind him, his buttocks naked and coated with dirt. The
old *patjao* charges like a wounded *bantang*, Loye thought to
himself as he kicked the priest once, hard, in the side of the
face. The *Boc* did not move. He has much heart, he mused,
just like an old *bantang*, but now he is dead. As three of his
men emerged from the shadows, he knelt beside the priest and

pried the crucifix from his hand, stuffing it into his own pocket. He was not a Christian, but such things were said to be powerful amulets.

Loye turned to his companions and made a stiff-wristed chopping motion across his throat. One of them, a half-caste Sadang, knotted his fingers in the priest's thick, graying hair and pulled back hard, exposing the dead man's throat. Then he began to saw through the windpipe and cartilage with his bushknife. The cartilage was tough and the man had to lean heavily on the knife to get it through. Another man knelt at the *Boc's* crotch and began to cut.

"You," Loye said to the third, unable to recall his name, "tear a piece of bamboo from the railing and stick it in the soft earth around the flowers. And see if the *Boc* has meat or fat in his kitchen. Cloth, too." They were short of these things. Fat was much needed for cleaning the mortar.

While the man with the bushknife was hacking his way through the neck-bone, grunting for emphasis with each blow, Loye tested the stability of the bamboo stake. It seemed strong enough.

"Done," said the half-caste, wiping the broad blade of the bushknife on his black shorts. "Shall I do it?" he asked.

"No, I'll do it," Loye answered, bending over and grabbing the head by the ears. His hands were sweating, the ears were small, and the head was surprisingly heavy. He had gotten it up only to waist level when it slipped from his grip and fell to the ground with a squelching noise, rolling aside into the flowers.

The other two men laughed.

"He resists," said one.

"He does not want to watch his hospital burn," said the half-caste.

"He will watch," Loye said. This time he grabbed the head with both hands by the hair, lifting it up until he had it centered on the end of the sharpened bamboo, blood draining from the neck in little spurts. Then he slid his hands down the sides of the *Boc's* head until he could grab each ear. He pulled down hard, lifting his feet off the ground so that he brought his weight to bear, and the head settled onto the bamboo stake.

"Oh, yes," Loye said, "the *Boc* will watch his hospital burn." With his knife he pried open the dead man's mouth, cutting the *patjao's* lip in the process, a thin trickle of blood flowing from the corner of his mouth, so that he appeared to be frowning. Without looking at the other man, he held out his hand, receiving the *Boc's* genitals, warm and slippery between his fingers. Breathing hard, sweat streaming across his naked chest, he stuffed the genitals into the dead man's mouth.

"He dines well," said the half-caste. Loye and the second man chuckled appreciatively. The man who had set up the stake came running from the priest's house, holding a large tin in his hands, three white cassocks trailing behind him.

"Only this," he shouted.

Loye nodded. The clearing was full of the crackling of the burning hospital, as the roof caved in with a shower of sparks. The church was burning, too. There were no more screams from the hospital. But the air was larded with the odor of burning flesh and the smell of blood, the light of the guttering flames flickering across the ruined flower beds. Down toward the labor lines of Notre Dame des Bois, Loye heard a single shot, and then another. He glanced at the head of the *Boc* priest impaled upon the stake, the ground at its base dark with blood. The *patjao's* eyes stared unflinchingly at the flaming hospital, the light from the fire dancing in his dead eyes, the obscene parts dribbling from his mouth. In the end, Loye thought, he was not afraid. The crucifix of such a one could not be an ineffective fetish. Well, it was done.

"Let's get out of here," he said quietly, and the men raced across the clearing in front of him, their shadows at their heels, into the quiet coolness of the rubber trees.

As he crossed the road, running hard, Loye heard from away to the north the delicate pop of an exploding grenade. Some of the troops had found the courage to come out. He wished he could have arranged the business of the sugar in the gas tanks. He would do it next time. From the direction of the other ambush, there was only silence. Still, he thought to himself, despite the movement to the north we are in good time. The whole operation had taken no more than ten minutes, perhaps twelve. It could be improved upon, of course. But as he ran, Loye felt pleased with himself and with his men. All had gone as he had planned. The beheading of the priest had been a good idea. The government troops would think nothing of it. It was traditional to mutilate the dead, who could, in any case, feel nothing. Yet Loye knew from his time with the French the effect such things had on the *Bocs*. If the *patjao* were truly a friend of Erohé's.

would the *Boc* not come to avenge him? Even if he did not come, he would hear about it and be angry; an angry man often was an incautious one. Erohé might be provoked into making a serious blunder in the hills. The only thing that caused Loye any concern about the attack was the two mortar shells he had expended. It was a great luxury to have a mortar but he had only thirteen shells, now only eleven. Since the closest government troops were those in the fortified posts guarding the road, there was no place in the hills where he could steal or buy more shells. He might have been wrong to waste two shells on the hospital. He would have to be more careful in the future. Still, it had been his first operation, and he'd wanted to be sure it was a success. It had been: Notre Dame des Bois was no more. The hospital building could be replaced, of course, and another *Boc* priest might be sent. But the fat, bearded one had worn a great name and he could not be replaced. No, Loye told himself, he had cause to be satisfied.

When he reached the shed where the rubber was cooked in huge metal vats and pressed into rough sheets, all his men were there except for the Chu Luc mortar crew and the two ambush groups.

"The mortar?" he asked.

"Gone on," replied Toa.

"Anyone hurt?" he asked.

"No."

"Let's go then."

"The big house?" Toa inquired. His instructions from Saigon had included the secondary objective of killing the *Boc* officer, if he could do so without endangering his attack group.

"Perhaps, but troops are coming. There's not much time. Move out in twos and threes and meet at the waterfall."

As he watched his men slip off into the night, Loye considered the situation. The problem was that the *Boc* certainly would have heard the mortar. And being a soldier, he probably had a gun. It was not worth taking too much of a chance. Still, it would be a fitting end to the attack.

As he ran after his men, across the lawn in front of the big plantation house, Loye wrestled with the idea. Suddenly he made up his mind, changed direction and ran through the flower beds, vaulting over the railing and onto the veranda. As his bare feet hit the wooden floor, a bright light flooded the veranda. Blinded, he raised his left hand in an attempt to shield his eyes and swung the machine pistol up in front of him.

"Loye," said a quiet voice in Rhadé, "you've come far from the Black River."

Loye spun on his heels to face the sound of the voice, dropping to one knee.

"Nothing stupid, Loye. You're too good a soldier for that."

Loye swore to himself. What a fool I've been! It was enough to have destroyed the hospital. The *Boc's* voice was confident, unafraid. Obviously he had a gun. And he knew how to use it. Loye remained crouched, playing for time while his vision returned to him. But the voice, which came from a darkened window opening onto an interior room, still had no body.

"What do you want, Loye? Your corporal's chevrons? I no longer can give them to you. Why kill me? It's not my war."

Loye relaxed a little. The *Boc*, he sensed, did not intend to harm him.

"I gave you your life once, *Boc*, on the Black River. Now give me mine in return."

"Father Dupleix?" the voice inquired.

"Dead."

"I taught you much, Loye, but never this." The voice had an edge of harshness to it now, Loye noted, a tinge of sadness, and a tone of death.

"That's why you lost, *Boc*, why we will win. But time is short. Shoot, or pay your debt and let me go."

"Yes. Never enough time in war, is there? One always is in a hurry, rushing to kill or be killed. Get out, then. Our score is settled."

Loye whirled and vaulted over the railing, landing spread-toed in the soft earth of the flower bed. He ran ten steps until he was clear of the light, then turned and sprayed the brightly illuminated veranda with his machine pistol, just as the light flicked off. As he fired, he sensed that the *Boc* had been unarmed. But he had no time to test this belief. He could hear trucks growling up the road and the sound of men shouting orders in Annamese. There will be another time, he thought, as he sprinted for the cover of the forest. Always there is another time. The work of this night was finished.

CHAPTER FOURTEEN

HAD EVER THERE BEEN such a feast before? Ilouha, sucking the marrow from a roebuck's shinbone, as she squatted with the other women over the dying embers of the cooking-fires, guessed that there had not. Nor in her lifetime was there likely to be another like it. Budop, the toothless one, the oldest of the Koho from Di-Linh to Dalat, had mumbled that he had seen nothing like it even in that misty, far-off time of his youth, before the *Bocs* had reached the highlands. And when Budop made an admission like that, it was worth something. Usually, according to him, everything had been bigger and better in those forgotten days. It was hard to imagine cranky old Budop as a young man, a hunter, a warrior, a pleaser of women. Always, it seemed, he had been old, his joints stiff and swollen, his gums bare, the muscles of his knobby chest fallen into women's breasts. If such a one as he could remember no such gathering of the chiefs, surely there had been none since the beginning of time.

The chiefs had been coming in for five days. No, six. Mouc, of the northern Koho, of whom she had heard but never thought to see, had been the first to come swaggering in. Mouc was rich beyond the telling, his women bragged. He had forgotten the names of his buffaloes, and his long-house held as many bronze gongs as a dog has fleas. Or so his women said. Two had come with him, his senior wife, an ancient, withered crone with breasts like tobacco pouches, and a fat, smiling girl who boasted of being Mouc's favorite. Although Ilouha knew that Mouc was a powerful chief, she was skeptical of the tales of his wealth and of his prowess as a hunter. The fat, young wife, she thought, boasts of Mouc's glory to give herself importance. *Aagh-ah*, yet was there one woman, Koho or Stieng, Mnong or Rhadé, who had a man, a *Boc* such as hers? A killer of men, his hair the color of beaten gold, his eyes like a dawn sky? A hunter slim as bamboo yet powerful as the great bull buffalo which was to

138

die this night? There is no other such as he, she thought to
herself complacently, and my belly swells with his son. She
had spoken of this to no one, except Hamon, the *patjao*, who
had studied the entrails of the forest fowl and assured her that
it would be a boy. It would be something she might hint of
to Mouc's fat wife. That one, she knew, had given Mouc no
children, although she had been his during the gathering of
three rice crops. Yes, she would tell Mouc's wife about the
seed within her, and feast on her envy.

So it had been six days since Mouc had strutted into the
village, two warriors at his side and two of his wives behind
him, carrying his great, silver-studded shield of buffalo hide,
his sleeping robes, and his weapons. The other chiefs, accompanied by their counselors, their warriors, and their favorite
wives, had come the next day and the next, until the forest
was filled with faces strange to her. Many Yé had known
in the days of his youth, when he had hunted the length and
breadth of the land, and some, whose villages were nearby,
Ilouha had seen at other gatherings. But never had there been
such a gathering as this. For not only had the Koho come
but other strange chiefs from far away, from the Stieng and
the Rhadé and the Chrao, some even from the villages of the
Jarai and the Bahnar, whose longhouses were many days'
march to the north. No chiefs had come from the Raglai or
the Chru or the Hroi. The Chru did not come, she thought,
because they are women and fear us. Many times Yé had
warred on the Chru, who lived to the east, and they feared
him. Why the Hroi and the Raglai chiefs had not come, she
did not know. Yé never had warred against them. Their
country was far away and they were savage, ignorant people.
She had heard it whispered among the women cooking rice
for the feast that the Hroi ate the flesh of men, which was an
abomination, and that the Raglai had tails like monkeys. She
wondered if this could be so and wished that their chiefs had
come so that she could have seen with her own eyes. It was
a great pity about the Hroi and the Raglai. But at least most
of the chiefs of the big tribes had come. Even old Cheo, the
great chief of the Rhadé, the friend of Yé's youth, had come.
She had thought that Cheo might stay away from the feast
because of Loye. In a time long ago, she knew, Cheo had
wanted her for Loye, and it had been promised. But she had
been only a breastless girl then and Loye had gone off to fight
with the *Bocs* against the Vietminh and had not returned.
Now Loye was back in his own country and leading men

against Erohé. She did not know if he was doing this because Erohé had taken her for his woman, but the possibility that this might be so did not displease her. Try as she could, she remembered Loye only vaguely, like a dream recalled at midday. His name, for her, conjured up only the image of a young hunter, lithe and strong, leaning on his crossbow, his eyes glad with the sight of her. But his face was dim in her mind. Now, they said, he was a great chief, leading the warriors of many tribes against the Annamese of Saigon, against Erohé. Loye had guns and he had men and this was wealth. But what wealth could there be to compare to that of Erohé, who had returned from the palace of the emperor in Saigon bearing guns and ammunition, gold dust and red blankets, bronze gongs and mirrors, copper wire and salt, gifts for everyone in the village and for every chief who might come to the great gathering? Still, it was no small thing to be desired by both Erohé and Loye. Mouc's fat, young wife could make no such claim.

It had taken a long time to assemble so many chiefs from so far away. As soon as Erohé had returned from the plains with the word of the emperor, Yé had sent runners loping over the forest trails. And now, weeks later, the chiefs had come, and a great feast was ready for them. There were great piles of rice, platters of river fish, heaps of succulent roasted francolin, crabs from the rice paddies, the flesh of pigs roasted whole over the four fires which danced at each corner of the clearing, chicken livers spiced with peppers, and great, cool jars of rice wine secured to stakes sunk in the ground, bamboo drinking-tubes sprouting from their necks.

The moon was high now and through the clashing of the gongs and the high-pitched shrilling of the flutes, Ilouha could hear the lowing of the great buffalo tugging at its tether to the sacrificial pole in the center of the clearing, its flanks stained with blood from the taunting stabs of the spearmen. Only once before could she remember an occasion so solemn that a bull buffalo had been slaughtered. That had been years ago, in the time of sickness, when every Koho village had sacrificed a bull to drive out the fever which was wasting the tribe. The sickness had died with the buffaloes and the fever had left the land. Tonight the death of the buffalo would kill the untruth in the hearts of the chiefs who had come together to decide this great thing of the fighting. No one, not Yé nor Mouc nor Cheo nor Erohé, could speak with a twisted tongue at such a time. For if he did, the buffalo's death would

be his own. She had explained it all to Erohé, speaking slowly
and carefully, like an old woman explaining to a young
one about the taboos of the blood, so that he might understand the greatness of the oath they were all about to swear.
Erohé had listened to her quietly, his face grave, nodding his
understanding.

The moan of the strings of the *brans*, strummed by the most
skillful musicians of the tribe, added a new note to the clash
of the gongs, the roll of the tambourines, and the squealing
of the flutes, and Ilouha knew that the men had feasted, that
it was time for the women to dance, and she ran from the
cooking-fires with the others, forcing her way into the firelight, her bare feet pounding the earth in cadenced tempo,
her hips swaying to the beat of the instruments, conscious
that the fingers of firelight were caressing her breasts, that
the eyes of Erohé were upon her. To the clash of the gongs
she danced, her lips slightly parted, aware that Mouc's fat,
young wife was dancing next to her, her body glistening with
coconut oil, swaying in front of Mouc, seeking his favor. And
so Ilouha danced as she had never danced before, conscious
of the jiggling of her firm breasts and the quivering of her
buttocks, stealing Mouc's greedy eyes, causing all to envy
Erohé, whose woman she was. Wearied by her great effort,
conscious of the tightness in her calves, of the sweat running
in rivulets over her breasts, and of the flashing, angry eyes of
Mouc's woman, she yielded her place and fell in with the
totality of the dance, becoming merely a part of its woman-
ness, seeking with her eyes beyond the firelight for Erohé.
She found him there, sitting cross-legged between Yé and
an ugly old chief she did not know, bare-chested, the light
of the fire playing on the gold of his hair, flashing from his
teeth as he talked, and in that time her heart went out to him,
and she was glad in him and in his seed which she bore within
her. I will tell him, she thought to herself, her eyes flitting
from him to the ranks of toothless crones on the edge of the
firelight, their gums red with betelnut juice, dreaming of the
dead days of their youth and fulfillment, I will tell him
tonight about his son. For she sensed the sadness that was
in him from another time, put there by another woman, and
she yearned to make him whole again. And then the gongs
clanged again and the time of the women was finished, and
Ilouha followed the others out beyond the firelight, falling
exhausted, her ribs heaving, behind the dreaming hags, among

the naked children, their eyes wide and glistening and full of
the mysteries which were theirs for the first time that night.

To a new beat of the drums, the young men stamped into
the clearing, shaking their spears, their heads held high in the
arrogance of their youth, gesticulating in front of the buffalo,
taunting it, stabbing at it, goading it into bellowing, the lie-
burdened bull charging on swaying knees to the end of its
tether, its great horns swinging in huge, weary arcs, seeking
the death beyond the rolling whites of its eyes. The night
was cold on Ilouha's moist back and she knew that it was not
long until dawn. The chiefs would have to talk soon, so that
each could have his say before the death of the buffalo, the
guarantor of the truthfulness of their hearts. So while the
young men danced, old women went among the chiefs, refill-
ing the great, earthenware jugs of rice wine, washing with
water the faces of those who had drunk too much, offering
final delicacies from the remains of the feast. Erohé, she saw,
was not drunk. His face was grave, his eyes steady, his pale,
white jaw, which once she had thought so ugly, firm and set
as he talked to the chief on his left, using his hands like a
potter to sculpture the substance of his words in the air.

Suddenly the music ended, and there was only the rustle of
the wind in the roof of the forest, the crackling of the fires,
and the plaintive bellowing of the tethered buffalo. As the
young men faded into the shadows, Yé stood up, swaying
slightly, his arms held high above his head, and there was
silence. All knew, even the children, that the words he was
about to speak were heavy ones.

"Never," said Yé, speaking slowly and very loudly, "have
so many chiefs of our people come together. This is well, for
what we must decide is a big thing. All of you know why
I have asked you to come to my village. Some of you have
come from very far, from Ankhé and even from Pleiku. The
road has been long and we welcome you, for we respect the
wisdom of our northern brothers."

The Bahnar and Jarai chiefs, pleased at Yé's compliments,
muttered among themselves and nodded. Ilouha smiled to
herself. They are like women, she thought, just like women.
Yé, in his wisdom, would feed their vanity, letting them preen
themselves with his words. Not for nothing had he the name
of the greatest orator among the southern Koho.

"I have called you here," Yé continued, "because there are
tigers in the forest." He paused to give effect to his words,
the firelight flickering on the tiger-bone amulet dangling

from his bull-like neck, the sparks from the fires rising into the night, the clearing silent except for the stamping of the buffalo.

"There are tigers in the forest," he said, "and there has come a time of choosing. When two tigers fight, it is the grass which suffers. We are the grass. One tiger is the Vietcong. Another is Diem, the Annamese emperor in Saigon, the friend of the *Bocs*."

A murmur of assent rose from the chiefs.

"Some say that this war is not ours," Yé continued, "that the men of the hills should have nothing to do with the quarrels of the Annamese, whether those of Hanoi or those of Saigon. I have said these words myself when first the fighting began years ago."

The chiefs grunted, remembering Yé's profitable neutrality in that earlier time.

"Now," he said, "I am not so sure. For some months a *Boc*, who speaks our language, has lived with us. We call him Erohé, the elephant. I know his heart. He has taken a woman of my longhouse to comfort him. He is one of us."

Ilouha's eyes sought Erohé and found him, his back erect, his eyes fixed on Yé, his fists clenched.

"Erohé," Yé went on, "has brought us guns and riches from the emperor in Saigon. Erohé is wise and he has words for us tonight. He is one of us. He understands the meaning of the buffalo which is to die tonight. He has spoken the truth before. He will speak it tonight. Let him speak now; hear him."

Ilouha saw Mouc, protesting, try to struggle to his feet. But another chief placed an arm on his bare shoulder and he relaxed again into a sitting position, his lips slack and moist in the firelight.

"Chiefs!" Erohé began, measuring his words carefully, "hear me. These are my words: that Yé is full of wisdom when he tells you that two tigers are fighting, that you will suffer like the grass if you stay in your longhouses. For if you do this, will not both sides suspect you? I bring guns and gold dust for chiefs who can see this. I bring words of truth for a people who have become my own. I ask that the men of the hills help me, fighting with the emperor in Saigon against the Vietcong, and in so doing, share in his victory over them."

Mouc was on his feet now, speaking loudly, facing Erohé.

"Why, *Boc*, why? Before you were born we suffered

under the old emperor at Hué. Now the emperor has moved to Saigon, but what have we to do with him? Or with the French, or with you, whose nose is long, whose skin is the color of the belly of a dead fish?"

"Why, indeed, Mouc?" Erohé replied. "Does no news reach the northern Koho? Because the Vietcong will break the power of the chiefs and crush the people, as they have among the T'ai. That is one reason."

A ripple of assent flickered around the seated crescent of chiefs. Not one of them, including Mouc, could help knowing what was going on in the T'ai country. Mouc started to speak again but Erohé raised his hands for silence.

"A second reason is this. I come from the emperor in Saigon and I bear a great word. This word is that if the chiefs of the hills will close the trails over which the Vietcong coolies come from the north, the emperor in Saigon promises that, as long as grass grows, the hill tribes shall rule themselves. I bring presents from Diem to show . . ."

Erohé's words were lost in a torrent of voices as several chiefs rose to speak. Ilouha saw that it was Cheo of the Rhadé, the father of Loye, to whom the chiefs were ready to listen.

"Hear me, *Boc*," Cheo was saying, his arms outspread. "These are words which have been said before. Always these words, these promises of freedom, have proved to be false. Why should we believe you now?"

"Cheo speaks true words," Erohé admitted. "There have been betrayals. This is not one of them. By Yé, my friend, and Ilouha, my woman, it is not. I have searched my heart and the heart of the emperor in Saigon. His words and mine are true. By this buffalo, with whom our lies die this night, this is true. I say it. Think and choose."

Once more the voices of the chiefs babbled like many brooks as Erohé sat down and Yé rose to speak again.

"I believe Erohé," he said. "Never has he spoken lightly of these things. He refused to say these words until he had gone to Saigon to speak to the emperor. His people are strong. They have guns and ammunition beyond the telling. A strong people does not lie. Erohé, who knows and respects our customs, would not lie on the death of a buffalo. My people do not love the emperor in Saigon. But we are not women, like the Chru. We are not grass to be trampled underfoot. We will fight the Vietcong. Who fights at our side?"

Mouc bounded into the center of the clearing, calling for silence.

"Yé has spoken well," he conceded, "now let the *Boc* act. Let him kill the buffalo. And hear me, Erohé: if you lie, if you betray us, may your bones grow soft and your sons turn against you, may the tiger make his home in your hearth and the wind blow always cold upon you, may you die alone, strangled by your own lies. Make this great oath and for the trust I have in Yé, I swear, on the death of the buffalo, to bring my people to the war."

The firelight playing on his muscular body, Mouc turned and hurled his spear sideways at Erohé, the point in the air, the shaft shimmering. Ilouha watched as Erohé rose, catching the spear midway down the shaft. Erohé walked slowly to the center of the clearing, his eyes on the ground, Mouc's spear balanced in his right hand. He turned to face the buffalo, the blood pumping out onto the animal's gray, leathery flanks, his eyes great and white, his muzzle flecked with foam, his bellowing loud in the chill of the pre-dawn air. Quietly, but loudly enough so that all could hear, Erohé spoke, seeming to address his words to the curse-laden buffalo tugging at his tether.

"I accept your curse, Mouc, knowing my words to be true."

Then Ilouha saw Erohé bound forward, his weight on the balls of his feet, the spear cocked back behind his head, the muscles of the arm bunched, the buffalo bellowing, and then the spear coming down in a great, thrusting arc, and the buffalo on its knees, blood and foam pouring from its nostrils, its tongue hanging out, and the dawn of a new day hemorrhaging along the ridges above the clearing. And the buffalo gasped and went down, Erohé standing in front of the dying animal, his eyes staring, and behind him she heard the roars of approval from the chiefs, for the buffalo had died from a single thrust and it was a good omen. Then she saw the chiefs shuffling into a dance and she knew that the thing was done and that Erohé had won, that the people were with him.

It was war.

CHAPTER FIFTEEN

THE SIGHT OF THE BROWN stain like dried blood on his desk blotter reminded Ngo Dinh Nhu of his anger. The memory of what he had done irritated him still further and he drummed nervously on the desk with his delicate finger tips. He had been wrong to lose his temper, to dash the cup of tea from the servant's hand. Even if the tea had been cold, it had been a stupid thing to do. He remembered the surprised look on the nameless servant's face and the thin tinkle of china shattering on the marble floor, the tea spreading across his blotter, soaking the files which littered his desk. He had risen halfway to his feet, watching the surprise on the servant's face change to fear. Did I really intend to strike him? He supposed he had. What an unworthy thing that would have been! With an effort of will he had regained control of himself, wordlessly slumping into his chair, flipping through the wet pages of the file upon which he'd been working. The sight out of the corner of his eye of the stoop in the servant's back as he knelt to pick up the pieces of broken china had further angered him. But anger was an emotion he could not afford. Anger was a luxury for little men. When one lost control of one's emotions, the advantage passed to one's enemies. And Ngo Dinh Nhu realized that he had many enemies.

He pressed the buzzer on his desk sharply and his secretary materialized at the door. The fool must have run from his desk. They all are afraid of me, he thought to himself, all of them. It gave him little satisfaction.

"Change this blotter. Immediately," he said.

"Yes, Excellency," the secretary replied, fumbling with the papers on the desk.

Nhu realized that he had been nervous and irritable for some days. Despite the nembutal, he was sleeping badly. It was not just the pressure of events, although God knew things were going badly enough. There was no one who could be trusted. He was surrounded by liars. They were afraid to tell him the truth. Those who were not liars were cowards and fools. Some were all three. And with men such as these he had to fight a war. It was clear, however, that he had underestimated the success of the Vietcong in infiltrating the pagodas. The situation, he had to admit, had deteriorated sharply. From the barred window of his office he could see the tanks parked in the palace grounds, the muzzles of their guns pointing toward the street. There had been three riots this week and, if the information of the informers was correct, one more was coming. The riots in themselves were nothing to be feared. The army, if it could not defeat the Vietcong, at least could handle street mobs. But the riots forced him to make arrests and he knew that this antagonized the army. Each of the arrested demonstrators, bonze or student or coolie, had relatives in the army. One day, if the riots continued, the army would turn on the government. Tric Dinh Trang, he felt, was safe enough. That fat pig of a general was happy as long as he was allowed to steal. It was the younger officers Nhu was worried about. Meanwhile, the Americans were becoming more and more childish and unreasonable, acting as if it were he who were personally responsible for the burning of a few fanatic bonzes. They were even talking of a suspension of non-military aid. Nhu did not fear this. The Americans were bluffing. They could not cut off the aid. They had no place to go. Their prestige was involved in Vietnam. They would grumble but continue to support the government. But talk of the possibility of the suspension of aid encouraged the Buddhists, strengthened the Vietcong, and undermined the President's position. It was extremely annoying.

He shoved the files aside, rose to his feet and paced up and down the brightly lit, austere office, studying the regular pattern of the perforations on the slabs of soundproofed material which lined the walls. The boy was the key. They had to crack the boy. It was clear from what other suspects had said that the boy . . . what was his name? Tran Dinh? No, Tric Dinh, perhaps. It didn't matter. It was clear that the boy had been in touch with whoever was directing the Buddhist agitation from the Xa Loi Pagoda. It was clear that he knew the real name of the man they wanted. The boy had to speak. He had to! They had offered the boy a great deal: money, a scholarship abroad, exemption from military service. In principle, Nhu objected to the use of torture. It

was ethically wrong to employ torture indiscriminately.
Stupid, too. It worked only on certain individuals. It was
not dependable, not scientific. Sometimes people lied under
torture, babbled anything in their heads in an effort to end
their sufferings, and this could cause serious mistakes. Although the use of torture could be justified ethically under
certain circumstances, persuasion almost always was better,
more reliable. Particularly when one had such oafs in the
Sûreté. Mong Le killed half of those under interrogation
before they could tell what they knew. He lacked subtlety
and a sense of pace. He was a peasant brute, but loyal at
least. That was something, but not enough. Nhu made a
mental note to have Mong Le transferred to a provincial
headquarters if he failed with the boy.

They had been working on the boy, in the small room
specially equipped for such affairs in the basement of the
palace, for nearly two weeks. Nhu had seen the boy twice.
Ordinarily he left such matters to Mong Le, who preferred
to work at his own interrogation room over at the Sûreté
building. He could sympathize with Mong Le. Always it
was annoying to have to work in a strange place where what
you wanted was not immediately to hand. But it was better
to have the boy in the palace, where a check could be kept
on Mong Le's enthusiasm for his work. In all the other cases,
Nhu saw only the reports containing the euphemism "the
subject admitted under severe questioning," knowing what
it meant, not wanting to know more. It was not the sort of
thing he enjoyed. But the boy was too important to be left
to Mong Le. Obviously, the boy was the key. If they could
wring from him the name of the man behind the Buddhist
agitation, the backbone of subversion in Saigon could be
broken in a single, decisive blow. It was useless to move
against the pagoda until that information was available.

Nhu stopped in front of the frameless mirror on the wall
and adjusted his tie. He wasn't looking well, no use denying
it. There were delicate shadows under his eyes and his skin
had a sallow, lifeless cast. Flecks of gray were beginning to
appear in his black hair.

The boy on the first occasion when Nhu had seen him,
had had a young, curiously unused look about him, as if he
had not been long in the world. Probably little older than
Le Thuy. Nhu lingered for a moment over the thought of
his daughter. A daughter was something special, more even
than a wife, because she had a part of you in her. Nhu put

aside the thought of Le Thuy. She had nothing to do with this.

He was not being sentimental in that final effort to save the boy from Mong Le. It was just that he was afraid the boy would not tell what he knew before Mong Le killed him. It had been unnecessary for him to identify himself to the boy. The boy had been very much afraid and in the terror in the boy's eyes, Nhu could see his own name written. The boy clearly had realized that the presence of Ngo Dinh Nhu meant he was to receive special treatment at Mong Le's hands if he did not cooperate. But he had only shaken his head dumbly, his lower lip between white, even teeth, tears welling up in his trapped animal's eyes when Nhu had asked him to tell what he knew. It had been with a real sense of regret that Nhu had left the room, telling Mong Le that he could proceed.

The second occasion had been four days ago. That had been extremely distasteful. Mong Le, in his ill directed enthusiasm for his task, had been very crude. The boy had been reduced to a quivering pulp of battered flesh and torn nerve ends. He began to whimper whenever anyone approached him but was no longer capable of coherent speech. It had been clear that the boy's life was little more then than a small, white bird fluttering in the red darkness of his broken body and smashed soul, seeking a way out, an ending. It had appeared likely that he would die before he spoke again. Nhu had been extremely severe with Mong Le. He had made it clear that the prisoner was there to provide information, not sadistic satisfaction to the animals of the Sûreté. He had ordered suspension of the interrogation for a day and medical treatment for the boy. But no rest. The klieg lights were to continue burning in the boy's eyes. He was not to sleep. It was the lack of sleep and the blinding glare of the lights which ultimately would break the boy, if he was going to break, rather than cruder forms of torture. Nhu felt sorry for the boy, and impatient with him. He, too, was tired. And it was the same problem, the identity of the man behind the Buddhist agitation, which was denying both of them sleep. The boy had only to speak a few words, a name, and they would find rest. This was the third day since Mong Le had returned to his work. Even with medical care, Nhu doubted if the boy could endure much more. He had a sensitive, girlish face and that type, if it did not break soon, had a tendency to die.

Nhu slumped down at his desk and noticed that the blotter had been changed. So absorbed had he been with the problem of the boy that he had been barely aware of his secretary's entry or exit. With a sigh he reopened the file dealing with the montagnard situation. What a troublesome people these *moi* were! Always it had been so but now with the flow of arms from the north over the Ho Chi Minh trail, what had been a minor vexation could become a major worry. It would be good to have a final solution to the problem. But the montagnard question held little interest for him. Essentially it was a military problem, and one remote from the immediate crisis in Saigon, the question of the Buddhists. He thought about the boy again and it annoyed him to find that he still regarded him as a person. He guessed this was because of the physical resemblance between the boy and his daughter, Le Thuy. He realized that in such matters one must cease thinking of the person under interrogation as a human being. One had to think of him as an intricate piece of machinery, as a mechanism about which one had a general understanding but no specific information. An able interrogator had to have a scientific mind combined with an artistic flare. Bao Duc had been such a man. A truly creative artist in his field. And then he had been found floating face down one morning in the Canal de Doublement. It had been a great pity. Now he had to rely on fools like Mong Le. Bao Duc had shown him that the human body and men's souls, and you were working with both in such affairs, had nerve points, buttons as it were, which you could press. Not every man reacted in the identical way to the pressing of the same button. But every man, and there were no exceptions to this, Bao Duc had insisted, had his crucial button. If you pressed it, psychologically or physically, he would tell you what you wanted to know. The problem was to discover as quickly as possible which button was the crucial one. In this Bao Duc had had no peers. It was wasteful to press the wrong buttons. If you pressed too many of them, the man died or lost his reason before he could tell you what you wanted to know. This was Mong Le's weakness: too frequently he pressed the wrong buttons and exerted pressure for too long. He lacked subtlety, finesse, understanding. At heart he still was a provincial policeman, a mechanic of the body rather than an artist of the soul. One Bao Duc was worth ten such men. Nhu picked up his telephone.

"Yes, Excellency?"

"Make a note. 'Mong Le.' That is all."

"Yes, Excellency."

"And get me some tea. Hot tea."

He returned the instrument to its receiver and tried once more to concentrate on the montagnard file. Almost immediately, the telephone buzzed gently. He picked it up.

"Mong Le on the wire, Excellency," his secretary said. "He says it's important."

"Put him through."

Nhu held the gilt telephone half an inch away from his ear, as if afraid that something distasteful might emerge from it, while the receiver buzzed and clicked.

"Excellency?" inquired Mong Le. He was breathing heavily, as if he had run to the telephone.

"Well?"

"Our bird has sung, Excellency!" The voice of the policeman was high pitched, excited, as if surprised by his own success.

"His name? The name of the man behind the Buddhists?"

"Cao Van Thuan, a bonze at the Xa Loi Pagoda. Some call him Thuc."

"You know of him?" Nhu asked.

"Yes, Excellency. We have a file."

"Good. Send it to me. Immediately. How is he?"

"Cao Van Thuan? Why I . . ."

"No, you idiot! The boy!"

There was a brief, pregnant silence. When Mong Le spoke again, a note of uncertainty tinged his words.

"He was not very strong, Excellency. Almost like a girl, in fact. He's dead, I'm afraid."

"You are a clumsy fool, Mong Le," Nhu said evenly, his voice edged with menace. "Had he died before he spoke, I would have sent you back to the provinces. Remember that."

"Yes, Excellency." The policeman's voice was mortified, hurt.

"Get rid of the body. And I don't want it found in the Arroyo Chinois or in some back alley. No one must know that the boy has been interrogated, that he is dead. This is vital. Do you understand?"

"Yes, Excellency. We have ways . . ."

"I'm sure you do. And get that file up here immediately. How old was the boy?"

"I don't know, Excellency, but I can find out."

"Never mind. It doesn't matter."

Nhu slammed down the receiver and heaved a great sigh. He was glad that it was over and relieved that he had not had to see the boy again. He was sorry about the boy but the information he had divulged, if it was correct, could prove decisive in the struggle for control of the city. When they had Cao Van Thuan in their hands, this could be determined. In any case, it was time to move against the pagoda. The risks, internally and internationally, were great, but the time had come to act. My brother, he thought to himself, is a wise man, a good man, a man not without strength. But he has no stomach for this sort of thing. I am necessary to him because of this. For a moment, Nhu bitterly resented his role of eminence gris to the regime, the fate that had given his elder brother the presidency and himself, the stronger of the two, the subordinate position. I do not like this Sûreté business, he thought to himself, any more than Diem. But I can and will do it and that is the difference between us. The fates make us what we are. Still, the boy could not have been much older than Le Thuy. He brushed aside the thought. What had been done was done. Now the thing was not to waste the opportunity bought with the boy's life. When his secretary pushed open the door, the file in his hand, Nhu shrugged off his resentment and doubt with his fatigue. He was ready to act and in action he knew he would find fulfillment.

He took the file from his secretary and flipped it open. The slightly out-of-focus picture which stared out at him showed a shaven-headed man in the robe of a bonze, his muscular left shoulder bare. His eyes seemed to glow with a burning intensity and his lips were thin and wide, his mouth hard. The file was brief: there had been no previous arrests but Cao Van Thuan, who had been educated at a university in the midwestern United States, was believed to harbor anti-government sentiments and was known to have contacts with both the American embassy and the corps of foreign correspondents. In ink at the bottom of the page were the words "surveillance for future action." Nhu scanned the single-paged file again, absorbing its details, and hurried out into the corridor. He strode down the hall of his brother's office, ignoring the salutes of the guards who lined the walls.

In the President's outer officer, the secretary rose to his feet but Nhu brushed past him and into the inner office, watching his brother's eyes flick upwards in irritation as he threw open the door. Trac Fon and Quang Tri straightened up from the folders they had open on the President's desk.

"Good morning," said Trac Fon, "we were just proposing . . ."

"Another time," said Nhu, holding the file behind his back, "I have important business with the President." There was no one who could be trusted.

"The Minister," Quang Tri offered, "was saying to the President . . ."

"Later," Nhu interjected. "I regret the interruption but this is important. The President's secretary will arrange another appointment for you."

The two men, frowning slightly, picked up their portfolios from the President's desk, and left hurriedly, bowing to Diem and then to Nhu as they passed. When they had gone, they left behind them an uneasy silence which separated the jowly, square-faced President from his younger brother, who remained standing in the center of the room, impatiently slapping the file against his thigh.

"Was that necessary?" Diem asked. "You are too abrupt. You deny their . . ."

"Yes. It was necessary. I have the name of the man behind the Buddhist agitation, the agent who planned the bonze burnings and staged the street demonstrations."

Nhu watched the President's eyebrows rise questioningly, his beady, black eyes coming to life.

"Who?" he demanded.

"His name is Cao Van Thuan. He is an American-educated bonze at the Xa Loi Pagoda."

"Is the evidence conclusive?"

"No, but it's sufficient. We were going to have to act anyway. We now have a focus, a prime suspect."

"What action do you plan to take?" Diem asked.

"Raid the Xa Loi Pagoda. Arrest Cao Van Thuan."

"Are you sure that's wise? Won't it provoke more rioting?" His elder brother leaned forward, his elbows on the desk, his square chin resting on his finger tips.

"Yes, it will cause rioting. But it's necessary. If the bonze is the man we want, there will be papers there, files which could crack the Vietcong in Saigon. The only way to get the bonze and the papers is to go in after them."

"You're sure? It will create difficulties with Washington." Nhu was beginning to become annoyed with his brother's caution, his Hamlet-like indecision. He bent over the desk, his eyes firmly on Diem's.

"It must be done," Nhu said. "You can prepare the Americans for it. But for God's sake don't compromise the action by telling them anything definite. They are not above warning the Buddhists."

"I don't like it," Diem retorted, pivoting his chair so that he gazed out over the tank-guarded palace grounds, "I don't like it at all."

"Nor do I. But it must be done. This is an opportunity which may not occur again. Surely you can see that?"

Diem did not answer. He got to his feet and walked slowly to the window, pulling back one of the gold drapes, staring into the garden, as if he might find the answer there. When he spoke again, he did so without turning around to face his brother.

"Yes," Diem admitted wearily, "I can see that. When do you want to move?"

"Give me three days," Nhu said. "It will take that long to organize it properly. I can't wait any longer than that, though. The Vietcong may get wind of it."

"All right," Diem replied, returning to his seat behind the desk. "What about the cabinet? General Trang?"

"Say nothing to anyone. I'll take care of everything."

"What about that montagnard situation? You were going to let me know about that."

"The orders have been issued. More than ever it is necessary now."

"I hope you're right about that," Diem replied.

"There is no choice. What about Englehardt? Will he be a problem?"

Diem shook his head and sighed.

"He knows about it," he said.

"Then that's all right?"

"Yes, you can go ahead on the montagnard thing. But I wish you'd think about this pagoda business a little."

"I've thought about nothing else for the past two weeks. We've got to do it. Now."

"So much is at stake. For all of us," Diem said, his eyes worried.

"I know that, my brother," Nhu said quietly.

"Go ahead, then. By the way, how did you find out about the bonze? An informer?"

"The mechanics of the thing would not interest you," Nhu replied, walking to the door, his hand on the knob. He was anxious to get started on the planning for the raid.

"Oh? Mong Le?"

"Yes. Mong Le." Nhu bowed slightly and closed the door as he left, leaving his brother staring after him, a troubled expression on his solemn face.

CHAPTER SIXTEEN

MAJOR GENERAL TRIC DINH TRANG sat sweating at his desk in his corps headquarters on the outskirts of Saigon. He was conscious of sweat running in rivulets over the roll of fat at the base of his neck, standing in globules on his wide forehead, staining his tunic under the arms. It had been the hottest summer he could remember. Or was it just that he was getting old and fat? No, it really was hot. The air conditioner the Americans had gotten for him was not working. The overhead fan, its triple blade turning slowly in the semi-darkness of the unlighted room, only agitated the hot air, rustling the papers on his desk, causing the small flags attached to the pins studding the large-scale military map, which covered one wall, to flutter weakly. It was better in the old days under the French, he thought to himself. Then at least a man could sleep in the afternoons. Now if you tried to sleep there would be someone from the palace poking around or one of the American colonels dropping in to ask stupid questions about the deployment of your troops. He liked the Americans, but they were a bother. As for the people from the palace, they always meant trouble.

He heaved his huge bulk out of the chair and tottered to the window, loosening his khaki tie and wiping his streaming face with a large handkerchief of purple silk. Outside, in the bright white sunlight of the parade ground, the new recruits were doing rifle calisthenics in their underwear. Trang liked to watch massed soldiers exercising with the rifle, to hear the commands of the drill instructor booming across the dusty parade ground. It reminded him of the old days, before the Japanese had come, when he'd been a slim young sergeant. He had come a long way since then; the army had been good to him. "Un, deux . . ." the instructor's commands rang out. The recruits were not too bad. Most of them were Cao Dai. A friend in personnel had stretched a rule or two to assign the Cao Dai to his corps. Trang felt more secure knowing

156

that the men in his headquarters regiment were of his sect. Nowadays, one never knew who could be trusted. And the cursed palace made it difficult enough for a general to build up a following by this constant shifting of commands. Trang had commanded the Saigon garrison for barely four months, yet a sixth sense told him another shuffle of assignments was in the wind. How could you do any business, let alone fight a war, if you were always being shifted from command to command? He knew the reason, of course: Diem and Nhu trusted nobody. They were afraid to leave a general in command of one corps for too long, afraid that ties of personal loyalty might be created between the generals and their men, and that this might make it easier to stage a coup.

Trang lumbered back to his desk and flipped the switch of the speaker on his desk. His aide's voice, young and crisp, filtered through the cloth of the speaker.

"Bring me a bottle of wine," Trang said, "the Chateauneuf-du-Pape."

Four months he had commanded the corps, and what had he to show for it? He was almost as poor as when he took over Saigon, the richest post in Vietnam. Almost, but not quite. The business of the batteries had been a profitable one, worth many hundreds of thousands of francs. And the money, less what he had given the quartermaster, who had marked the batteries "lost in transit" and indented the Americans for more, was safely in Switzerland.

General Fung Lao always had been a fool and a scoundrel; he deserved to rot in a Central American embassy. Selling arms to the Vietcong was carrying things a bit too far. One had to maintain a sense of proportion, of honor. The batteries were quite a different matter. Trang knew where the batteries would end up, but this did not bother him unduly. One had to be realistic. He knew the Vietcong would find someone to sell them batteries. By not selling them himself, he was not depriving the Vietcong of the batteries but only assuring someone else, less worthy than himself, of the profit. In any case, he had not sold the batteries to the Vietcong. Nobody could accuse him of that. He had sold them to a Chinese dealer in Cholon. What the dealer did with them was his concern.

There was a knock at the door and his aide, erect and cool looking in his well-starched uniform, came in carrying a bottle of wine, a glass, and a bowl of ice.

"Another glass, Wang. Sit down. Join me."

"Thank you, sir," said Major Wang. He clapped his hands and called for another glass, which an orderly brought. As Wang cooled the glasses in the ice and then poured the wine, General Trang studied him through half-closed eyes, his hands locked together behind his head, his chair tilted back under his great weight.

He did not know how far he could trust Wang. Nhu had his spies everywhere. His old aide had been taken from him and sent to a commando battalion in the Camau peninsula after that slight miscalculation in the pay accounts. Even if he was not one of Nhu's men, Wang was difficult to understand. He seemed honest, which meant he was either high principled or lacking in initiative. Perhaps both. He kept his own counsel, which showed he had sense, but made him no easier to gauge. Trained at Fort Benning in the United States, he was of a new and different breed. A good soldier, but still a question mark in the matter of loyalties and ideals. With all this talk of a coup d'etat in the air, it was essential to know where one's officers stood.

"Hot," said General Trang, sipping his wine. Now was as good a time as any to try to sound out Wang.

"Very hot, sir. I'm doing my best to get that air conditioner replaced."

"I know you are, my boy, I know you are. You always do your best. That's one of the things I like about you."

Wang smiled politely. General Trang was not sure just how much he ought to say to Wang about the coup. He had not yet made up his own mind about it. His personal participation in the plot was essential to its success. A rebellion which lacked the support of the commander of the Saigon garrison could not succeed. As such, he was in a good bargaining position. He could afford to wait. But if he waited too long, and a new shuffle of commands took place, he would lose this happy situation.

Nor was he completely convinced that a coup would be a good thing. If the plotters failed, and this was possible, even if he threw in his lot with them, there was much to lose. Position, money, life. The Ngo Dinhs were not a family to be trifled with. Trang was a realist, so he did not concern himself unduly with the question of honor. Honor, as the Americans spoke of it, had gone long ago. Now that he thought of it, the Americans did not prattle much of honor. They were a pragmatic people, interested primarily in results.

It was the French who spoke so incessantly of honor. If the coup did succeed, however, he would be in a position to profit by it. His command of Saigon and his influence within the Cao Dai stood to buy him a place on the junta. The opportunities for doing business from such a vantage point would be immense. Nearly two million dollars a day in American aid was flowing into the country. He would be in a position to demand the job of liaison officer between the aid program and the government, with all which that implied.

Still, it was best to proceed cautiously. Much depended on the feelings of the younger officers such as Wang. The soldiers and the regimental commanders would do what they were told. But he was not so sure about these young, American-trained officers, many of whom were the battalion and company commanders.

"The men look good," Trang said, waving his glass in the direction of the open window, through which came the shouts of the recruits, counting in unison as they went through their rifle calisthenics.

"They're coming along pretty well, sir," Major Wang replied. "They need action, though, something they can get their teeth into."

"Action? They've been out on the streets three times this week, Major."

"I don't mean that, sir. Not riot control. They need action against the Vietcong."

"They'll get plenty of that."

"Perhaps, General. But they're soldiers, not police. I don't think . . ." Wang's voice trailed off into silence. He's afraid, Trang thought, he's afraid to be indiscreet.

"Yes? What do you think, Wang? Go on, I'm interested."

"Nothing, sir," said Wang, putting down his wine glass.

"Come on," said Trang encouragingly, "spit it out, man. Off the record."

"I don't think it does the troops' morale much good to be used against civilians, sir, their own families, people who are supposed to be on their side." The words came tumbling out in a rush.

What a business, Trang thought. In my day, we did not speak of morale. One obeyed orders and that was all there was to it. With the Americans, of course, it was another thing. But the Americans, from whom Wang had gotten his ideas about morale, were a different kind of people. What the Vietnamese soldier wanted was strong leadership and victories.

Most of all, victories and the fruit of victories: loot. The general, once having been an enlisted man himself, sympathized with the common soldiers. It was not right that everything should go to the officers. While the common soldiers could not hope to sell batteries by the thousands to Chinese merchants, they had a right to expect a bit of loot. They were getting precious little in this war.

"I hadn't thought of it, but you may be right, Wang."

"I'm sure I am sir," Wang said, earnestly, picking up his glass again. "We waste too much energy fighting the wrong people. School children! Half the country's held by the Vietcong and we fight school children!"

"Well, these are difficult times, strange times. It's hard to know what to do."

"The generals could talk to the President, sir, convince him that things are going wrong." Wang's earnest face was unsmiling. He was serious in what he said. Trang laughed.

"None of us have much influence with the President, Wang. We've tried it before. But he prefers his family's advice."

"Something's got to be done. Anything."

"Do many of the young officers share this view?" Trang asked. There was no need for either of them to talk treason. They could understand one another.

"Yes, General. I believe they do."

"Well, Wang, we're all in this together. When the time comes, we'll know what to do." Trang lifted his glass toward Wang and then drained it. The younger officer finished his wine and put down the glass.

"Yes, sir, we'll know what to do. Thank you for the wine, General. Now if you'll excuse me, I've a lot of work." Wang rose to his feet and stood at attention, waiting for permission to withdraw.

"Certainly, Wang, certainly. Business before pleasure always has been my motto. Pleasure to talk with you. Always glad to have your ideas."

Wang saluted, turned and walked to the door. As he was opening it, Trang spoke.

"By the way, Wang, I hope you'll keep me informed as to what the younger officers are thinking. All unofficial, of course. These are difficult times and we can all help each other."

"You can depend on me, sir," Wang said with a smile, closing the door.

He has not told me much, Trang thought. But a little, a

little. It seemed apparent that there was a certain amount of dissatisfaction among the junior officers. With the course the war was taking, if not with Diem himself. Yet things had reached the stage where the war and the government and the Ngo Dinh family were inseparable. If you criticized one, you were criticizing the others. Major Wang was a Buddhist, of course, as were most of the officers, and this was important. Even nominal Buddhists, and most of them were only that, were unhappy about the self-immolation of the bonzes and the student arrests. Also there was a certain amount of careerism. Many of the Buddhist officers felt that their Catholic colleagues were given preference over them in the question of promotions and responsible jobs. At the same time, many of the generals toying with the idea of a coup were Catholics. While some Catholic officers looked on Diem as their protector, others felt that their own long-term survival depended on his overthrow. The motives of the plotters, Trang knew, were in fact very mixed. Many feared Nhu and his secret police. Others felt that Diem's actions in the current Buddhist crisis were unwise and eventually would lead to a Vietcong victory. A few felt Diem had lost his drive and no longer was capable of active prosecution of the war. All resented the interference of the Ngo Dinhs in military affairs, the unwarranted rebuffs, the constant shuffling of commands. A few wanted power for power's sake. Whether they themselves ruled or a more pliable civilian held the presidency did not much matter, as long as they controlled the palace.

Trang shared many of these sentiments. But he was by nature a cautious man. He had won his general's stars not by achieving great victories but by avoiding terrible defeats. If the coup succeeded it might weaken the country to the point where the Vietcong could take over. It would not happen in a day but it could happen. One coup inevitably led to another, as the victors quarreled over the spoils. While Trang was willing to sell batteries which the Vietcong eventually would acquire, he did not want to see them victorious. He did not believe he would have much future in a united and inevitably Communist Vietnam. In this sense, he thought to himself, I am, as the Americans would say, vigorously anti-Communist. What was really in his personal interest was a continuation of the war, the maintenance of a state of permanent stalemate. Really this was in the interest of all the generals. As long as the war lasted, the power and prestige of the generals would remain high, more American money and U.S. equipment would continue to flow into the country, there would be countless opportunities for a clever officer to make himself a wealthy one.

That is the paradox of our situation, Trang thought to himself: we succeed only if we neither win nor lose. Victory would be almost as unfortunate as defeat. In the end, always there was the prospect, if one did well and was not too greedy, of a good ambassadorship or retirement to France. The general liked France. He had been there many times and he liked it very much, particularly the south of France, where the weather was good. But it required a great deal of money to do it properly.

But although he was no revolutionary, he would sleep better if Nhu were out of the way. He knew that he, like the other senior generals, was under constant surveillance by Nhu's agents. He knew who most of them were and he always made it a point to be financially helpful to them. They were family men with children to provide for and Trang sympathized with them in their difficult, unremunerative duties. Some of his best friends were Nhu's agents. He himself had told Nhu that more than one officer was politically unreliable when the officers concerned had had the temerity to question some of his financial dealings. It was a good way of dealing with troublemakers. But he would feel more at ease if Nhu's agents were not around. That was one point. Another was whether or not Diem and Nhu, through their policies, were ensuring a Vietcong victory. He did not think this was the case, at least for the moment. But if it did appear that this was so, he would owe it to himself as well as to his country to join the conspiracy.

The plot, of course, might come to nothing. Always there was some sort of coup in the air. It was just a way of expressing dissatisfaction with the way things were going. There were a few transfers, perhaps an arrest or two, and everybody forgot about it. Projected coups were not things which a senior general took too seriously. Coups were the recreation of hot-eyed colonels and zealous majors. On the other hand, as a form of insurance, it was necessary to know what was going on so that one was protected in the unlikely event that such a coup not only took place but was successful. Trang appreciated that he had risen from the ranks precisely because of his legendary ability to maintain a position of benevolent neutrality in almost any situation. He was a modest man and to him it seemed quite simple. One simply refused to commit one's self in the early stages of any conspiracy, while at the same time assuring the plotters and those plotted against of one's unequivocal loyalty. When it was clear which side was going to win was time enough to commit one's self. He was not going to be rushed into anything, particularly not now when some of his business ventures were beginning to bear fruit. But he had to admit that the current conspiracy seemed to be better organized and more far-flung than most of the abortive coups. The plot would bear watching, particularly if he was right about Wang and the other young officers.

Thinking of Wang reminded him about the problem of his own nephew's disappearance. Trang was childless and hence inordinately fond of his sister's only son. He confessed that he spoiled the lad. The lad was a university student and Trang was very proud of him. If all went well, Trang hoped to buy the boy an appointment in the diplomatic service. No one could accuse him of not fulfilling his familial responsibilities. He had bought the boy his draft exemption and was paying his way through the university. He would have liked him to be a soldier, but there was too much of his mother in Tric. In any case, it would be a good thing to have a diplomat in the family. There had been nothing but trouble, however, since the boy had entered the university. Tric had gotten himself involved with the Communist wing of the Buddhist Students' Association. Trang did not object to this on ideological grounds. He rather approved of someone in the family having a foot in the other camp. That way you had at least a minimum amount of insurance no matter which side won. But Tric had been stupid and Trang was very worried about him, as was his mother. He had been arrested once during a street demonstration and it had taken all of Trang's influence to keep him from being conscripted and sent to the delta in a punishment battalion. The boy had been unrepentant and Trang, with his peasant shrewdness, had understood immediately that his nephew was more deeply involved with the Vietcong than he cared to admit, even within the walls of the family.

Now he had failed to come home for more than a week. His mother was frantic with worry and had made Trang's life not worth living. At a time when he had the crucial decision to make about whether or not to join the conspiracy, with several important business deals hanging fire, he had the job of trying to find a lost boy in a city of two million people.

It was not wise to ask too many direct questions about missing people, but always there were ways of finding out whom the police were holding. But his inquiries, always made through a fourth or fifth party, had produced nothing. In his heart, Trang feared that the boy had inadvertently fallen afoul of the Vietcong hierarchy and been liquidated for some minor disciplinary reason, his body disposed of. If this turned out to be the case, he promised himself, it would go hard with the Vietcong prisoners in the stockades within his corps area. Tric was all he had and he would be avenged.

Meanwhile, he had a final approach to make. He finished his wine, picked up the telephone, demanded an outside line, and dialed a number.

"My friend," he asked, as soon as he recognized the voice at the other end of the telephone, "you know who this is?"

"I know," replied the voice.

"I have a favor to ask."

"Ask it. Nothing is too much."

"You know the son of my sister?"

"Yes."

"He has been missing for more than a week. I want you to get a friend, a discreet friend, to make inquiries at the Sûreté, keeping my name out of it. Inquiries at the highest level. Your friend must ask for Colonel Mong Le."

"Nothing more?"

"Nothing. And thank you."

When he hung up, General Trang, although worried, was pleased with himself. He had done all he could for Tric.

CHAPTER SEVENTEEN

HARRY WAS IN A GOOD mood as he strode down the forest path toward the low hills that marked the southern boundary of the Koho country. Yé was setting a comfortable pace and the going was easy, the sun warm on Harry's back. The two of them were making adequate time to reach Sans Souci before dusk. Harry was glad to be going back. It would be good to see Marc and Father Dupleix again. He had been worried about them ever since he'd heard about the Vietcong attack on Notre Dame des Bois. The information he'd received had been sketchy. Only that the mission had been attacked and that there'd been some damage. Harry sensed that Yé had not told him all he knew about the incident, although there seemed no reason why the chief should conceal the facts. Harry's first reaction had been to lead the montagnards down into the rubber to see for himself what had happened. But Yé quickly had dissuaded him. The news they had was both contradictory and stale. There might be nothing to it, in which case much time and effort would have been wasted. In any case, it might be a trap laid by Loye to lure them out of the Koho country. Finally, Yé had said flatly that the Koho warriors were not interested in leaving their hills to embroil themselves in a quarrel which did not concern them. Harry had considered going by himself but on reflection had decided against it. The news had come as the chiefs were gathering for the buffalo ceremony and he could not risk the success of the whole montagnard rising on what was fundamentally a personal matter. Yé had seemed greatly relieved when he'd told him of his decision. Now Harry realized it had been a correct one. The chiefs had been true to the pledges made over the dead buffalo. The northern Koho were out under Mouc who, for all his braggadocio, was proving to be an effective leader. The Stieng, Chrao, Jarai, and Bahnar had sent their young men against the coolie trains. Only the Rhadé had refused to send men. Harry could understand Cheo's attitude. Yé had

told him that the Rhadé had suffered greatly at the hands of
the Vietminh because of their support of the French. With
Loye, Cheo's son, leading the Vietcong, it was too much to
expect the Rhadé to come in. The best that Harry could hope
for was, through a judicious combination of threats and presents, to keep the whole Rhadé tribe from actively supporting
Loye. Many of their young men, he knew, were with the
Vietcong leader now.

All through the hot weather Harry and Loye had groped
blindly for each other in the hills, each seeking a decisive
encounter on his own terms. Harry nurtured a grudging but
growing respect for Loye as an opponent. The Rhadé had
that uncanny sixth sense about his flanks which characterizes
all fine small-unit commanders. You could not hem him in
against a river or pin him in a valley. Loye slipped through
your fingers like a shaft of moonbeams slanting down through
the forest. You tracked him down and thought you had him
and then he wriggled out of your grasp, leaving you nothing
to show for your sweat but a spot of blood on a leaf, a few
expended cartridge casings, a footprint in the mold of the
jungle's floor. Yes, Harry had to admit that Loye was good.
Nor were Loye's skills entirely defensive. Twice Loye had
turned the tables on him. Harry still shuddered when he recalled that midnight ambush in the pouring rain. The storm
almost had been their undoing, then had become their salva-
tion. He and Yé, with a strong party of montagnards, had
been stalking what they took to be Loye's main body through
a savage little range of densely forested hills. The rain had
killed the Koho scouts' sense of smell and dulled their hearing.
They had not realized that Loye had turned back on them,
like a wounded buffalo lying up in a thicket, until the trap was
sprung. Had the rain not hampered Loye's riflemen and ruled
out the possibility of an effective pursuit, the Koho losses
would have been heavy. As it was, they'd left four dead in
the dripping forest. The second time had been during an
attack on a coolie train. As Yé had put it later, a tone of embarrassed respect in his voice, Loye had used the coolie train
the way a clever hunter lures a tiger with a fat she-goat.
There had been many coolies and the supply train had been a
target which Harry could not resist. They'd scattered the
train, but Loye had been waiting for them in the forest after
the attack, when the Koho were dispersed and careless. They
had extricated themselves only with great difficulty, losing
three men killed and four wounded. Still, Harry guessed he

could not complain. His primary objective was to stop the flow of arms and men down the Ho Chi Minh trail into the Mekong delta, and in this he and his montagnards had been relatively successful. In the past month alone they had destroyed two supply trains and scattered three others. To the best of his knowledge, only one large batch of coolies had passed through his country unscathed in the past month. It was not a bad record.

Ultimately, however, he was going to have to catch Loye and defeat him. And he sensed that neither Yé nor Mouc nor the rest of the montagnards, particularly since the two near-disasters, had much stomach for this. He couldn't really blame them. It was much more profitable from their point of view to attack the lightly-guarded coolie trains, operations which offered at least the possibility of loot, than to track well-armed, skillful, fighting men. Yé and Mouc had little interest in provoking a blood feud between the Koho and the Rhadé, who now provided the bulk of Loye's men. When the war was over, the Koho and the Rhadé were going to have to live together in the hills. The supply trains were a different matter, since most of the coolies were northern Annamese. Harry almost suspected that on more than one occasion, when he had been close on Loye's heels, Yé had led him off on false spoors. Although he was now far more skillful in the forest than he once had been, Harry could not be sure of this. But he suspected it. He had not had it out with Yé because Loye eventually would come to him. As long as he could keep hitting the coolie trains, Loye would have to seek him out. When all the conditions were favorable, he would meet Loye and destroy him, despite Yé and Mouc. Harry had information that Loye now was far to the north, organizing a covering screen for a big coolie train assembling in Laos. Loye and the coolies would not reach the place where he wanted to attack them, at the gorge of the Se Nang, for another ten days. There was plenty of time to get down to Sans Souci and back. By taking only Yé with him to Marc's, all the fighting men would be fresh and ready when it was time to lay the ambush.

No, Harry had to admit that, despite the additional complication of Ilouha's news, his problems were not too great. He had to laugh at the way she had broken it to him. They had been eating their evening meal and she had asked him out of the blue if he'd given any thought to taking a second wife. Although the montagnards were polygamous, the question had rather startled him. He'd laughed and said he hadn't. She'd then proceeded to give a detailed recital of the virtues of Hamon's youngest daughter, a girl still almost a child. The idea had seemed preposterous to Harry, despite the political advantages of a tie with the *patjao's* house, and he'd told her so. Ilouha had pouted and made it patently obvious that she was displeased with him. When he'd asked her why, she'd told him about the child. Under tribal custom, she'd explained, he could not sleep with her again until the child was weaned at the age of two or three. So he would need another woman. In any case, there would be much more work to do and she couldn't handle it all. If he had any consideration for her at all, he would see to it that another pair of hands was there to help. In any case, she'd insisted, he was a man of great consequence and his position demanded more than one wife. She would be shamed before all the other women if he did not take another. He had tried to laugh her out of it but she had been adamant. Finally he'd said he'd think about it and let her know. One child was going to pose enough of a problem, he reckoned, without his building a harem and scattering the seed of his loins through all central Vietnam. He really hadn't thought out what he was going to do about Ilouha, and the child certainly would complicate matters. Day by day he grew more and more attached to Ilouha, but he couldn't take her back to Virginia. He had to admit that much to himself. Yet he certainly wasn't going to abandon her and his child. If things went well, he might be able to get a more or less permanent posting to Saigon. There, with a little tutoring from an Annamese woman, Ilouha might be able to fit in. The child, of course, could go to one of the good French-run schools. It was something he was going to have to sort out.

Meanwhile, he was glad to be walking toward Sans Souci, a cool beer, and a good dinner. The going was easy, the land falling away beneath him, the sun friendly. Harry wondered about the lack of game. Strange. They had not seen so much as a monkey all morning. At midday they halted in the shade of a thicket, the back of the day's walk broken, and Harry slumped to the ground with an exaggerated grunt, grateful for the rest. Yé untied a packet wrapped with leaves.

"Food?" he asked.

"Thanks," said Harry. "It's good walking today."

"Yes. The trail is good."

"We should be in the rubber long before dark."

"Yes." Yé kneaded the rice into sticky balls and handed one to Harry. He popped it into his mouth and chewed slowly.

"Why is there no game?"

"I do not know," Yé replied. "I wondered if you would notice. We should have seen *bantang,* or at least wild boar."

The two men chewed in silence, enjoying the shade and the rest.

"Things are not going too badly, Yé."

"No, the fighting goes well."

"Not well enough. Too many coolies are getting through to the delta."

"My people have stopped the big trains, Erohé. And it is hard without the Rhadé."

"It's not that so much. It's this business of not being able to smash Loye."

Yé held up his hand for silence and cocked his head to one side.

"There are words on the wind," the Koho said. "The sound of a tree falling."

Harry listened for a minute and then shook his head.

"I can't hear anything. This business of Loye: if we could destroy him, the problem of the coolie trains would take care of itself."

"How is this?" Yé asked.

"We can't attack the coolies with any confidence as long as Loye is dogging us. With him gone, it would be another matter."

"What about the soldiers with the coolies?"

"They're few. They'd have to bunch together into bigger groups to defend themselves. Then I could call for air strikes from Saigon."

"This is something of which I have no knowledge," Yé replied. "But Loye is wise and brave and he has guns. When we fight him, we lose many men. The Rhadé are not women like the Chru. It is better to attack the coolie trains."

Harry laughed.

"And there's loot," he said.

"And there is loot," Yé repeated, with a chuckle.

"Sometimes I think you lead me on cold trails when it comes to tracking Loye," Harry said.

Yé's crafty old face assumed such an expression of injured innocence that Harry could not restrain a smile.

"I, Erohé? Would I do such a thing?" he inquired indignantly.

"Never mind, my father. Loye and I will meet despite you."

"Soon you will have a son," Yé said suddenly. I was right, Harry thought, the old devil can't wait to change the subject.

"Yes. How are you so sure it will be a son?"

"It will be a son. Hamon has said it."

Harry laughed and shook his head in disbelief.

"Only fools laugh, Erohé. You *Bocs*, who think yourselves so wise, are ignorant of things the most stupid *patjao* knows. And Hamon is not stupid."

"Sorry, Yé. Hamon's got a good set of bones. If he's rolled them and it's come out a boy, a boy it'll be."

"Who will you take for a second wife," asked Yé, mollified at Harry's admission of Hamon's powers.

"This a thing I have not decided."

"You owe it to Ilouha and to yourself to do so."

"Maybe."

"Or is it that you will leave us when the fighting is done?" There was no note of criticism in Yé's voice. He asked the question as he might have inquired about the prospects of a forthcoming hunt.

"I don't know, Yé. She wouldn't be happy with me in my own land. It's too far."

"Perhaps not; but her place is with her man."

"It's something of which we'll have to speak," Harry conceded.

"There is room here," Yé said, making a broad sweep of his arm to encompass the surrounding hills. "When the tribes are at peace there is rice enough, and roebuck and *gaur*, and fish from the streams."

He's inviting me to join the family firm, Harry thought to himself, affection for Yé warring with bitterness at his own duplicity; he's offering me a cottage on the family estate. How could he ever explain it to Yé, much less to Ilouha? Later, when he had thought through it all carefully, he would have to try.

"We'll talk of this another . . ."

Yé was holding up his hand again, his lips pursed in concentration. Harry could feel a breeze fresh on his left cheek. He could hear nothing, but the wind, he could see, was bringing some sound to Yé's ears.

"What is it? What do you hear?" Harry demanded. Yé rose to his feet in a half crouch and sniffed the air apprehensively, glancing around him.

"I do not know. But the wind brings me noises from over there," Yé said, pointing to the southwest. "It could be elephants feeding. Or it could be men. Many men."

"Can you smell them?" Harry asked. His own sense of smell was virtually useless. He guessed it was because he smoked.

Yé shook his head. "No, the wind is not strong enough."

"Can't be elephants this low in the hills. Nor tappers. We're still miles from the rubber."

"It is not tappers I hear. It is the falling of trees."

"What do you think?" Harry asked.

"You slide down the valley, following the trail. I'll work around that ridge to the right. One of us should be able to see whatever it is I hear. Do you see that large, black rock, shaped like a man's head, halfway up the slope?"

Harry nodded.

"Meet me back there when you hear the call of the *Ko-el* bird."

Harry nodded and began a careful descent of the valley, keeping off the trail, moving cautiously, trying always to keep bushes between himself and the direction from which Yé had heard the sounds. He was pleased that Yé had enough confidence in his bush-craft to send him off by himself. Three months ago, he thought, Yé would have told me to wait under the bush where we ate. It gave him a curious sense of pride. He slipped off the safety on the .45 automatic. The Browning was too heavy for long trips.

When he had covered perhaps a quarter of a mile, Harry caught a fragment of sound borne on a gust of air. He could not identify the sound. The wind was blowing fitfully. One minute he heard something. The next, nothing. But something definitely was there. By now Yé, working up the ridge, probably had a pretty good idea of what it was. Harry worked his way forward carefully, moving slowly but steadily from bush to bush. It was erratic movement, he knew, which betrayed you in the bush. If you moved steadily and carefully, you could make yourself almost invisible.

The sounds became more distinct and constant. Once he thought he heard a burst of laughter, then the sound of an axe striking wood. Finally, there was the sharp, obvious clang of metal scraping on rock. Montagnards clearing the forest for a paddy, he thought. But montagnards did not have metal tools. They burned down the trees when they cleared. He moved more slowly, keeping always away from the sun, on the shady side of the trees. There were voices, many voices. Suddenly Harry saw the two men. He froze in his tracks, involuntarily sucking in his breath. They had not seen him. Keeping his arms stiff at his sides, he backed slowly behind the tree, went down on his knees, and from there to his stomach. Worming his way forward again around the shady side of the tree, he crawled into a bush, parted its leaves and looked out.

The valley fell away steeply beneath him and opened out into a small glade, through which passed the trail he and Yé had been following. At the edge of the glade, on a fallen log, sat two Vietnamese soldiers in animated conversation. Harry blinked his eyes incredulously, half expecting the green-uniformed men to dissolve before his eyes. No government troops had been this far into the hills in years. These two, whatever their business might be, were here in direct contravention of Diem's undertaking. The Koho tribal lands ran right down to the edge of Marc's rubber. These men were interlopers. They might, of course, be deserters hiding out in the forest. Yes, that probably was it. They were deserters. While he was telling himself that this was so, Harry knew it to be a lie. There was nothing furtive about the Annamese soldiers. They were laughing and joking. They had the confident air of men going about their authorized business. What then? As he tussled with the problem, afraid of what the answer might be, Harry heard the deep, reverberating thud of an axe biting into a large tree, and, far away, the rumble of a jeep's engine. Through the screen of trees beyond the glade, he could see sunlight glinting on axe-heads as they flashed in the noonday sun. He could hear the woodsmen shouting to each other. No, these were not deserters.

Harry wriggled backward out of the bush and wormed his way around the edge of the glade, by-passing the two sentries, working his way forward until he reached a position where he could get a clear view of what the axemen were doing. He knew what he would find but he had to see it for himself. From his new position, the panorama unfolded before his eyes. The woodsmen were government troops, stripped to their underwear, their dungarees, rifles and helmets laid out in neat piles near them. They were widening the narrow trail to a breadth of twelve feet. Behind them other soldiers were working with picks and shovels, leveling the trail, while they traded obscenities with the guards leaning against the trees. At the far end of the trail he could see what he had thought was a jeep. It was a small bulldozer.

They were combat engineers clearing the way for the infantry. The Vietnamese army was cutting a road into the Koho hills. The army was moving into the montagnard country in force. That was why he and Yé had seen no game. Harry couldn't believe it. That meant Englehardt had lied. It meant Diem had broken his pledge. It meant his own word to Yé, to Mouc, to the other montagnards was worthless. Cheo had been right. This was just another betrayal. Why? Why had Englehardt done it? The man of Dos Lobos, Kiernan's savior, had sold him and the montagnards down the river. What a fool I've been, he thought. Ilouha, the child, the resistance movement among the hill tribes, everything that he had worked for was finished, in ruins. Slowly, in measured fashion, under his breath, he whispered every obscenity he could think of. The smiling little soldiers were still chopping busily away at the trees when he opened his eyes again.

"*Ko-el*," came the mournful cry of the ground cuckoo from far up the hill to his right, "*ko-el*."

Yé. What was he going to say to Yé? How could he explain away what to him seemed senseless? Weren't we doing enough? We'd stopped most of the coolie trains. Now everything had been thrown away. He didn't want to face Yé. He realized there was an excellent chance that the Koho chief would try to kill him. Harry had an almost irresistible desire to stand up and walk into the Annamese road camp, leaving Yé and Ilouha and his shame irrevocably behind him. Instead, he wriggled backwards until he could turn around, crawled until he was out of earshot of the road gang, then rose to his feet and walked slowly toward the black rock the shape of a man's head.

Yé was squatting in the shade of the rock, his eyes flinty, the burp gun cradled across his knees.

"I wondered if you would have the courage to come," Yé said. He spat copiously. "I thought you would go to them. That is why we came today, is it not?"

"No, it isn't why we came. You saw them?"

"I saw."

Harry walked over to Yé and squatted beside him, placing a hand on his bare shoulder. Yé removed the hand as if it were something distasteful.

"I didn't know, Yé. I swear to you I didn't know."

Yé grunted, his flinty eyes hard on Harry's.

"You don't believe me? You think I'm lying?"

"No. You are lying, *Boc*. Like all the others."

"Listen, Yé: we're in this together. I've been betrayed as much as you. I . . ."

"There is nothing together for us any more, *Boc*. Everything is finished. The war, all things. I curse the day I gave Ilouha to a man with a serpent's tongue. May your child be born dead."

Harry shoved Yé roughly and jumped to his feet, reaching for the .45. Yé continued to regard him coldly, the burp gun still in his lap.

"Don't say that, damn it, Yé. Don't say it."

"Are you going to shoot me now, Erohé? Is that what you have come back to do?"

Harry replaced the pistol in its holster.

"No. I'm going back to Saigon and find out about this, to stop it if I can. You'll see, Yé. I didn't betray you. I didn't."

"I should kill you. But I don't want your carcass defiling my hunting grounds. Yes, go back to Saigon, Erohé. And keep your feet from the soil of these hills, or it will go hard with you."

"Yé, I . . ."

"Go, before my heart hardens against you, *Boc*." Ye's expression had not altered. His face showed no emotion. But his eyes were flinty and he kept his lips close together as he talked, spitting out the words as if they had a bad taste.

Harry started to say something but thought better of it. He turned and walked back down the slope toward the road camp, his eyes moist, his chest heavy with anger, sorrow, and disbelief.

When he looked back, Yé was still squatting where he'd left him, his eyes on the ground.

Part Four

THE JUDAS-GOAT

CHAPTER EIGHTEEN

MARC'S BUSH JACKET was tight in the shoulders and Harry felt strange in the tapered French trousers. He could have waited for his own clothes to be washed and dried but already he'd wasted one night with the Vietnamese combat engineers and another at Sans Souci and he wanted to get on to Saigon. He had the feeling, as he hurried down the Catinat, that people were turning to watch him. Not the Vietnamese. The purposeful, antlike scurry of their lives was such that they had no eyes for him as he shouldered his way down the crowded sidewalk, past shops cluttered with silks from Shantung, cheap Japanese transistor radios, Chengmai cottons, and black-market tape recorders from the American PX. But the Americans turned to watch him and one had sworn at him when he'd jostled the man in his haste. It might have been better to go to the Caravelle, change into a suit, and take a cab to the A.I.D. mission. But that would have taken too long. Already he'd wasted two nights. He wanted the truth from Englehardt and he wanted it now. He had walked from the Chasseloup Laubat school, where he'd parked the car, in the hope that the exercise would burn away his anger. He wanted to be cool and rational when he talked to Englehardt. But it was not working that way. Lies, lies, lies. The whole montagnard movement had been built on lies. Diem's lies, Englehardt's, his own. In retrospect, he could see that he had sensed the betrayal when Englehardt had made the pledge at the Capriccio. Why had he not faced the matter then and there? He guessed it was because he had wanted too much to believe in Englehardt and in the future of the montagnard movement. He had shut his suspicions out of his mind, rejected his better judgment. Yé had been right. Harry Coltart was the greatest liar of them all because he would not permit himself to see the truth and to speak it. Yé, Ilouha, his own son, all who believed in him, they were the ones stuck with the bill. Like the T'ai, the Koho would pay with their freedom if not with their lives for placing their trust in a white man. Marc had warned him that it would be so, but he hadn't listened to Marc. Now everything was falling apart. Father Dupleix, that good man whose weakness was love, had been killed. Loye's work, Marc had said. So in a sense that, too, Harry thought, is my responsibility. Many others would die if the government troops moved into the hills in force. Why? Why? That was what he didn't understand. The montagnards had kept their half of the bargain. The coolie trains were being hit. Since Mouc had come out with his men in the north, the movement had been gaining momentum. Now they had been betrayed and everything was finished, dead. Why? He meant to find that out, to reverse that decision if he could.

A Vietnamese flower peddler got in his way and Harry shoved the man aside. A hand gripped Harry's elbow. An American in a loud sports shirt, his eyes serious, concerned.

"That's no way to treat somebody, fellow. Causes a lot of bad feeling."

"Get out of my way," Harry muttered, shouldering his way past the American.

"Damned drunk," the man said to his companion. "They shouldn't let that type out here."

Harry hurried on, walking fast, threading his way through the crowd, bolting across the side streets, almost oblivious to the hooting of horns and the squealing of tires, his head pounding with anger. The man was right. They shouldn't let my type out here. We kill everything we touch. God damn it, God damn it!

He turned sharply through the gate and into the A.I.D. compound, sending a pair of secretaries fluttering, and bounded up the steps.

"Englehardt," he said to the Marine guard. "I want to see Englehardt. Harry Coltart."

"Fill out an appointment slip, please."

It was not the same Marine guard as before, but he had the identical, hard, young eyes, the same aloof, disciplined face. Harry was aware of the Marine's eyes studying him as he hastily filled out the slip and thrust it across the desk.

The Marine glanced at the slip, dialed a number and spoke into the telephone, leaning back in his chair, his eyes never leaving Harry.

"I guess you can go up," he said.

Harry vaulted up the stairs, knocked twice on the familiar

door and turned the knob. The secretary was not at her desk. He walked without knocking through the door into Englehardt's inner office. Englehardt was sitting at his desk in his shirtsleeves, his eyes on the door. He smiled faintly but did not get up.

"Hello, Harry," he said. "What're you doing here?"

"You know why I'm here." Harry had had enough of deceit, enough of fencing with words. He just wanted to talk facts and he was going to make the fat man with the tired eyes do that whether he wanted to or not.

"I don't know. I'd like to. I'd like to know why you left your post without authorization. Sit down and tell me."

"You son of a bitch." Harry spoke the words evenly and without emotion.

Englehardt rose from his chair, a flush on his cheeks as he leaned forward across his desk, his clenched fists on the polished wood.

"Who are you calling a son of a bitch?" he demanded. "If you've got something to say to me, sit down and spit it out. But don't forget who you're talking to, Coltart. Don't you forget it for a minute."

Harry remained standing.

"The road. You lied about the road."

"I lied about nothing. I said you had to go along with Diem. And you did. What else was there to do?"

Englehardt sat down again, his arms crossed in front of him. Harry dropped into a chair, some of his anger dissipated with his outburst.

"But you knew Diem was lying. You knew he had no intention of giving the montagnards what they wanted."

"Maybe I did. And you would have, too, if you hadn't gotten yourself emotionally involved. I tried to warn you about that, Harry."

"Yes. You warned me. But why?"

"Why what?" Englehardt inquired.

"Why did Diem lie? Why is he sending troops into the hills? The tribes kept their part of the bargain."

Englehardt spoke gently, as if trying to teach a slow child the mysteries of mathematics.

"Look, Harry. What Diem did was necessary and right. He couldn't give in to the montagnards without making other concessions to the Buddhists. And he's got to cut the Ho Chi Minh trail."

"But we were cutting it," Harry insisted.

"The hell you were. Stuff's still getting through. The montagnards aren't strong enough to stop the Vietcong by themselves. That's why the army's going in."

"Then why did you make me lie to them? If the army was going in anyway, there was no need to betray them."

"Diem wasn't ready. You were a stopper, Harry. You and your montagnards had to hold the Vietcong until the army could get this thing set up. A large-scale operation takes time to plan. You did that and all of us are grateful to you."

"Thanks. And me?"

"You? Murkland would have sent you a signal in plenty of time. Didn't I get Thompson out of Laos after his operation was compromised? I thought you knew me better than that."

"I didn't mean that. I meant what am I supposed to do now that I've given my word to a people, lied to them? Doesn't it occur to you that there's a moral question involved?"

"Tom Kiernan again? Listen, Harry, you're just as wrong now as Kiernan was in Budapest in 1956. Sure, I covered for him, because he was a good agent and I didn't want him drummed out of the Agency. But he was wrong and I sent another man to Budapest to do the job he wouldn't do."

"And Dos Lobos?"

"The same. What's moral about this war? Nothing. It's just one we've got to fight because the world is what it is. People get hurt in the process. You should know that."

"I guess I should. I suppose I never thought about it in terms of people you lied to, of playing with people's lives. I wish you'd told me the truth that night at the Capriccio."

"I wish I could have afforded to. When you spoke of the montagnards as *your* people, I knew that no longer was possible. Too much was at stake."

"And what do I do now? Just say to the hill tribes, 'I'm sorry it was necessary to betray you'?" Harry could feel his anger rising again within him. He had been a fool to trust Englehardt.

"You'll be going home, Harry. There's nothing more you can do in the hills. You're tired and you've got a lot of leave coming. Once you're back in the States, you'll feel better about it. All of us get a bit on edge out here."

"Yes, we get on edge. It's terrible for us."

"Cut it out, Harry."

"It's final then? Nothing can be done?"

Englehardt shook his head.

"Sorry, Harry. It had to be. I'm just sorry it was you and I who had to do it."

"You're sorry."

"Don't get snotty, Harry. I'm trying to be pleasant about this. You'll get over it. Leave, a new assignment . . ."

Harry had had enough. He smashed his open palm down on Englhardt's desk.

"There isn't going to be any new job," he blurted. "I'm finished. I'm going into some clean business like . . . like . . . like dope peddling."

Englehardt rose to his feet.

"I think you've said enough, Harry."

"Enough? I haven't said half enough! You . . ."

"Get out of here, Coltart, before I have you thrown out. I'm having new orders cut for you. They'll be at the Caravelle tomorrow. Maybe when you're back in the States you'll . . ."

Harry slammed the door behind him, cutting Englehardt's sentence in two. He crumpled up the pass and tossed the wadded paper on the Marine's desk and strode out into the streets, looking for a taxi. The States! He was damned if he was going to run out on the Koho.

He paid off the taxi at the school and jumped into the Deux Chevaux, revved the little car's engine and roared out of town on the Thudaumot road, leaving behind him the neat, suburban villas of Saigon, the country changing to truck gardens and then to rice paddies and ahead of him the long, low line of blue hills which shielded Sans Souci from the monsoons. As the shimmering rectangles of the paddies whipped past the windows hour by hour and the hills grew more distinct, his anger slowly drained out of him. The dirt road was rough and the physical effort of driving the car at high speed absorbed some of his bitterness. As far as he was concerned, Englehardt had ceased to exist, if only because he was not the man Harry had thought him to be. It had been a case of mistaken identity. When you thought about it, nobody had a real identity except to himself. Other people saw you through a smoke screen of their own suppositions. You could not blame a man because you had failed to perceive what he was.

The road struck straight as an arrow across the paddies toward the hills and Harry drove fast, not seeing the scenery, conscious only of the exhilaration of the speed and the straining of the car. Now that it was over and there was nothing more to be done in Saigon, he felt better about it. The thing was to find Yé. Together they could work something out. He wasn't sure what that might be; he only knew he had to go back, to share the fate of the montagnards, the fate which he had helped to shape. His place was with Ilouha, with Yé, even if Yé tried to kill him. It had to be because for him now there could be no other place. The burden of what he had done was too great to be taken back to Virginia with him. In the hills, he thought, Yé and I will think of something.

It was late in the day and he was very tried when he reached Sans Souci, the red dust pluming out behind his spinning tires as he careened up the driveway toward the mound of bougain-villaea which was the plantation house. He must have heard me coming, Harry thought to himself. Marc was there, stand-ing on the veranda, the familiar, mocking smile on his twisted face.

"Back so soon?" Marc inquired.

"Yes. Got a beer?" Harry threw himself into one of the rattan chairs, wiping the dust from his eyes with the back of his hand.

"Of course. What news?"

"Bad. More government troops are coming."

Harry gulped the beer thirstily. Marc frowned, gave a low whistle and dropped into a chair.

"So much for the montagnards," he said. "I warned you, Harry."

"Yes. I thought Englehardt and Diem meant what they said."

"Nobody means what he says any more. Lying has become a congenital disease of our time. In a hundred ways we each betray each other every day. You know that."

"It's not what I wanted, Marc."

"No, it's not what you wanted. You were just the Judas-goat."

"Judas-goat?"

"Haven't you ever seen domestic animals shipped off to be slaughtered? The quickest way to get them into the freight cars is to discover the Judas-goat, the one they trust, and send him first. Then they all follow."

Was that, Harry wondered, what he really was? A pro-fessional Judas? Perhaps Marc was right. Perhaps that was his principal stock in trade, an ability to inspire confidence in others, the better to betray them. But it couldn't be left at that.

"And what now, Harry?"

"Englehardt's ordered me home."

Marc paused for a moment, and put down his glass.

"Perhaps it's for the best."

"I'm not going."

"What? What do you mean?"

"I want a guide, Marc."

"A guide? What for?"

"I'm going back. To Ilouha, to Yé."

The Frenchman started to his feet.

"You're out of your mind, Harry. Yé would as soon kill you as look at you."

"I have to go back, Marc. I have to. Will you help me?"

"No, Harry, I won't. I won't help you to commit suicide. It wouldn't change anything. Haven't you done enough to them, even if you don't care about yourself?"

"I thought it all out in the car. I'm asking you to help, Marc."

"The answer is no. It's insane."

Harry drained his glass of beer, got to his feet and walked to the steps, looking out over the neatly clipped lawn to the ranks of rubber trees and the river beyond.

"That's the way it is?" he asked quietly.

"That's the way it is, Harry."

"Well, I'll be on my way then. May I borrow the car?"

"Of course. Look, Harry, there's nothing you could do to help them now. You can see that."

Harry opened the door, climbed behind the wheel, flicked on the ignition, and started the car.

"Sure. Thanks, Marc, for everything. You'll find the car at Notre Dame des Bois."

As he let out the clutch and put his foot down on the accelerator, Harry saw Marc's mouth open, but his words were drowned in the roar of the engine.

As the Deux Chevaux rattled down the rutted, dirt road to the mission, Harry thought about what he had to do. The important thing was to get back to Yé before the Koho chief made contact with Loye. Once that took place, he knew he would have no chance.

At the mission, a group of Annamese workmen were squatting on the beams of the new hospital, thatching the roof under the supervision of a young priest in a dirty white cassock. Beads of perspiration pebbled the priest's wrinkled forehead. He was shouting instructions up to the Annamese. Harry got out of the car and shook hands.

"I'm Harry Coltart," he said in French.

"Ah, Mr. Coltart. I'm Pére Jean. Marc Michaud has spoken of you."

"I'm sorry about Father Dupleix."

The young priest clasped his hands in front of him and inclined his head slightly, as if to acknowledge a compliment.

"Yes. He was much loved. These are terrible times."

Harry nodded his head.

"Look, Father, I need help. I want a guide. Someone who knows the Koho country."

The priest's eyebrows rose, questioningly.

"The Koho country?" He paused. "You're working there, aren't you?"

"Yes. Will you help me?"

"I don't know. Since the attack, we've been trying to discourage coming and going between here and the hills. It's too dangerous."

"Please, Father. It's important, very important. To a lot of people. I'll pay the guide well."

"Hmmm. Where do you want to go?" The young priest studied him carefully.

"Just to Yé's village. It's not far, but I'm not sure of the way. Please."

"Well, I know Father Dupleix thought well of you and you're a friend of Marc's. Why not one of his men?" he asked, nodding at the Deux Chevaux.

"His montagnard tappers are working on the other side of the plantation," Harry lied, "and I've got to leave immediately. It's a matter of life and death."

"I see."

"In the name of God, Father," Harry pleaded, "if you've got someone, let him take me."

The priest pursed his lips and ran a dirty hand through his tousled brown hair.

"I have such a man," he admitted. "If he's willing to go, it's all right." The priest turned and cupped his hands, shouting up to the men on the roof beams. "Long," he said, "send for Mi Tang."

Harry heaved a sigh of relief. The two white men stood talking together and smoking, until the guide could be found. Finally, a tall, thin man returned with the worker called Mi Tang.

"This *Boc,*" the priest said, addressing the new arrival, "wants to go to the country of the Koho, to the village of Yé. Will you take him?"

"Yes, I will take him, if he will pay me," the man said slowly, studying Harry. "When do you want to start?" he asked.

"Now. Right away," Harry said. He noticed that the few hairs at the end of Mi Tang's chin were gathered into a wispy goatee. The last two fingers of his left hand were missing.

CHAPTER NINETEEN

FROM HIS POSITION behind the tree, John McWhorter could see the tank shudder as it fired, the muzzle-blast a thin jet of orange flame in the fading light. Almost immediately the projectile burst against the facade of the Gia Long Palace, punching a narrow hole, smudged at its crumbling edges, in the cream-colored wall. Other tanks parked among the shrubbery of the formal garden opened fire, the explosion of their shells against the building shrouding the palace in a cloud of dust. The rebel Marines, red kerchiefs knotted around their throats to distinguish them from loyal troops, clustered behind the tanks and fired long bursts of machine-gun tracers at the palace. The tracers, glowing like fireflies in the dusk, made long, graceful arcs as they converged on the palace, struck the masonry and glanced off at crazy angles, as if a part of some extravagant Fourth of July display. From the darkened windows of the palace came answering spurts of flame as the Palace Guard and the Vietnamese Special Forces troops returned the fire, drowning out the martial music from the palace public address system which had followed Diem's most recent exhortation to the palace's defenders to continue their resistance. Loyal troops, the President had promised, were on their way. This, McWhorter knew, was a lie. Diem was through. All the generals were in on this one. Fat, old General Trang had told him so in the smoking ruins of the naval headquarters earlier in the day. All of them except General Huynh Van Cao in the delta. But this time General Cao could not save Diem. There would be no troops coming from the south, as there had been during the abortive 1960 coup. All the boats, Trang said, had been seized and taken by rebel troops to the east bank of the Mekong. McWhorter could not imagine what had led Trang to join the conspirators. The fat old bastard owed his general's stars to his refusal to get involved in politics. Obviously something had been eating Trang, but McWhorter didn't know what it was. Somebody

186

said Trang had a personal grudge against Diem, something to do with his family. McWhorter knew no more than that. But when Trang turned on you, it was a pretty good sign that nobody was on your side.

Around the corner of the palace trundled a pair of loyalist tanks, awkwardly pushing their way through the flower beds. Their advance was almost comical. They looked like fat, hesitant dowagers, aware of their clumsiness and afraid of crushing the flowers. The tanks rumbled forward, squat and low slung, their turrets rotating slowly, the ugly snouts of their cannon probing the air like the antennae of grotesque, prehistoric insects. The first loyalist tank braked sharply in the middle of the flower bed, as if startled, and fired almost immediately. The shell whined through the air and exploded in front of a rebel tank, showering it with bits of dirt and rock which struck sparks from its armor. The rebel tank's gun barked hoarsely, hitting the tank stalled in the flower bed, from the turret of which shot a sheet of flame followed by the explosion of its ammunition, dark lumps hurtling from its broken shell. The second loyalist tank stopped, hesitated for a moment and turned toward its injured mate as if to help, then backed up quickly and retreated around the corner of the palace, pursued by a hail of tracer bullets and the derisive shouts of the Marines.

McWhorter rolled over into a sitting position, his back against the tree. He badly wanted a cigarette but he was afraid he might draw fire from the palace if he lit one. The air was full of the angry humming of bullets. He did not intend to take any unnecessary chances. It was too close to the end to be careless. He fought the desire for the cigarette and thought instead of what he had seen that day. It had been a day to remember.

He'd been sweating on his bed in the Caravelle when the first desultory crackling of small-arms fire had rippled like summer thunder down the shaded noonday streets. He had run to his window and seen sidewalk peddlars hastily disassembling their stands, shopkeepers slamming down the metal shutters in front of their stores. In less than a minute the streets had been deserted except for a lone peddlar dashing for cover, bullets striking sparks from the pavement at his heels. McWhorter had picked up the telephone while dressing hastily, but the switchboard had not answered. The elevator was not working and he'd had to use the stairs to reach the lobby, where the reservations clerk lay flat on his stomach behind the desk. He'd tried to find out what was going on but nobody had known any more than was obvious, that fighting had broken out in the city and a coup was under way. As he'd broken from the door of the Caravelle, running bent over and close to the building, McWhorter had seen an Annamese police officer struggling wildly in the cramped back seat of a Renault, trying to get out of his white uniform. If the police officer was any gauge, things did not look well for Diem.

Down the Catinat, red kerchiefs tied around their necks, the rebel Marines had come in small groups, firing at anything that moved. High overhead, four fighter planes had circled slowly, wing-tip to wing-tip. From time to time, one of them would peel off in a long dive, the wind screaming over its wings, its cannon hammering as the plane came whistling in low over the red tile roofs of Saigon. McWhorter, hearing heavy firing from the direction of the Quai le Myre de Vilers, had run toward the river, hoping to God that the rebels would see he was a white man and hold their fire. The firing had been heavy in the dock area, and with ricochets whining around him, he'd ducked gratefully into the doorway of the old Hotel Majestic. The lobby had been empty, the upset chairs testifying to the hurried exit of its occupants. Miraculously, the old-style birdcage elevator had responded to the call button, and he'd been able to get to the roof. There he'd found Houghton of the *Guardian,* a foppish little man who prided himself on the fact that, even on Saigon's hottest days, he never was without his coat. McWhorter didn't like Houghton, with his Fleet Street airs, but he'd been glad to see him, comforted by the sight of a familiar face.

"What're they after?" McWhorter had asked.

"The planes? Naval headquarters. The sailors are putting up a jolly good fight." Houghton had sounded as if he were commenting on a soccer match.

"Captain Quyen?"

"Dead. They got him in the streets. I don't know who's in charge."

"The palace?"

"There's fighting there, according to Halberstam. And the airport's sealed off. I think they've got old Diem this time."

Two of the planes had made a long, lazy loop to the east and come in low across the treetops on the far shore of the river, their wings sparkling as their machine guns fired. From

the smoking wreck of naval headquarters and from two
frigates moored in the river had come ack-ack fire, black
mushrooms of flak sprouting in the air around the oncoming
planes. One of the puffs had seemed to sprout on the edge of
one wing of the leading plane. The aircraft had hung there
for a moment in the sky, then veered off slowly, turning to
show its white belly, like a shark attacking, until it disappeared
into a cloud of spray in the river, the other plane coming on
fast, dumping its bombs on the smoking building, rising
sharply on the hot air of its own exploding bombs, then
roaring off, its wings waggling, to rejoin its circling comrades. The Marines had gone with the bayonet into the
shattered building after the bombs had fallen and there had
been heavy firing, and then silence, and then a single, final
shot.

It had been that way most of the day. The Sûreté, the
Ministry of the Interior, the telegraph office, the radio station,
all had fallen to the rebels. Few had put up as much of a
fight as the naval headquarters. The rebels had been very
clever. The movement of the rebel troops into the city had
been cleared by Nhu himself as a fake coup designed to smoke
out enemies of the regime. By the time Nhu had discovered
the deception of the rebel generals, it had been too late. Now
all that remained was the palace. Looting already had begun
in the city, McWhorter knew. That was a pretty good sign
that Diem was going to lose. Lodge had refused help, they
said, and advised Diem to resign and accept the rebels' offer
of safe-conduct out of the country. The story went that
Diem had rejected the American ambassador's advice with
coldness and contempt. But if the temper of the people was
any gauge, McWhorter thought, Diem would have done
well to have followed that advice. The statue of the Trung
sisters had been pulled down; homes and shops belonging to
government officials were being looted and burned. Over the
city hung a gray pall of smoke. Soon Diem would be finished.

As he sat slumped against the tree, McWhorter realized
that the rebel guns had fallen silent and that there was no
firing from the palace. An end-of-day quiet lay on the palace
grounds, the fading light broken by the burning loyalist tank,
which cast weird, flickering shadows on the scarred lawn.
Through the shadows flitted the shapes of servants fleeing
from the palace, taking advantage of the rebel offer of safe-
conduct. A rebel officer clambered up on top of a tank,
pointed a transistorized loud-hailer at the palace and ha-

rangued its defenders in Annamese and French, demanding
that they throw down their arms. In answer, a single rifle
shot reverberated from one of the building's darkened windows, the bullet whining high over the officer's head. He
jumped quickly from the tank, shaking his head in disbelief.

"Soldiers!" boomed a megaphone from the palace, "this is
your President speaking. Do not obey traitorous officers!
Loyal troops even now are arriving from the south. The
Seventh Division is coming! Defend your President!"

The old bastard's got guts, McWhorter conceded, as the
Marines hooted at the voice, drowning it in their gunfire. All
night long, McWhorter lay cramped and tired behind his tree
while the tanks fired, slowly pounding the palace into rubble.
Flames licked from the ruins and the frosted glass of the
cupola atop the palace roof, miraculously unbroken, glowed
like a live coal. As the night wore on, more and more troops
crowded into the palace grounds, men from the Fifth Division,
Trang's recruits and the hard-bitten veterans of the elite Sixth
Airborne Battalion. McWhorter didn't mind the cramps. He
could put up with them. He had waited a long time to see
the fall of Diem and Nhu and he guessed he could wait a few
hours more. It was something he didn't want to miss.

After the palace falls, he thought to himself, I must get
over to the A.I.D. building and talk to Cao Van Thuan. With
Diem's arrest, the bonze no longer would need the diplomatic
immunity which refuge in the building afforded him. Cao
Van Thuan had been damned lucky to get over the wall and
into the A.I.D. compound when Nhu's goons had raided the
Xa Loi Pagoda. Now the bonze would be going back to the
pagoda. After that, McWhorter thought, he'd have to see
about getting his copy out. The telegraph office was closed
and censorship had been imposed. The rebels, damn them,
weren't acting any more democratically than the fallen regime.
The coup was, in fact, a hard one to figure out. The rebels
ran the gamut from holy men like Cao Van Thuan to old
war lords of General Trang's stamp. It was hard to say which
way the country might go or who might rule it, although
they said that General Minh, "Big" Minh, was the chief
conspirator. McWhorter wasn't going to worry about that.
That was somebody else's problem. He'd been right about
Diem's fall and he'd be going home to reap the rewards that
went with being right. He'd even had a bit to do with Diem's
fall himself, he thought proudly. It was up to the next man
to worry about Vietnam's future.

As dawn began to break, McWhorter saw that the palace grounds were jammed with troops. Other soldiers were clustered on the roofs of nearby buildings. More than twenty tanks, by his count, ringed the smoking Gia Long Palace, the snouts of their cannon trained on the ruined shell of the building. Firing had died out in the rest of the city. It was quiet in the garden and McWhorter suddenly realized that he had not eaten since noon the previous day and was very hungry. The rebels had cranked up another bull-horn.

"Ngo Dinh Diem! Ngo Dinh Nhu!" demanded the electronically amplified voice from the cover of a rebel tank. "This is your final chance! Surrender, and you will be allowed to leave the country. Resist, and you die!"

In reply, a machine gun stuttered from a palace window and, as if on signal, all the rebel tanks fired together. Under the impact of the volley, the palace seemed to McWhorter to shiver like a wounded beast. The rebel riflemen and machine-gunners added their fire to the fusillade, pouring their bullets into the building. Mortar shells were bursting on the roof, showering the terrace of the palace with broken tiles. As each mortar shell exploded, the rebel troops shouted encouragement to the mortar crews. A white cloth appeared in a ground-floor window and fluttered frantically. The rebels stopped firing. But more shots came from the dust which swirled around the base of the palace and the rebels renewed their cannonade with increased violence. Again, someone waved the white cloth from the palace window, this time with an almost comical enthusiasm. There were no more shots from the palace.

Slowly a young Marine, his red insurgent's kerchief knotted around his helmet like a bloody bandage, rose to his feet. He stood there in the growing light, his rifle held diagonally across his chest. Another Marine, older and more cautious than the first, made as if to stand up but remained bent over in a half-crouched position. Nothing happened. The smoking palace remained silent and dead. Another Marine rose and then another until all the rebels were on their feet. And from their throats came a yell of triumph as they ran toward the palace, the tanks lumbering after them, the hatches of their turrets open, the tank captains' bodies bobbing and swaying as they sat braced high in the open hatches. Running forward with the rebels, McWhorter heard himself whooping.

McWhorter bounded across the terrace, the broken roof

tiles and shards of window glass crunching under his running feet. The main door of the palace had been hit by a tank shell. It hung crazily from its hinges, its panels shredded into splinters. The building was smoking fitfully, like a city dump. As the rebels poured into the palace, men of Nhu's Special Forces and Palace Guards bolted past them, tearing off their uniforms as they ran. Some of the Marines stopped to club down with their rifle butts the unarmed, fleeing men. But most of the rebels ran on into the palace, laughing and yelling, anxious for their share of the loot.

The great reception hall was a shambles. Rebel soldiers were tearing down the golden drapes, chopping at the gilt furniture with their bayonets, pulling books from the shelves and stuffing them into the fronts of their tunics. A sergeant was prying at a gilded light fixture with the butt of his rifle, trying to jerk it intact from the wall. In one corner of the hall, a soldier from the Fifth Division held four Special Forces troops up against a wall, their hands clasped behind their heads, while another rebel emptied their pockets. The great reception hall echoed with shouts and laughter and the brittle tinkle of breaking glass. From another room ran a chuckling soldier, six bottles of brandy cradled in his arms. It hadn't taken them long, McWhorter thought, to find the wine cellar.

General Trang, surrounded by a knot of young officers, their pistols drawn, burst into the reception hall from the terrace. The general's beady, piglike eyes flitted around the room, taking in the scene of the looting. He smiled broadly, hesitated for a minute, as if he might join the plundering and then, with a grace and lightness which so many fat men have, bounded up the curving staircase, taking the stairs two at a time, his aides at his heels, McWhorter behind them. At the top of the stairway, two soldiers were beginning to cut the carpeting from the stairs with their bayonets. Other rebels already had reached the second floor. The doors of the offices were open, their floors littered with glass and plaster from the shelling. A dead officer of the Palace Guard lay in the corridor, half of his face torn away by a shell splinter. General Trang stepped delicately over the body and puffed down the hall toward the President's office, McWhorter trailing along behind the knot of officers. The reporter shouldered his way past the last officers and into Diem's office. A handful of rebel Marines were systematically dismembering the room. One had pulled all the drawers from Diem's desk and the carpet was covered with a snowfall of documents. Another was sweeping ashtrays, a clock and mementoes off the desk and into a knapsack. A third, his eyes rolling wildly, his lips flecked with foam, was stabbing at the cushions of a leather sofa.

"Out of here!" Trang shouted in French, "get these canaille out of here!"

The general's aides, waving their pistols in the air, hustled the young Marines from the room, slapping hard the one who had been stabbing at the sofa, the men resisting and resentful.

"What is this piece of offal?" Trang demanded as a pair of officers emerged from an adjoining room, dragging a cowering Special Forces sergeant between them. The officers answered in Annamese, both of them talking at the same time.

Trang swore mightily and delivered a swift, well-aimed blow to the captive's groin. The sergeant doubled up in pain, hanging from the officers' arms.

"Take him to my headquarters," Trang shouted, hurling his bulk into the President's chair, pounding the desk with frustration.

"What's happened?" McWhorter shouted. "Where's Diem?"

"Our birds have flown, Mr. McWhorter," Trang said slowly, his eyes hard. "Diem and Nhu got out last night. That switchboard operator has been putting our telephone calls through to them at the place where they're hiding, somewhere in the city."

"Shee-it," exclaimed McWhorter.

CHAPTER TWENTY

THEY HAD BEEN WALKING hard all day, putting country behind them, and Harry was almost done for, his breath coming in short, rattling gasps, the muscles of his legs tight as drums. His wrists were raw where they were bound with strips of hide and the cut flesh stung as the sweat ran down his arms into the sores. But it was not his wrists or his leg muscles or his lungs which bothered him so much, or his head, where the blow had fallen. It was the business of having to walk fast over rough country with his hands trussed behind him. Harry could not have imagined how difficult it was to do this. With his arms tied behind him, he had no sense of balance and the going was hard even on level ground. He'd fallen many times. Not being able to break his fall with his hands gave him a curious sense of helplessness. Each time, Loye had jerked him to his feet by the cord knotted around his neck and he'd stumbled on, gasping for breath, the redness before his eyes. Harry finally had persuaded Loye to loosen the cords around his wrists, but the Rhadé had refused to remove them. That was foolish of him, Harry thought. Harry knew that his helplessness was slowing them up. He was worried about that. He had been trying hard to keep up because he was afraid Loye would kill him if he could not maintain the pace.

Ever since they had seen the small plane, Loye had been in a hurry. They had been skirting the edge of a forest clearing that morning when the plane had appeared suddenly, at treetop level, flying north, the sound of its engine trapped among the ravines. Loye had yanked the rope, pulling Harry choking to the ground. Yé had jumped on him, the tip of his knife pressing against Harry's neck just under the ear lobe. Ilouha and the other five men had been ahead, under the canopy of the forest. Only Harry, Loye, and Yé had been caught on the edge of the clearing. But the pilot had not seen them. Harry knew that. Otherwise he would have

circled to take a closer look. But he had flown on to the
north, never varying his altitude, keeping just above the treetops. The plane had been a small, single-engined, U.S. Army
job, the type used for artillery spotting, the kind the French
call mouchards. The pilot had flown on to the north, the
plane shrinking to a small, black dot on the horizon, the roar
of its engine gradually fading away. Only then had Yé rolled
off him and Loye jerked him to his feet again. Since then,
they'd stepped up the pace. The plane had made Loye uneasy
and he seemed in a great hurry to get where he was going.
Where that might be, Harry didn't know. Since his capture
two days before, they had been marching roughly north by
northeast, putting country between themselves and the mission. He was very tired and afraid that Loye would kill him
if he could not keep up. He guessed they would kill him anyway, when they had gotten what they wanted from him,
but, for the moment, he wanted to live.

He'd been foolish to trust Mi Tang. Marc had told him
that there were many Vietcong among the people of the
district. But Harry had needed someone to take him to Yé
and it had not occurred to him that an employee of Notre
Dame des Bois might be a Vietcong agent. He had made the
three-fingered man walk in front of him. He and Mi Tang
had traveled for a day into the hills of the Koho. Early on
the morning of the second day, as they were passing through
a thick grove of bamboo, Loye and Yé had jumped him. As
he'd reached for his pistol, arms had pinned his own to his
sides, and a blow on the side of his head had brought the
ground rushing up fast to meet him, knocking the air whistling
from his lungs. Harry had awakened to find his arms bound
behind him, the halter around his neck, Yé and Loye squatting
in front of him, speaking in monotones. Harry had spotted
Ilouha with the other men, but had not had a chance to speak
to her. As soon as Loye had seen that he was conscious, he'd
jerked him to his knees and then to his feet, and they'd set
out on the long march to the north. Yé had not spoken to
Harry on the day of his capture or on the next, the present
one, and whenever Harry had tried to attract Ilouha's attention, Loye had jerked the halter, pulling him forward faster.
The men were Loye's and it was clear that the Rhadé, not
Yé, was in command.

Ilouha had kept her eyes averted, avoiding Harry's gaze.
She was beginning to be big with his child but she moved
rapidly and with great grace, the strength of her youth show-

ing in her muscled calves and erect back. At noon on the first
day they had stopped for a while beside a stream. Ilouha had
given him water from a calabash, and fed him a little rice. He
had not tried to speak to her then because Loye's eyes had
been fixed on him. Nor had there been an opportunity that
night, which they'd spent in a forest of *dau* trees.

Later, Harry thought as he plodded along, perhaps tonight,
there might be a chance to speak to her. It had to be tonight.
He knew from the direction in which they were walking that
they were getting closer to country held in force by the Vietcong. After tonight, he conceded, there would be no chance
of escaping. Tonight, if Ilouha would help him, he would
have to try. With luck, both of them might make it. But
once they had gone much further beyond the Koho country,
it would be hopeless. Nobody would be trailing them. Harry
sensed that they had made a wide loop to avoid the troops
cutting the road into the hills. And Loye had sent his main
body off to the west, keeping only Yé, Ilouha and five of his
men. If by any wild chance troops had tracked him from
Notre Dame des Bois, they would have followed the larger
group. There were, Harry knew, no regular patrols this far
north. No, there was no chance of rescue. It was better to
walk as fast as possible and stay alive. Later, Ilouha would
help him.

Earlier that morning, the day after the mouchard's visit,
while they had been resting beside a stream, three big, troop-
carrying helicopters had flown over, heading north. But
there was no chance that the helicopters had seen them. Harry
knew that. The forest canopy was too thick. It was agonizing
to think of Americans being so close. Harry had fought an
urge to leap to his feet, to shout, to wave to the helicopters.
But he'd known it would do no good. He'd sat there quietly,
not even looking up, until the sound of the helicopters had
died away to the north. Even Loye had not been worried
about the helicopters. He'd looked at Harry, his mouth
twisted into a crooked smile, and jerked his head in the direction of the choppers, as if to say, "They won't do you any
good."

Since the midday rest, the little party had walked hard for
almost five hours. The going was tough because they were
walking against the grain of the land, not following the tilt of
the country but climbing up hills only to dip down into deep,
stream-creased valleys choked with bamboo and lianas, humming with insects which tortured Harry, unable because of

his bound wrists to flick them away. The going down was much harder than the climbing because of his lack of balance and Harry was about played out. If we have to go down and up one more time, he thought to himself, the sweat streaming down his face, I won't make it. Even if Loye threatens to kill me on the spot, I won't be able to get up again. You've got to make it, you son of a bitch, he swore to himself. You lying bastard, you've got to make it. Somehow, the cursing seemed to help and he plodded on.

Finally, when Harry felt he couldn't go a step further, Loye had held up his hand and spoken to the men ahead of him.

"It's enough," he'd said in Koho to Yé, "we'll sleep here."

Yé had looked doubtful for a minute, maintaining they had not covered enough ground, but finally had agreed. Harry had dropped to his knees and then fallen over on his side, his eyes closed, weary beyond belief. Yé had untied his hands then, fastening the neck halter to a tree and using the thongs taken from his wrists to hobble Harry's ankles. He'd signaled to Yé that he wanted to talk, but the Koho chief, inclining his head in Loye's direction, had indicated that the time for this would be later. When he had rested for an hour and restored the circulation in his arms, Harry felt better. He waited until Loye had gone off with one of the other men to look for water before calling out to Yé. The old chief had shambled over to him and looked down at him with an expression which conveyed both distaste and lack of interest.

"This is no good, Yé," Harry whispered.

"I have no words for you, *Boc*."

"Look, Yé. I'm asking nothing for myself. I'm just trying to tell you that the Koho are finished if they go over to the Vietcong. Many government troops are coming. You know what that means."

It would be the final madness, Harry thought, if the Koho resisted. The Vietcong might slow the advance of Diem's troops into the highlands, but the Koho country lay closest to the road. The initial thrust of the troops would carry them through that portion of the hills, even if they were stopped beyond that. If the Koho resisted, the troops would ravage their country like a swarm of locusts. He had to make Yé understand that.

The old man nodded.

"I know what it means. It has happened before. You swore it would not happen this time."

"I did my best," Harry protested. "They lied to me, Yé. I tried to make them stop the road but they wouldn't listen to me."

Yé grunted in disbelief.

"We'll fight the troops, *Boc*, for two reasons: there is nothing else to do and we are not women. Why did you come back? It was very foolish, for I told you we would kill you."

Harry was silent for a moment. Why had he come back? To talk Yé into surrendering? To try to rebuild the alliance? To bring Ilouha out? He wasn't quite sure in his own mind.

"I had to come back, Yé," he said simply. "I got you into this and I wanted to do what I could for you."

"There is nothing to be done, *Boc*. There have been too many betrayals. This, I think, will be the last."

"What are you going to do with me, Yé?"

"Do with you?" The idea seemed to surprise Yé. "That is for Loye to say. I would have killed you when we caught you but Loye would not have it. He will decide when and how you are to be killed."

"Help me. Yé. Help me to get away. I never lied to you about the road. I just didn't know."

Suddenly, urgently, Harry wanted to live. He knew now that, as Marc had said, there was nothing more he could do for the montagnards But he wanted to live and he begged for his life. Yé shook his head and spat a stream of betel nut juice into the dust.

"The time of talking is finished, *Boc*," he said. "You belong to Loye."

Harry slumped back against the tree to which he was tethered, the hope draining out of him as Loye and the other man returned. It was the end of the road for Harry Coltart. According to Hollywood, he should have a hollow ring containing a capsule of cyanide. It was not going to be that easy. Nothing about it looked as if it would be easy.

While Ilouha prepared the evening meal, Loye and Yé and the other men squatted together under a nearby tree, talking of the war. Harry lay against his tree, his eyes half-closed, aware that Loye was watching him. Finally, the Rhadé rose to his feet and sauntered over to Harry.

"What are you thinking about, *Boc*? About the manner in which we will kill you? About how you will escape?" It was the first time since his capture that Loye had spoken to him. He had a pleasant, mellifluous voice which matched his handsome, open face.

"Let me go, Loye," Harry whispered urgently. "I'll make you a rich man. My people will pay . . ."

The young Rhadé threw back his head and laughed, displaying a row of even, stained teeth.

"You cannot buy your freedom, *Boc*. For you, it's finished. Perhaps you think Ilouha will help you? She is mine now. Your son will be one of us."

"You dirty, yellow . . ." Harry's lunge was caught short by the tether, which pulled him choking onto his side, his hobbled feet lashing out at Loye.

As Harry lay gasping for air, Loye kicked him once, carefully, in the side, turned and walked back to the other men, who laughed and joked at the sight of the trussed American squirming on the ground.

When it was growing dark and the other men had eaten, Ilouha brought Harry a handful of rice and some water. Loye had strolled off into the bushes to relieve himself. Harry knew it was his last chance. He wolfed the rice and then spoke.

"Ilouha," he said, "you've got to help me."

"What is it you want?" she whispered. "Does it hurt where he kicked you?"

Harry shook his head, placing his hand on hers.

"No, it doesn't hurt. But you've got to help me, Ilouha. Tonight. We've got to escape tonight. We'll go away together. You know the way."

Ilouha looked at him curiously, as if he were a stranger who had entered the longhouse at night, one she was seeing now for the first time in the light of day. She shook her head, gently running her free hand across his forehead, smoothing the hair away from his eyes.

"That I cannot do," she said. "You are no longer one of us, Erohé. You betrayed us and now I belong to Loye."

Harry could not bring himself to believe that she would not help him, that she would give herself voluntarily to Loye. He could not accept that.

"But, Ilouha," he continued, "you and I . . ."

"That was before, when you were one of us. Now it is Loye and I. You could not stop being a *Boc*. You tried, but it was not possible."

"It's finished, then?"

"Yes, Erohé, all is finished for you and me. Rest now, for tomorrow the trail is long."

She took her hand from his and turned away from him, as if to get to her feet and go.

"Ilouha?" he said.

"Yes?"

"Thank you. That which we had was good. Thank you for that."

"Rest now," she said softly.

"What is Loye going to do with me?" he asked, as Ilouha rose to her feet. She looked down at him, her eyes troubled.

"He is taking you north," she answered, "through the mountains to Hanoi."

Hanoi! And then? But that was a question he did not have to ask.

CHAPTER TWENTY-ONE

NGO DINH DIEM SAT quietly beside his younger brother in the third pew from the front of Cholon's St. Francis Xavier Church, the communion wine a small, warm glow in the pit of his stomach. Diem was at peace with himself and with his God. He felt only a tremendous sense of relief, knowing that it was all over. He had seen more than enough strife in his lifetime; now there was to be only peace, the peace of God which passeth all understanding. Diem and Nhu were alone in the dimly lighted church. The young Annamese priest, his acolytes, and the few worshipers had hurried away at the end of the service. A few at the back of the church had slipped out even before the benediction. Diem smiled as he remembered the shaking of the young priest's hands as he had offered him the Host. Diem was glad he had been able to take communion, to receive for the last time the eucharistic wafer and the wine, the body and the blood of Christ, Redeemer of all men. Yesterday had been All Souls' Day, a day of obligation. But there had been the American admiral and his delegation in the morning, and then the fighting had broken out at noon. There had been no time to attend Mass. That is not quite true, he confessed to himself. You could have made the time to hear Mass but you put it aside, because in your pride you thought there still was a chance to win.

Yet a man reached a point where it no longer was worth much to win. What was the point of victory if you were surrounded by traitors and hated by the people? The escape from the palace had been incredibly easy. When he'd learned that there was no chance for General Cao to break through from the south, he and Nhu had followed the tunnel out under the palace grounds to the garage where the two unmarked Citroens were kept. He'd taken one, Nhu the other. By prearranged plan, they'd met later at Ma Tuyen's house in Cholon. The switchboard operator at the Gia Long had simply plugged the telephone calls from Lodge and the rebel generals through to him at Ma Tuyen's, thus preserving the fiction that he was still in the palace.

The finality of his defeat had been forced home on Diem when Ma Tuyen had said politely but firmly that it was impossible to get a junk to take him and Nhu to the delta. When a Chinaman turned down such a huge sum, it was clear that all was lost. He did not blame Ma Tuyen. Their host was, after all, a businessman. If the proposition did not make sense, if the risk appeared to outweigh the profit, you could hardly blame him for saying no. But if I could have reached Cao, Diem thought, we could have marched on Saigon together with the Seventh Division. The Seventh always had been loyal. And Nhu's Civil Guard would have come out for me. The city could have been regained. He shoved the thought aside. It would not have been worth the trouble. It was finished now, all finished. Diem did not want to think about such things any more. Not much time was left. He wanted to be ready when they came.

Diem concentrated his thoughts on the lean, alabaster body, with its crimson wounds, hanging from the cross above the altar, brooding upon its significance, aware only of the play of colored light on the body, as the wind outside rustled the leaves of the trees which stood between the stained glass windows and the sun. He sensed rather than heard his brother rise from his knees, his prayers finished. His heart went out to Nhu. As the older brother, he was responsible for Nhu. Had he failed Nhu? Perhaps, for he sensed that his younger brother was not yet at peace, that his restless spirit had not accepted that which he must surely know was to come.

"Don't worry, Nhu, it will not be hard," Diem said.

The younger man covered his eyes with his hand, as if to spare his brother the sight of what was written there, shook his head and spoke very quietly.

"It's my children," he said.

"They'll be all right. No one will harm them. They are at Dalat?"

"Yes. The Special Forces group guarding them has instructions to take them into the forest at the first sign of trouble in Saigon. But they may have gone over to the rebels."

"At least you know that Tran Le Xuan and Le Thuy are safe. Be grateful for that." It was a paradox that Madame Nhu and her eldest daughter should live precisely because the coup had caught them in the very bosom of their enemies, in America. Thuc, too, was safe; he was in Rome for the

Ecumenical Council. And Ngo Dinh Luyen, the youngest brother and the weakest, was safe at the Vietnamese embassy in London. It was not much with which to rebuild a dynasty.

"Yes," Nhu said, "thank God for that. But what about the boys and little Le Quyen at Dalat? She's only four. Only four."

The President placed his arm around his brother's narrow shoulders and gave him a pat.

"You mustn't worry. Trust in God and He will save them."

"And Can?"

Diem chuckled.

"Don't worry about Can. He'll take care of himself. Hué may still be loyal."

Diem didn't really believe that. If all the generals were in on the plot, then the troops at Hué would follow the rebel lead. But it helped to pretend that everything had not been lost in a single day. By any lights, the Ngo Dinhs had fallen on evil days. Of six brothers, Diem thought, the Communists killed the eldest and his only son. And now these swine will kill Can, Nhu and me. That will leave only celibate old Thuc and Luyen, the playboy, of all the Ngo Dinhs. It was essential that Nhu's two sons should be smuggled out of the country. They were all that would remain of the family. Diem had decided that he would not go into exile. His purpose in trying to bribe Ma Tuyen into providing a junk was not to escape, but to carry on the fight from the delta. Nor, he suspected, would Nhu accept the ignominy of exile. It was as important for a ruler to know how to die as it was to understand how to live. That way, if they did get out, Nhu's sons could carry with them a heritage of pride.

Diem was startled out of his thoughts by the pounding of Nhu's hand on the back of the pew in front of them.

"It was my fault," he exclaimed furiously, "all my fault!"

"Nonsense! It was not your fault. Our friends and our enemies conspired together to bring us down." Or had there been something else, Diem wondered. A flaw in his own character? Too much mandarin pride? Nepotism? Stubbornness carried too far into obstinacy? Scepticism deformed into unreasoning suspicion? He considered these possibilities and rejected them. He had done what he thought best for the country.

"Those pigs Trang and Nguyen Giac! I should never have been caught asleep by Operation Bravo," Nhu said.

"Yes. We both were foolish about that." I should have

had Giac shot when he made his ridiculous demand to be
Minister of the Interior, Diem thought. But he had never
dreamed that the young general would have the stomach to
stage a coup. And Trang! That fat, old bandit had fooled
them all. Who would have thought that he, cautious and
venal as a moneychanger, would join the rebels? In retrospect, Diem could understand about Giac; but Trang, no.
It didn't add up. Trang must have had a personal reason for
joining the conspirators, something that did not tally with
the rest of his character. The insurgent troops had moved
into the capital under the cover of Operation Bravo, a fake
coup authorized by Nhu and designed to bring into the open
secret enemies of the regime. But Bravo had turned out to be
in earnest. It had been too late when he and Nhu had
realized that.

"But it makes no difference, brother," Diem continued, "if
they were all against us, it would have come some other way."

Nhu half turned in the pew to face his brother, the guttering light from the altar candles playing on his lined, tired
face. Diem breathed deeply. How rich was the scent of the
incense! For one who once had thought of entering the
Church, it was perhaps fitting that the end should come in
such a setting.

"Let's try again," Nhu urged. "There are other men with
ships. If we can't reach Cao in the delta, perhaps we can get
to Hué. If Can is still alive, it will be possible to organize
something there!"

Diem smiled and shook his head.

"No, Nhu, no. For me, it's finished, although you are free
to go. There's nothing more for me except to ask God's
forgiveness for my sins and to try to die with dignity."

"I won't leave you," Nhu replied.

"No, I didn't think you would."

"Still, it was my fault. It was me the Americans were after.
I should have gone into exile."

"I would not have permitted it. I needed you then, as I
need you now. You did what you did for me."

"How I detest the Americans!"

"You know, Nhu, I don't think they really understood
what they were playing with. They'll have ample opportunity
to regret their stupidity. There's no need to hate them. Not
now, so close to the end."

Diem know it would not be long. He was surprised that
the troops had not come already. They were very inefficient.

It was no wonder the war was being lost. Still, he could imagine, even in the cloistered silence of the church, the state Saigon must be in. They would be along soon. There was no need to rush toward death. He wanted the little time left to compose his thoughts, to prepare for what was to come. He placed his hand on his brother's and fixed his eyes once more on the cross. All Souls' Day, the day upon which the Church glorifies God for all His saints, known and unknown, a day with a vigil of fasting and abstinence, a fitting day for the fall of a Christian ruler in a pagan land. Was it the Pantheon in Paris or the one in Rome that was dedicated to Our Lady and all the martyrs? Rome, he thought. Rome made him think of Thuc and of what lay ahead for himself and Nhu. He could not tolerate being taunted by fools like Giac and Trang, generals so incompetent they couldn't put down a peasant rebellion with all the money and guns in the world. Suppose he were dragged through the streets or made to endure a mock trial by a rebel tribunal? He could not, would not stand it. How much easier it would be, Diem thought, if we were not Catholics. Suicide would have been a fitting end. But it was out of the question. The Ngo Dinhs had been Christian since the seventeenth century. They would keep the Faith. But if it be Thy will, he prayed, let them kill us quickly, let them not make a spectacle of us. Defend us from our own weakness, oh God.

Diem was unprepared for the manner of their coming. He had imagined the wailing of sirens, the rumble of trucks, perhaps the screams of an infuriated mob. There was none of this. The great, oak door of St. Francis Xavier creaked on its hinges and opened slowly, filling the church with the morning light, turning to flecks of gold the particles of dust which hung in the air, dissipating the richness of the incense. Diem half turned in the pew, resenting the unwanted interruption of his reverie, and saw the silhouette of the soldier framed in the doorway, the light glowing behind him. The soldier, Diem saw, was in combat uniform, wearing a helmet, a pistol in his right hand. The soldier took a few hesitant steps down the aisle, the pistol held out in front of him, his eyes obviously troubled by the gloom of the church. Other soldiers carrying rifles and submachine guns fanned out behind the first one, flitting down the side aisles. The time had come. Diem gave his brother's hand a gentle squeeze.

"God save you and keep you, Nhu," he whispered.

Diem stood up slowly, stiff from his long vigil, and turned to face the officer walking down the aisle.

"You're late," Diem said. The officer stopped but said nothing. He's unsure of himself, Diem thought. He doesn't know what to do.

"This is a holy place," Diem continued, "put your guns away. Take off your helmets. We will not hurt you."

The officer said nothing but motioned with his pistol to the troops moving down either side aisle. Then he walked forward again, slowly, his eyes fixed on Diem, as if he expected him to disappear in a puff of smoke.

"Didn't you hear the President?" Nhu demanded. "Do as you're told, you swine!"

Nhu's shouted words seemed to awaken the young officer from his daze.

"Seize them! Seize them!" he yelled to the soldiers. "Search the back. There may be others there."

"You need not be afraid," Diem said, "we are alone."

Two soldiers ran toward Diem, their wide, peasant faces excited and filled with awe, their arms outstretched to grab him. The President pushed the first of them away, the sound of their hobnailed boots on the stone floor echoing loud in his ears. Then he turned and walked down the aisle toward the officer, Nhu at his heels. The two soldiers fell into step behind them. The officer slowly raised the pistol until its aperture was level with Diem's chest. Diem could see the barrel swaying from side to side in the officer's hand. He's very nervous, Diem thought.

"You are Ngo Dinh Diem and Ngo Dinh Nhu?" the officer demanded.

"I am the President of Vietnam," Diem replied.

"I arrest you both in the name of the revolutionary government. You will come with me."

"You are a filthy traitor," Nhu shouted over Diem's shoulder. The President turned and placed a hand on his brother's shoulder.

"We will come with you, since we have no choice," Diem said quietly.

Out on the sidewalk, a small crowd had gathered around the clumsy bulk of an M-113 armored personnel carrier. Diem did not look at the crowd, although he realized that some of them were shouting at him. He could not tell whether the shouts were of praise or hatred. He no longer cared. He walked to the curb and looked uncertainly around him, blink ing in the sunlight. He had expected a car of some sort. But there was only the personnel carrier. He turned and walked toward the front of the vehicle but the officer placed his hand against his chest.

"No," he said, "in back!"

Diem shrugged, brushed the man's hand away, and walked back to the double-doored rear entrance. Nhu already was climbing in. Diem never had been in such a vehicle. He peered inside curiously until his brother had disappeared into the murky interior. Then he clambered in, aware of his awkwardness, and sat down opposite Nhu. The officer took a submachine gun from one of the soldiers and climbed into the personnel carrier, slamming the thick door shut behind him. As he did so, a single light bulb, guarded by a wire shield, went on overhead. The motor coughed and turned over and Diem could feel the vehicle bouncing over the cobblestones. It was very hot in the personnel carrier and Diem realized with distaste that he was sweating. The officer sat at the back of the truck, the submachine gun cradled in his arms. They'll promote him for this, Diem thought. They'll make him a major. Somehow it struck him as very funny and he had to control himself to keep from laughing.

"Where are you taking us?" Diem asked the officer.

The officer shook his head, his teeth clenched together, his eyes burning, the snout of the submachine gun pointed at Nhu's stomach. The realization slowly came to Diem that the officer was going to shoot. There would be no humiliation for him, no torture for Nhu. He thanked God quickly, not knowing how much time he had. He could sense from the way the nerve in the officers cheek was pulsating, from the whiteness of his knuckles as he gripped the barrel of the gun, that the officer was working up his courage to shoot.

"Nhu," Diem said quietly, "don't worry about the boys . . ."

Nhu must have read what Diem had seen in the officer's face for he began to curse the man, slowly, vividly, with a richness of vocabulary which rather astounded Diem, taunting the man for lacking the courage to do what he had been paid to do. Nhu's voice, low at first, barely audible, rose slowly until he was almost shouting, the officer's eyes starting out of his head, his lips turned back in a snarl. He's going to do it now, Diem thought. In a minute it will all be over. They say it doesn't hurt at all. Yes, he's going to shoot. He's finally found the courage to kill a Ngo Dinh. Now. Now, he's going to shoot. He's going to do it now.

"Pater noster . . ." Diem began. And then his ears were bursting with the incredible reverberations of the shots in the confined area and his nostrils were full of the acrid, bitter smell of burning powder and he saw Nhu double over and fall forward toward the officer, his arms outstretched, his fists clenched, and then Diem felt his own body slammed back against the steel wall of the vehicle by the leaden blows pummeling him, driving the breath out of his body. Diem tried to speak to Nhu as he fell forward on his brother's body but the blood surged up in his throat, choking him, and a great light exploded in front of his eyes, blotting out forever the smoking aperture of the submachine gun and the terrified face behind it.

CHAPTER TWENTY-TWO

HARRY HAD GIVEN up hope. There was no way out. That morning they had splashed across the slow-moving, Black River which marked the northern boundary of Koho country. They were in the Rhadé hills and there no longer was the faintest chance of their stumbling across a government patrol. Here the Vietcong was the government. Saigon troops had not penetrated the Rhadé country since the days of the French, even on punitive expeditions. He could not buy his freedom from Loye, and both Yé and Ilouha had refused to help him. So it was finished. Soon, Harry suspected, Loye would be handing him over to the Viets who were to take him north to Hanoi. There would be no reason for Loye, Yé, and Ilouha to make the long march. Somebody else, perhaps cadres going north for training, would do that. Soon the last links with the past, Ilouha, Yé, and Loye, would disappear. It was going to be a long walk. Harry did not want to think about Hanoi. He did not want to think about what was in store for him. He had never been very good at standing pain. But Marc had been right: always it was better to live. Later, after the North Vietnamese and the Chinese interrogation officers had gotten out of him all he had to tell, he might be exchanged. It was a slight chance but he knew he must cling to it, nurture it. It was all he had. He had to concentrate on the business of the walk to the north. He had to try to keep up. Harry knew what would happen if he couldn't. He knew that not a single French or native soldier captured with an abdominal wound at Dienbienphu had been repatriated by the Vietminh. They hadn't been able to keep up on the march to their prison camps; they'd all been bayoneted. At least he wasn't wounded. He could do it. He was going to do it.

It was not only the fording of the river that told him they had passed from the country of the Koho into that of the Rhadé. It was the way Loye acted. The Rhadé leader had become more relaxed, almost jocular. He had loosened the

thongs around Harry's wrists and helped him to his feet once
after he'd fallen on a slippery piece of trail. The two flankers
and the point man had been called in and the whole party
walked together in single file with no effort at concealment.
Loye had handed the tether rope to Ilouha and dropped back
to joke with Yé and the other men. Ilouha was setting an easy
pace, her shoulders swinging, the tether rope hanging slackly
from Harry's neck. He had tried to tell her what the having
of her had meant to him. But the Koho tongue was so limited.
It contained no word for love. He could only tell her that
he had wanted her and had found her good, pleasing to his
heart and to his body. Ilouha had nodded her head at his
words and smiled shyly at him, started to say something and
then stopped, looking away, walking on in front, the tether
tightening. But she had promised she would try to get word
to Marc that he had been taken to North Vietnam. Harry
was sure she would do that. She had said she would and
Ilouha never had lied to him. None of the Koho ever lied.
They were a very primitive people.

The hand grenade had come just after that. Ilouha had
been leading him by the tether, her eyes on the trail. The
grenade seemed to hang in the air for a moment, blotting out
the sun, before it plopped moistly onto the trail a few yards
in front of Ilouha, like a fat partridge going to cover. As the
grenade hit the ground, Ilouha stopped and looked up at the
noise, unaware of its source, her back straight. Instinctively,
when he had seen it black against the sun, the word "grenade"
had flashed across Harry's mind, his muscles had bunched
involuntarily and he had shrunken into himself. But for an
instant his body could not accept totally what his mind told
him. "Down, get down!" came the signal from his mind and
he threw himself forward, clumsily because of his bound
wrists, Ilouha's name on his lips, catching her in the small of
her back with his shoulder, knocking her sideways off the trail
at the moment of the explosion, the air filled with the whirring
of many locusts, the deafening crash of the concussion mixed
with the short, sharp stab of pain in his shoulder and the
sickening impact of the up-rushing ground. Momentarily
stunned, Harry heard the bark of the machine gun behind
him and saw Yé double up and fall forward, one hand clasped
to his belly. The machine gun continued to chatter in short,
sharp bursts as Loye bounded by, dodging from side to side,
his body bent low. He had almost reached the cover of a
bamboo thicket when Harry saw him turn and hesitate.

Ilouha, down on one knee, blood pouring over her breasts from a jagged wound in her chest, was calling to him.

"Loye," she cried, her voice thin above the fusillade of the shots, "Loye!"

Loye looked quickly into the forest and then back to Ilouha. Then he turned and ran back to her. Circling her waist with one arm and throwing her left arm around his neck, Loye dragged her toward the cover of the bamboo. He had gone only a few steps when the stutter of the machine gun cut him down. As the bullets struck Loye, Harry saw him drop Ilouha, lurch forward for a step and then collapse. He did not get up. Harry began to inch his way toward the fallen pair, pushing with his toes, rolling across the ground toward them.

"Ilouha," Harry shouted. "Ilouha!"

Before he could worm his way over to her, the firing died out and there was only the groaning of the wounded and a thrashing in the grass behind him, where Yé was fighting the stomach wound. Slowly a circle of Vietnamese soldiers in camouflaged dungarees and berets materialized at the edge of the forest, their carbines held at the ready. One of them shouted a command and the rest ran in among the wounded, clubbing them with the butts of their carbines. Harry watched as a soldier kicked Ilouha aside and smashed his weapon into Loye's face as the Rhadé struggled to rise from the ground to shattered knees.

"You bastard," Harry shouted, "you bastard!"

And then he felt someone tugging at his bound wrists and turned, kicking at the man.

"Hold it," the man shouted, "that's enough of that." It took a moment to sink into Harry's consciousness that the man towering over him, who wore a captain's bars, had spoken in English, that his face was that of a white man. But an American couldn't be in Rhadé country!

"You Coltart?" the man demanded, slipping the thongs from Harry's wrists.

"Yes, I'm Harry Coltart. How did you . . ." Then he remembered what had happened and scrambled over to Ilouha, pushing aside the Vietnamese soldier who was going through Loye's pockets.

"Ilouha," he said, cradling her in his arms, pressing his hand gently against the quivering flesh of the great wound in her chest, "Ilouha."

"Erohé," she whispered, her parted lips forming the words with difficulty, "Erohé, it hurts so . . ."

"Don't talk," he said gently, "don't say anything."

Looking wildly around him, Harry spotted the American. "Bandages," he shouted, "have you got a field dressing?"

Harry snatched the dressing out of the American's hand and pressed it against the jagged hole, the cotton a terrible white against the brown of her skin, the scarlet of her pumping blood.

"The boy," she whispered faintly, "the boy . . . had hair gold like . . . yours . . . great chief . . . Hamon promised . . ."

A tear squeezed itself from the corner of her right eye and ran quickly down her cheek. Harry started to speak, to comfort her, but choked, his own tears flowing into his filthy, three-day beard. Ilouha's body stiffened suddenly in his arms and she half raised herself from the ground.

"Dark," she muttered almost inaudibly, "very dark . . . sun . . . too late . . ." and then her head fell against his chest and Harry felt her blood pumping from her breast, soaking through the dressing, warm on his hand, and he held her tight against his chest, rocking backwards and forwards, holding her as if he might never let her go.

Later he allowed the American to lead him away from her, to push him gently to the ground. Harry took the proffered canteen, tipped it up, choked and then drank, letting the water run down over his chin. The American lit a cigarette and handed it to him. Harry inhaled deeply, twice, trying to put together everything that had happened.

"How'd you get here?" he asked.

"Choppers. That spotter plane saw you lying in the clearing. Me and these commandos came in here yesterday and set up the ambush. Sorry 'bout that grenade. One of these guys goofed on that one. Reckon he thought he could pick her off without getting you."

"Yé," Harry said, "how's Yé?"

He got to his feet and looked around him. The commandos had herded the wounded men together. Yé was lying on his back, his eyes closed, a small, blue hole in his stomach just above the navel. Next to him sat Loye, his wounded legs stretched out in front of him. Blood was flowing from Loye's nose and he was picking bits of broken tooth from his smashed mouth.

"Who's Yé?" the American asked, "their leader?"

"No, he's not their leader," Harry said. "He's not Vietcong. He just got caught in the middle."

Harry walked over to Yé and knelt beside him. He could tell that the wound was bad. Right in the gut. Yé was conscious and Harry realized that the black, crafty eyes were studying him carefully, asking a silent question.

"How is it, Yé?" he asked. "Bad?"

"The wound is not so bad, Erohé. But bad enough."

A Vietnamese officer, jaunty in his black beret, walked over and studied the four wounded men. Two dead Vietcong lay on the trail where they had fallen. That meant one had gotten away. Harry did not know which one had escaped.

"Which is their leader?" the Vietnamese officer asked in Annamese, directing the question at Yé. The Koho chief hoisted himself onto one elbow and pointed at one of the dead men.

"That one," he said in Koho. "His name is Xuan."

"What's he say?" the American officer asked.

"He says that one's their leader," Harry replied.

"Is he?" the Vietnamese officer asked.

Harry's eyes shifted to Loye. The Rhadé continued searching in his bloody mouth for pieces of tooth, but he looked up. There was no emotion in his eyes, no entreaty, no fear, only mild interest. Somewhere in the bushes, a Ko-el bird cooed.

"No," Harry said slowly, "he's not the one. That man there, Loye, he's their leader." He pointed at Loye. The Rhadé said nothing. Yé slumped down onto his back again. Suddenly Harry felt confused, unclean, angry. The Vietnamese officer said something and two commandos seized Loye, binding his arms behind his back with garrotes of piano wire.

"What'll they do with him?" Harry asked as they dragged Loye off into the bushes.

"Interrogate him, I guess," the American said.

"But that man's wounded. Can't it wait until we get back?"

"He won't be going back. No room in the choppers."

"You mean . . . ?"

The American captain nodded and drew the forefinger of his right hand across his throat in a slicing gesture.

"They'll get what they can from him here. None of these Charlie Chans will be going back."

Harry studied the frank, young face of the American officer. This was what it always came to.

"Look," Harry said evenly, "that man's a prisoner of war

and you're an American officer. If you let them torture him in his condition, I'll see your ass court-martialed."

The American regarded him with flat, blue eyes.

"You won't get anybody court-martialed, Coltart. I don't know who you are or what your game is, but my orders are to place you in custody and bring you to Saigon. Seems you're the one, not me, who's got some explaining to do. You behave yourself, now, and let me have a look at that shoulder of yours."

"Never mind my shoulder. You can't do this. You . . ."

From the forest came a long, drawn-out screech, an involuntary cry, as if torn from an animal in pain. They were starting on Loye.

"Look, Coltart. This isn't my war. I didn't start it. I'm a professional soldier practicing my trade. Here I don't give orders, just advice. That man's Captain Nguyen's prisoner, not mine. He can do with him what he wants. I couldn't stop him if I wanted to. I don't see nuthin', I don't hear nuthin'. It's better that way."

Yes, Harry thought, like the man says, it's better that way. It's better not to see too much, or feel too much, or want too much. In the end, they always took it away from you. Eventually you found that the only way to get through was to shut your eyes to what's going on, to pretend it didn't matter, that it never happened. That was what he was going to have to do about Ilouha, about Yé. He could learn a lot from the American officer, if he wanted to. He closed his ears to the screeching from the forest.

"Go ahead and dress the shoulder," Harry said, "I'm sorry."

"That's better, friend, much better. None of us likes what we got to do, do we? But we got to do it. Right? That girl, that native girl, she something to you?"

The officer jerked his head in the direction of Ilouha's body as he tore away Harry's shirt, dusted the wound with penicillin, and expertly tied the dressing.

"Yes," Harry said, "she was something to me."

"Sorry about that. We thought she was just a Vietcong joy girl. I mean the way she was leadin' you by that halter and all."

"No, she wasn't a joy girl."

"Well that's too bad. I'm real sorry. We'll bury her, if you like."

"Yes, I'd like that."

The American shouted in Annamese to two of the commandos. They laughed and one said something which Harry didn't get. The American officer shouted at them again, louder this time, and they shrugged their thin shoulders, strolled over to Ilouha's crumpled body, and began to scratch at the ground with their entrenching tools.

"Thanks," Harry said. "Can you let me have another dressing for him?" He pointed at Yé. "He's her father," he added.

"Sure. Won't do no good though. Maybe you'd like to do it," he added, handing him the dressing. "But make it snappy. We've got to get out of here. This jungle's stiff with Vietcong. Don't know why Nguyen's taking so long with that gook."

Harry slipped one arm behind Yé's shoulders and propped him up against his knee, pressing the dressing against the wound. There wasn't much blood, since it was a stomach wound, but some of the light had gone out of the Koho's eyes, the way the colors of tropical fish fade when you take them from the water.

"Ilouha?" Yé asked.

"Dead. They're burying her."

Yé nodded, his eyelids fluttering.

"I'm sorry, Yé," Harry said. "Sorry about everything. I didn't mean it this way."

"It would have been better if you'd stayed in your own land, Erohé. Better if all *Bocs* had done that."

"Yes."

Loye had stopped screaming. Harry saw the Vietnamese officer and the two commandos walk out of the forest. They were laughing and wiping their hands on their dungaree trousers.

"And Loye?" Yé asked.

"Dead. He was just a terrorist, Yé."

"He was a man, Erohé. Once he . . ." Harry felt a shudder ripple through the old chief's body. A rattle began deep down in his chest, his body stiffening, his head falling back, his broken fingernails gouging the flinty soil of his hills, as if in death he had found it very dear.

"Come on," the American officer was saying. "Haul ass. There's nothing more we can do here."

Harry lowered Yé's body to the ground. He took from the Koho chief's neck the greasy, leather pouch containing the tiger's floating collarbone. The power of the fetish was gone. It had failed Yé. He stuffed the amulet in his pocket, closed Yé's eyes, and limped down the trail behind the tall, young officer, past Ilouha's shallow grave scraped from the forest floor. At the edge of the forest, Harry stopped for a minute and looked back at the raw, red earth of the grave. When the rains came, the grass would come back and Ilouha's resting place would disappear. He turned and walked away, aware that he was weeping.

Behind him he heard two quick shots. The choppers' load factor would be correct.

CHAPTER TWENTY-THREE

"AM I UNDER ARREST?" Harry asked, toying with Yé's amulet.

"No," Fowler replied, "but you're flying out tonight. To Manila. You'll have some explaining to do there."

Harry was so clean that he felt as if he were somebody else. The doctor had dressed the wound, picking out the grenade fragments, and bandaged the shoulder. Afterward they'd put him to bed between crisp, cool sheets, so fresh from the hospital laundry that the creases were still ironed into them. A pretty young nurse had sponged him down and given him an alcohol rub. Another had shaved him. He'd asked for a nail file, the nurse had brought him one, and he'd worked for a long time on the broken stubs of his nails, trying to get the dirt of the hills out from under them. He had felt better about it all when the last of the dirt was out. Harry Coltart, Judas-goat, was a dirty, unshaven man, stained with the dust of the hills. This man, alcohol rubbed and shaved, was a very clean man. Therefore, he could not be Harry Coltart, Judas-goat. It followed, it was perfectly logical. You could go on from there to solve anything you wanted.

"I don't care about the explaining," Harry said. "I'm getting out. I've had enough of this business."

Harry resented Fowler's bursting in on him like this, interrupting the cleaning of his nails with talk of flights to Manila. Before Fowler had come, the small room with its very white metal bed, its bedside table and single, straight-backed chair, its lime-colored walls, had been a private place, remote, cloistered, restful. Harry would have liked to keep it that way, but Fowler had come strolling in as if it didn't matter at all.

"You may not have much choice in that, Harry. You disobeyed a direct order, you know."

"Did I? I suppose I did. Which reminds me: where's Englehardt? I'd like to see him."

Now that it was over and the people he had cared for were

dead and the thing he had worked for was wrecked, Harry felt curiously relieved, detached, almost light hearted. He would have no more moral judgments to make. It seemed almost possible to him that Ilouha and Yé and Loye never had existed, that that time in the Koho hills had been a dream, a terrible, beautiful vision induced by a hallucinatory drug. Yes, he wanted to talk to Englehardt. Englehardt could give focus to his perceptions. Englehardt could help him to know the truth.

"Englehardt's gone," Fowler said.

"Gone? What do you mean, gone?"

"Relieved. I thought you knew. I've taken over from him. He'll be retiring, I expect. He got emotionally involved and staked too much on Diem."

Harry almost laughed out loud. Englehardt emotionally involved! But there was something Harry didn't understand.

"I don't get you," he said.

Fowler stared at him, an expression of incredulity spreading across his thin face.

"Are you trying to say you don't know about Diem?"

"What about him?" Harry asked.

Fowler slapped his forehead with his open hand, smiling broadly.

"He's dead. Nhu, too, the whole gang. The army took over two days ago. There's a junta under 'Big' Minh."

"God. I didn't know. What touched it off?"

Harry couldn't believe it. Diem and Nhu dead. The government swept away. Englehardt gone. Father Dupleix, Ilouha, Yé, and Loye dead. It seemed impossible. Harry was not sorry about Diem and Nhu. They had played for big stakes and lost. They had betrayed others and been betrayed in their turn. McWhorter had been right after all.

"I guess the raid on the Xa Loi Pagoda was the final straw," Fowler said. "Nhu's goons sacked it. They almost caught Cao Van Thuan but he got over the wall into the A.I.D. compound."

"What about McWhorter?" Harry asked.

"Who?"

"John McWhorter, the Washington *Express* correspondent."

"Left for the States last night on the same plane with Englehardt. He got that editor's chair."

All the lines were breaking down. New cards of identity all around, but Harry didn't care. He didn't care at all. From now on, he was going to be numbered among those not present. He was going to be neutral. He felt at peace wearing the clean, institutional, hospital pajamas in the comfortable, metal bed with its spotless coat of white paint. The shoulder wound had been cleaned and tightly bandaged and it did not hurt at all. Not a bit. The nurse had given him a shot of something and he was suffused with a warm, pleasant drowsiness, the soft, sweet scent of the flowering mango tree flowing gently through the open window, the war very far away, in another place. Somewhere out beyond the mango tree, remote from the hospital's quiet, bee-filled garden, on the far side of the cobbled street, there was a war. But no longer was it his war. He would go out to it no more. His war was finished with those he had loved who had fought it. Each generation had to mourn its own dead. Some new, ersatz Lawrence, some freshly minted Don Quixote would have to go out to that virgin war beyond the garden wall. New promises would have to be made and broken, but he was going to be neither the quisling nor the betrayed. For Harry Coltart, it was finished. The Judas-goat was going away, bearing with him his burden of blood and guilt. He could not carry any more. There came a point when the load on the A-frame became a little too heavy for even the strongest coolie to straighten up under.

He realized that Fowler had been speaking to him.

" . . . getting back to the office," Fowler was saying. "I'll see that your stuff gets sent along to Manila. Anything else you want?"

Harry thought for a moment. No, there was nothing he wanted that Fowler had to give. Nothing at all.

"No thanks. Can I get out of here?"

"I'm afraid not. Eisenberg will take you to the airport at nine. But you've a visitor. Michaud. I don't suppose it would do any harm."

"Thanks. I'd like to see him. I promise not to give away any state secrets."

Fowler gave his noncommittal, second-in-command's smile, reached across the bed and shook hands. At the door he stopped, his hand on the knob, raised his eyes to the ceiling and snapped his fingers in mock exasperation.

"I almost forgot," he said. "I've something for you from Englehardt. He left this for you."

Fowler pulled a small, worn Bible from his coat pocket and

handed it to Harry. Inserted in the Bible was an envelope.

"So long, Coltart," Fowler said. "Sorry about all this, but good luck in whatever you do. I'll send up Michaud."

Fowler closed the door behind him, leaving him in lime-colored peace. Harry tossed the little Bible beside him on the bed and tore open the envelope. The note was written in Englehardt's rounded, old-fashioned script. It read:

"Diem was my Yé, Harry, so we're both in the same garbage-scow with no land in sight. It probably won't be much comfort to you, but read Ecclesiastes I, 7. Sincerely (if I may use the expression), Ramsey Englehardt."

That's rich, Harry thought. Englehardt was a fine one to be quoting from the Bible. He and Englehardt were in it together though. Englehardt was right about that much. The war beyond the garden wall wasn't Englehardt's any more, either. There was more than one Judas-goat. Harry flipped through the flimsy rice paper pages of the little book, through Esther, Job, Psalms, and the Song of Solomon, turning back to Ecclesiastes. Harry moved his finger across the tightly-printed page with its burden of too-heavy type until he found the verse.

"All the rivers run into the sea," he whispered aloud, "yet the sea is not full; unto the place whither the rivers go, thither they go again."

Harry read on a little further and then snapped the Bible shut. He was not in the mood. "All the rivers run into the sea," he thought to himself. Graceful, poetic words, but did they mean anything? What was Englehardt driving at? That the judgment of their acts would have to await another time? That men were condemned to echo their promises and their betrayals? That the shattered lives really did not matter within the context of a tortured century? Harry didn't know. It was something he knew he was going to have to work out someday. So many lives had flowed into the war. Ilouha's, Yé's, Loye's, Diem's, Nhu's, countless thousands of others, the unknown, unmourned dead, human fuel for the meat grinder. Yet the sea of blood and guilt was not full. It could take more. The endless process had to be repeated. It had become a meaningless ritual, a dirge sung by a mute priesthood to a deaf congregation. And for what purpose? Harry didn't know and he didn't want to think about it any more, at least not now. Later would be soon enough. He slipped the Bible under his sheet when he heard the light tap on the door.

"Come in," he said.

The door opened and Marc clumped into the room, filling it with his controlled presence, driving out the cool nothingness.

"Well, Harry," he said quietly.

"Well, Marc."

Harry had a feeling he would not be seeing Marc again for a long time, and he was not sorry. Marc reflected too much of his own life. They shared too many victories and defeats, had done too much together. There was much to be said for bland, blank, unfamiliar faces. Harry wanted no more memories paraded before him.

"And how goes it?" Marc asked gently.

"How did you know I was here?"

The Frenchman hesitated for a moment, chewing his thin underlip, and sat down in the straight-backed chair next to the bedside table before he spoke.

"I should tell you, Harry, that it was I who informed Englehardt that you were heading for the Koho country."

"Merci."

"It was necessary, Harry. Necessary for you and for the Koho. You could do nothing more for them. And to die is not interesting."

"No, it's not at all interesting. You know that Ilouha and Yé are dead? Loye too."

"I didn't know. I'm sorry."

"Everybody's sorry, Marc. You're sorry. I'm sorry. Englehardt's sorry. President Kennedy's sorry. But the others, they're dead and they don't care that we're sorry."

"No, the dead don't care. It's a dirty business, Harry. Get out of it while you're still in one piece. And I don't mean just physically in one piece."

"You can't just forget what you've done."

"No, but you can sign a separate peace with yourself. You can leave Vietnam to us, to the people who have no place else to go. Go home and marry the girl next door."

"There is none, I'm afraid."

"Nonsense. All Americans have a girl next door and always she's beautiful. Raise battalions of children. Teach them baseball and have the neighbors in for backyard barbecues. Build walls around yourself and don't come out to places where you're not wanted. Go home, Harry, go home."

Harry nodded his head, his eyes on his friend.

"I'm going, Marc. This Judas-goat is leaving Vietnam. But not for home. There is no such place any more. Not for me."

"Balls, mon ami. You'll be all right once you get to the States. Forget Ilouha. Be honest enough to recognize that there could have been nothing meaningful for you with her. She was Koho, a primitive, the daughter of a savage. And you are an American, not a Frenchman. Forget her."

Marc jumped to his feet and paced up and down the narrow room, his hands clasped behind his back, his expression stern, the way Harry had found him that morning when they had walked among the rubber trees and swum in the pool of icy water. Forget her. That was good advice. But that raw piece of new earth in a jungle clearing was engraved upon Harry's memory and he knew it was something he never would forget.

"She was going to have a child."

"I'm sorry about that, Harry."

The Frenchman stopped his pacing and walked slowly to the open window. He looked out and inhaled deeply.

"It's going to rain," Marc said, "soon."

"Don't you want to know how Loye died?" Harry asked. "He was your corporal, wasn't he? The one you left behind at the Black River?"

"Yes, he's the one. How?"

"I betrayed him. He was wounded. The commandos tortured him to death."

"He was a good man, Harry. There are many such with the Vietcong. They fight for what they believe to be right, just as we do. Perhaps we're both right, or both wrong, depending on how you look at it. But forget about Loye. He tried to kill me and he would have killed you with no compunction. Remember Father Dupleix?"

"Remember? That's my problem, Marc. I'll remember it all. I can't leave everything that has happened in Vietnam, like a worn-out suit you give to your servant, when I fly out of here tonight. Those thoughts and those faces are coming with me. They won't fit in at the barbecue. They won't fit in at all."

Marc nodded, still staring out the window.

"We're the walking wounded, Harry. Oh, I'm not talking about these little souvenirs, this pretty face of mine, that hole in your shoulder. These are only the outward and visible signs of an inward and spiritual gangrene. Stein called that other generation lost. Ours is not lost. We're still among the living, but secretly maimed, empty and dry, like corn husks in a frozen December field. Through experiencing too much of love and betrayal, we've lost the capacity to care. This, I think, is another name for death."

"You're good at speeches, Marc, but . . ."

"It's true, Harry. All of us who've played this game for too long are emotional ambulatory cases. We'll make it, though. We're tough. Yes, very tough. We'll laugh, drink martinis, make love, breed children, recreating our own emptiness, forging new human instruments of betrayal. No, don't worry about Loye. Don't mourn for trust. All of us betray each other every day, Harry. Trust would have no value if there were fewer betrayals."

"Shut up will you, Marc. I don't want any more of your Gallic philosophy."

"Philosophy is all that's left to us, Harry. We must be on our guard not to care too much. It's through our caring that we've destroyed ourselves and others. We're dangerous."

"Goodbye, Marc. I'm tired. I've had enough. Will you please leave now?"

The Frenchman stubbed out his cigarette and touched Harry gently on his good shoulder.

"Of course. Forgive me. One talks to ease one's own burden. It was selfish of me."

"Goodbye," Harry said.

Marc opened the door and stood there for a moment, his weight on the good leg, his lean body erect, the later afternoon sun kind on his destroyed face.

"Come back one day, Harry. You'll find me at Sans Souci. Like Abdullah of the Caravelle, I've become part of the scenery. Goodbye . . . and luck."

Marc waved and closed the door behind him, leaving Harry alone in the antiseptic quiet of the hospital room. The sedative was taking effect and Harry felt an immense weariness creeping over him, soothing him, calling him away. Through the open window, with the scent of mango blossoms, came the slow tolling of the angelus and a low mutter of thunder, the rain falling slowly at first and then pelting down in big drops which clattered off the tin roof and fell hissing into the dust of the garden, leaving the leaves of the mango shining and new, washing the room with the odor of new rain. From somewhere out beyond the garden wall, Harry heard a Vietnamese woman singing, her voice plaintive and sad.

"Ilouha," he whispered, feeling the tear on his cheek, "Ilouha."

The woman chanted on, her voice rising through the drumming of the rain and the tolling of the church bells. It was a song Harry guessed he would not forget, for she mourned for him, for all of them, the quick and the dead.